Stacie relaxed and let herself enjoy the feel of Trish's body grinding against her. The music never stopped but blended smoothly into one composition. At some point, she became aware of a second pair of hands around her waist and a pelvis grinding against her ass. A wave of desire shot through her. As the stranger's movements became more insistent, Stacie slid one hand behind her and encountered the bare flesh of a thigh. A hand grabbed Stacie's and guided it beneath what she suspected was an extremely short skirt.

Visit

Bella Books

at

BellaBooks.com

or call our toll-free number

1-800-729-4992

On The
Wings of Love

Megan Carter

Bella
BOOKS

2005

Printed in the United States of America on acid-free paper
First Edition

Editor: Christi Cassidy
Cover designer: Sandy Knowles

ISBN 1-59493-027-9

Dedication

Martha
You make it all possible

Acknowledgments

Martha—Thanks for all your support and encouragement. You never complain about my need to brainstorm at three in the morning, not even when those brainstorming sessions require driving around for hours. You know how to make a road trip fun.

PJ—Thanks for taking the time to read the manuscript, your valuable suggestions and for just being there to listen when I needed to grumble.

Linda Hill—Thanks for helping make a lifelong dream come true.

Christi Cassidy—Thanks for all your hard work in helping to bring this manuscript to life. And even though I'd rather have a root canal than go through the long tedious days of revisions, your suggestions never fail to make the manuscript better.

About the Author

Megan Carter lives in Texas. She enjoys hanging out with friends at the coast and taking long, romantic road trips with her partner. *On the Wings of Love* is Megan's first novel.

You may e-mail the author at mcarterbooks@aol.com.

Chapter One

"This is your last chance, Stacie," Jack said as he closed his office door behind them.

Stacie wished she had taken time to grab a cup of coffee, but she hadn't even made it to her desk before Jack spied her and called her into his office. Now she would have to wait until he completed his monthly lecture on punctuality. She was too tired to play the *you boss, me peon* game today. She decided to try to derail his attempt. "I'm only a couple of minutes late."

"You're a half-hour late, and that's not the only problem. You blew the interview with Congressman Manchester and left us in a bind last night. You knew we were holding space for your copy." He ran a hand over his shiny bald head. At forty-three, he had given up the losing battle with hair loss and shaved his head.

The calm resolution in Jack Conrad's voice concerned her more than his dire warning. He wouldn't dream of firing her. After her recent string of successes, her future with the *Voice of Texas* was guaranteed. The *Voice*, as it was more commonly known, was a small Austin daily newspaper. Now that the name Stacie Gillette was practically synonymous with the word *exclusive*, he wouldn't fire her over something as asinine as being late a few times a week. She fought to extinguish the tiny flame of doubt that threatened to ignite. She was the only person on the staff, including the senior editor Jack Conrad, who could boast of the national wire service picking up three of her articles within a two-month period.

During her first exclusive, she convinced the mega pop star Roz to make a public announcement of her lesbianism. On the heels of this was her scoop in the prostitution scandal that was still causing shock waves within the Austin capital. That story had proved relatively easy. Following up on a tip from one of her rapidly growing team of informers, she waited outside the hotel room with a camera until the high-ranking state representative stepped out with a scantily clad, sixteen-year-old prostitute clinging to his arm.

Stacie's crowning glory was the exclusive interview with Robert Hinson, the infamous serial killer known as the Yellow Scarf Strangler. He had strangled six women before the Austin police finally captured him. During his arraignment, Hinson refused to speak to anyone from the press. Stacie used a pair of tickets to a sold-out concert to bribe a jail guard to get her in to see Hinson. After getting to him, it was surprisingly easy to convince him to tell her his story. A small quiver ran through her as she recalled the first time she saw his eyes. They weren't the cold, hollow fisheyes she anticipated, but instead a soft baby blue. Hinson was twenty-nine, only two years older than her. He was cursed with the same stubborn cowlick that tormented Stacie's younger brother, Danny. During the course of the interview with the soft-spoken Hinson, she found herself wanting to slick it down as she had so many times for Danny. It took two trips for her to get all of Hinson's story, but what a story it was.

On the heels of her success came the petty jealousy of resentful coworkers. Peter James, the senior staff reporter for the *Voice*, whined for days about how Stacie had blown the opportunity of a lifetime. He threw around words like *weak writing, sensationalism*, and droned on ad nauseam about her stealing a once-in-a-lifetime opportunity from a real reporter who could have turned the interview into a Pulitzer.

Stacie understood he was pissed because she had shown more balls than he ever would. They were all jealous of her youth and talent. Sure, there were things she still needed to learn, but she had graduated summa cum laude from UT Austin. Unlike Peter and several other staffers who were already well over forty, there was still plenty of time for her to make it to the big leagues.

She swallowed the smile threatening to betray her. Where would Jack Conrad ever find someone to replace her? She could smooth over the Manchester incident as she had others. What did it matter if she was occasionally late for work, or if she blew a few of the bullshit assignments Jack insisted on sending her way? It wasn't as if she needed to do any major kissing up. She wouldn't be with the *Voice* much longer. It was only a matter of time before an editor from one of the larger newspapers noticed the increased visibility of the Stacie Gillette byline. She felt certain she would be receiving an offer before the year's end. But, she cautioned herself, until then, it might be wise to keep things cool, just to keep Jack from freaking out. She lowered her head in what she hoped Jack would perceive as remorse.

"You really should work on a different act," Jack said as he pushed back from his desk. "Your humble pie imitation is getting old."

"Oh, come on, Jack! You don't honestly expect me to believe you wouldn't have told Manchester where to get off, had you been doing the interview."

She saw the slight tightening in his jaw and knew she shouldn't continue with the line of thought but couldn't stop herself.

Jack had given her the assignment with the incumbent Congressman Ralph Manchester along with an admonition to keep her opinions to herself. The interview was supposed to explore Manchester's views on the new school funding proposal,

3

but Stacie kept directing her questions toward the congressman's refusal to take a stand on gay marriages. If she could get him to take a public stand either for or against the issue, the larger Texas newspapers were sure to pick up her story.

However, Manchester proved to be a tough old politician who deftly evaded her attempts. To add to her frustration, twice she caught the crafty statesman manipulating her.

When it finally became apparent that Manchester didn't intend to answer her questions, Stacie tried to bully him. Wasn't that what hard-nosed journalists were supposed to do? How many times had her journalism instructors pounded it into her? *Do whatever it takes, but don't lose the story.*

She pressed harder. Each time she asked a question on gay marriage, he would start talking about school funding, and she would in turn interrupt and ask another question on gay marriage. This continued for several seconds until Congressman Manchester suddenly stood.

"I'm sorry there seems to be some misunderstanding. I came to discuss the school funding issue, but you don't seem to be interested in what I have to say." With that, he and his aide walked out of the room.

Smarting from the abrupt dismissal, and not to be outdone by his walkout, she had stormed out behind him. It wasn't until she was halfway across town that she remembered that space was being held in that night's run for her interview. Pride kept her from going back and begging the pompous old windbag for a second chance. No one really wanted to read another article about school funding anyway. After almost three months of arguments over the issue, the public was probably as tired of hearing about it as she was. She didn't feel like going back to the office and facing Jack. It took every ounce of her courage to dial his number, but for once, things went her way. The call went to Jack's voice mail. She left a quick message, telling him Manchester had been called away before the interview could be completed, and turned her cell phone off. Jack would try to call her for more details, but since it was already after five, she told herself she was officially off work, and there was nothing wrong with being unavailable.

"Stacie, you didn't complete the assignment," Jack interrupted her thoughts. "You knew we needed it for the run, but you allowed your ego to get in the way. Your adolescent temper tantrum left several people scrambling last night to fill the space saved for you. To say nothing of how unprofessional you were. Congressman Manchester called me extremely upset. He thought I deliberately misled him on the topic of the interview."

She glanced around his office to give herself time. Trains were everywhere. The man was almost obsessive in his love for trains. She was tired and her patience was growing thin. It wouldn't hurt some of the slugs who called themselves reporters to do some real work for a change. If that old fart Manchester had just answered her questions on gay marriages, Jack would be kissing her ass this morning. She couldn't wait to get away from this joke of a newspaper.

A yawn escaped before she could stifle it. She hadn't gotten much sleep the previous night. Depressed by the thwarted interview, she had stopped by the bar for a quick beer after work. While she sat there mentally berating the congressman, a leggy, dark-haired woman with gorgeous hazel eyes and firm breasts that begged to be noticed took the seat beside her. An hour later, they went to the woman's apartment, and sleeping hadn't been on the agenda.

Jack was still raving about Manchester. Tired of listening, she said, "Jack, there was no story. Manchester is an old—"

He held up his hand. "I don't intend to discuss this. I've already called Congressman Manchester and he's agreed to meet with us again."

"It's a dead-end story. I don't want to—"

He interrupted her. "I've given the assignment to Peter."

She frowned and started to protest. She didn't want to do the interview, but she certainly wasn't going to stand by and have Peter snatch her story away.

"Stacie, I'm warning you. The best thing you can do now is keep quiet."

The look on Jack's face stopped her. There was something different about this ass-chewing. She swallowed her argument. It really wasn't worth the energy anyway. Let Peter take the lame assignment.

Jack pulled his chair back up to his desk. "I have another assignment for you. I want you to interview the author Cheryl Wright. She's moving here from L.A. She has a reputation of shying away from the press, but her publisher has assured me she's willing to give us a short interview. Call her and set up a meeting." He handed her a sheet of paper. "Her latest romance novel is sitting at the number two slot on the *New York Times* best-seller list. Make sure you read it before the interview."

"I don't read romance novels."

"Well, read this one," he ordered.

Another nowhere assignment. Stacie decided it would be wiser to hold her complaint and reluctantly pulled a battered pad from her hip pocket. She didn't intend to waste her free time reading the drivel of a romance novel. Stacie glanced at the paper Jack had given her. Written beneath the author's name and phone number was a list of titles. One of them caught her attention. "Is she the lesbian writer who wrote the book that caused all the controversy a couple of years ago?"

He nodded. "Yes, it was a fictional romance not so loosely based on the relationship between Dwight Eisenhower and his female driver, Kay Summersby. A lot of people didn't appreciate her digging up old dirt."

Stacie rolled her eyes. "Sounds boring."

"A couple of million readers didn't think so, and don't use the term 'lesbian writer.' It's offensive."

She waved him off. The last thing she needed was for him to get on one of his twenty-minute soapbox lectures.

He sighed and continued, "She has experienced a few unpleasant scenes with the press and doesn't care much for us, so don't try to make this more than it is. A simple human interest story is all I'm looking for." He glanced up at her. "Just to be sure we're on the same page here, what I mean is, don't push your own agenda."

"There is no gay agenda."

"I didn't say there was. I said don't push *your* agenda."

Stacie started to retort but realized she probably didn't have a right to do so. She felt a small sense of relief when he moved on.

"You'll have to meet her somewhere; she doesn't want the interview to be held in her home. The only information I have on her is a listing of titles, she's thirty-four years old, a graduate of Wellesley, and she recently moved here from Los Angeles."

Stacie experienced a small spark of interest. "What does she look like?"

"I don't know. As I said, she's gun-shy with the press. She appears to be something of a recluse. There are no photos on her books, and we haven't received a press packet on her."

Stacie made a barking noise, the brief spark of interest gone.

"That's disgusting. Why do you do that?" he asked.

"What?" she asked, looking up from her notes, genuinely puzzled. "If she were gorgeous her photo would be everywhere."

He shook his head. "Get the story." He flipped opened his desk planner. "I'm scheduling this for Tuesday's paper, so I want it on my desk no later than four on Monday. Take a camera with you and try to get a couple of shots, if she doesn't mind." Again, he looked at her. "Don't push if she doesn't want the photos taken."

She stood. "No problem, I'll have it Monday morning."

"That'll be great if you can. Just make sure you do it and do it right. Don't forget you've got your regular pieces."

"I haven't forgotten. How could I possibly forget *What's Happening Around Texas* and everyone's favorite, *Texas Moments in History*?" She started for the door.

"Stacie."

She stopped with a loud sigh.

"I mean it. This is your last chance. You have the potential to make a top-notch reporter, so don't blow this."

7

Without replying, she left. "What a waste of time," she mumbled as she closed the door behind her. What was so great about this author anyway? She decides to move to Austin and Jack thinks everyone is dying to read about her. "Not likely." How much could there be to say about a romance writer anyway?

It was the third week in July. The weather bureau was predicting temperatures in the mid-nineties by the afternoon. She wasn't looking forward to running around all over town just to talk to this woman. Maybe she could do the interview over the phone. She groaned when she remembered that Jack wanted photos. *Just another of the many drawbacks of working for a smaller publication*, she thought. *You had to be a jack-of-all-trades.*

Photos meant she would have to go request a camera from Marianne Dexter in the supply department. Stacie hated having to deal with Marianne, who made her sign in triplicate for every little item taken out. She had been even worse since Stacie lost a tape recorder.

"It wasn't even a new one," Stacie grumbled as she made her way to the back stairs. As she trudged down to her dungeon office, she stopped suddenly and smiled. Most of the information she needed could probably be found on the Internet. If she was lucky, maybe there would even be a photo.

After racing to her office, she settled before the battered desk that filled her tiny workspace. Water pipes above her head clanged and rattled. Two years ago, the cramped space and pipe noise had nearly driven her nuts; now she rarely noticed either.

As she logged on to access the Internet, she dreamed about the large corner office she would have someday after she went to work for a real newspaper. The position would be in a large city. She didn't particularly care which one, as long as it was big, her salary grotesquely high and her office twice the size of Jack's modest space.

Who knows, she mused as she began typing her search request, *with the stories I've been writing, I could be leaving this second-rate rag even before the end of the year.* That thought brought on a glow of anticipation that was only slightly dampened by the poor results brought about by her search request on Cheryl Wright.

She glanced through the few items gleaned from the search and quickly discarded them as useless. Most were gushy reviews of Cheryl's previous romance novels, while the rest were the usual list of book dealers. After closing the connection, she yawned and began to spin her chair in slow circles. She hadn't told Jack, but her two ongoing weekly assignments were completed. Had she told him, he would have sent her out to cover some rinky-dink women's social event. With nothing to do, she didn't feel like sitting in the dungeon all day.

As she continued to spin, an idea grew. She would call Cheryl Wright and schedule the interview for lunch. Then she could write off her lunch as a business expense. She'd ask the writer a few stock questions and then skip out for the rest of the day. Jack wouldn't know how long the interview took. She would have time to go home and sleep before meeting her best friend, Brenda, at the bar for their weekly Thursday night get-together.

She grabbed the paper Jack had given her with the contact information for Cheryl Wright and dialed the number.

The voice that answered the phone sounded gruff, as though picking up the receiver had caused her a hardship.

"Stacie Gillette. I'm a reporter with the *Voice of Texas*." She paused and let the statement hang. She loved the sound of the words. No matter how many times she said them, it always gave her a thrill. The pause usually produced another effect she enjoyed immensely. People couldn't stand silence. As soon as she stopped talking, the person on the other end would rush to fill the quiet.

Rather than the usual rush of greeting, all she heard was a frantic clacking noise. It took her a second to realize she was hearing the clatter of computer keys.

"Hello," Stacie said.

"Just a minute."

More typing followed. *Of all the arrogant . . .* Stacie's impatience got the better of her. "Look, if you don't have time, I've got other interviews to do."

"Fine."

Stacie's jaw dropped as the phone went dead. She slammed the receiver down. Who did this woman think she was, anyway? So her book was on the *New York Times* best-seller list. It was a romance novel. Did Cheryl Wright think reporters were waiting in line for an opportunity to interview her? Stacie wadded the paper with Cheryl's number and tossed it toward the trash can. She reached inside her desk drawer for her contraband CD of computer games. The newspaper's computer geek had made her remove the games from her PC, but she could still access the games directly from the CD. She would play Solitaire until lunch and then invent some excuse to take off. She hadn't gone home sick in a few weeks; maybe she'd develop some mysterious illness in the next couple of hours. As she pulled out the CD, she remembered Jack's final words. She didn't believe he would fire her, but it probably wasn't cool to ditch two interviews in as many days. With a weary sigh, she tossed the CD back into her desk and swallowed her pride as she redialed Cheryl's number. She gritted her teeth as the phone rang several times before clicking over to voice mail. *I am not leaving a message for this self-centered, arrogant bitch.*

Stacie was in the middle of her Solitaire marathon when her phone rang. She glanced at the phone and wished for the umpteenth time they would give her a set with caller ID. It was probably Cheryl Wright calling back. She answered the phone in what she considered her best "I'm in charge" voice.

"Hey, big sister. Do you always sound like you're about to rip off somebody's head, when you answer the phone?"

She smiled. "That's my professional voice," she teased. "Why haven't I heard from you lately, little brother? I was starting to worry about you."

"Oh, you know, I've been busy."

"How's school?" Danny was in his final year at Texas A&M.

"Fine. What have you been up to?" Was it her imagination or had he hesitated slightly before answering?

"Are you sure you're okay? You're not sick or anything, are you?" she asked. Finances were always a constant source of struggle for him. Even with the money she was able to send him and

10

what he made with his part-time jobs, there never seemed to be enough. "If things are getting tight, I could send—"

"I'm not calling about money. I just called to see how you're doing."

"I'm glad you did. I've missed talking to you." Because finances were so tight they didn't talk nearly as long as Stacie would have liked. It wasn't until after he had hung up that she realized he had said very little about himself. As she sat staring at the phone, she wondered if he really was all right.

Stacie spent the remainder of the morning playing Solitaire. She dialed Cheryl's number several more times, to no avail. Jack sent her an e-mail just before lunch informing her that he wanted everyone in the conference room at three. Human Resources wanted to do the yearly overview of the Code of Ethics. With her escape plan destroyed, she skipped lunch and caught a couple of hours' sleep at her desk. She spent the remainder of the day browsing the Internet. If anyone questioned her access time, she could explain it away as research.

It was a little after four when the meeting with Human Resources ended. Stacie phoned Cheryl Wright one final time. When the voice mail kicked on, she started to hang up but suddenly had an idea. The simplicity of it made her smile. "Ms. Wright, this is Stacie Gillette with the *Voice of Texas*. If you're still interested in doing an interview, I will be at Hav-A-Java tomorrow morning at nine-thirty." She quickly left the address to the coffee shop and hung up.

She chuckled at her brilliance. The coffee shop was only a few blocks from her apartment. She could sleep in and still make it in plenty of time. If Cheryl Wright appeared, fine, she'd do a quick interview. If she didn't, it was still all right. She could tell Jack with all honesty that she had tried to do the interview, but the author hadn't shown. He couldn't blame her for the acts of some quirky writer.

Satisfied that she had done everything possible to secure the interview, she grabbed her car keys. It was time to have some fun.

Chapter Two

There were fewer than a half a dozen cars in the parking lot of Rosie's when Stacie arrived. The place wouldn't start rockin' until much later. She and Brenda liked to get together before the crowd arrived. That left them free later in case they got lucky.

As she stepped inside, a frigid wave of stale cigarette smoke and the pounding bass beat of an early Madonna song engulfed her. She hesitated just inside the door to allow her eyes time to adjust to the room's dim interior. She and Brenda met here every Thursday to catch up, and occasionally they would return together on the weekend. Usually Stacie had better things to do with her weekends than catching up on gossip with Brenda.

As soon as her eyes adjusted, she saw Brenda waving to her from their favorite table, front and center of the dance floor. Stacie waved back before heading to the bar to order a beer.

The bartender, Zoey, a tall, back-to-nature dyke with short, slicked-back hair gave Stacie a nod as she approached. "What'll you have?"

"Corona."

Zoey reached into the cooler for the beer. As she popped the cap and slipped a wedge of lime over the lip of the bottle, Stacie discreetly studied Zoey's never-changing wardrobe of a well-worn denim work shirt with sleeves neatly rolled and jeans.

Zoey was something of a legend around Austin. At one time or another, she had tended bar at most of the women's bars, and everyone knew that if Zoey was on, you didn't try any crap. Start a fight and you'd find yourself banned from the place for weeks. Stacie had seen Zoey literally throw a woman twice her size over her shoulder after the woman went ballistic at finding her girlfriend's tongue swabbing someone else's tonsils.

Stacie couldn't understand why, but women flocked to Zoey. Even Brenda had dated her for a few weeks. Stacie couldn't see the attraction. She preferred women who were more feminine, and thankfully, there were plenty of those.

Stacie dated a lot, but she made sure each woman knew right up front that she wasn't in the market for happy-ever-after. Her career came first. She told herself that once she was firmly entrenched in her dream job, then maybe she would consider settling down, but for now there were far too many beautiful women to limit herself to only one. Why go to an all-you-can-eat buffet and only have a salad?

Zoey set the frosty Corona crowned with a tangy wedge of lime on the bar with a gesture that Stacie always thought of as a chin wave; the head goes back as the chin snaps up in acknowledgment.

Without intending to, Stacie mimicked the gesture and instantly felt as stupid as she probably looked. To cover her embarrassment she tossed some bills on the bar. "Keep the change," she muttered as she scurried away to where Brenda waited. As she left, she thought she heard Zoey's deep rumbling laugh.

Stacie and Brenda became friends while they were attending UT Austin. Stacie was majoring in journalism and Brenda in nursing. No one, least of all them, understood their friendship. They were complete opposites, and there had never been any sexual attraction between them. While Stacie had often been told that she was almost too self-confident, Brenda was in constant need of being reassured about practically everything. Stacie's life moved in a straight line. She never completely left one opportunity until a better one was available to take its place, but Brenda changed jobs more often than most people changed the oil in their car. She currently worked at a nursing home and was lucky enough to have landed a day shift.

"Hey, Stacie. You're here early."

"Yeah, I had a pisser of a day, so I cut out as soon as I could get away," Stacie said. "Let me tell you—"

"I've met the coolest, sexiest woman," Brenda interrupted. "Do you think she'll be the one?"

Stacie swallowed her groan. Her hopes of venting her own problems and the injustices heaped upon her the last couple of days evaporated. If a new woman was in Brenda's life, nothing short of a national disaster would shut her up. Brenda didn't allow Stacie time to comment before launching in on the attributes of her new love interest.

Stacie sat down and took the tiniest sip of her beer. She had long ago developed a talent for nursing a drink for hours on end. In truth, she didn't even care for the taste of beer, but all her friends drank it, so she followed suit.

Brenda was telling her something about green eyes. Stacie turned on her best *I'm all ears, tell me everything* face before tuning Brenda out and beginning her discreet perusal of the other bar patrons. No one caught her attention, but it was still early.

Brenda was so engrossed in her story that she didn't seem to notice Stacie's lack of attention.

It was a good forty-five minutes later when a woman walked in wearing a dark military uniform. *Now that takes balls*, Stacie thought. She sipped her beer and eyed the woman's shapely legs that seemed to go on forever before disappearing beneath a skirt that Stacie suspected was much too short to meet military standards.

The woman stopped just inside the door and scanned the room. *She's looking for someone or this is her first time here and she doesn't know the layout of the room*, Stacie decided. A few seconds later, the woman made her way to the bar.

Stacie resisted the temptation to tell Brenda to be quiet as she strained to hear the woman's voice. A quick glance around at the other bar patrons let her know she wasn't the only one interested in the new arrival. Only Brenda, who was talking about her new girlfriend's dimples, seemed oblivious.

A familiar warmth began low within Stacie as she made a slow visual inspection. The uniform jacket accentuated all the right places, and the skirt hugged slim hips that tapered into those long, slender legs. Her dark hair was short but styled in a deliberate tousled look that suggested a hint of wild abandonment.

Their eyes met as the woman turned. She held a bottle of water. The dim lighting from behind the bar allowed Stacie to see the slow welcoming smile tease the corner of the woman's full lips. They continued to maintain eye contact until the stranger chose a table and sat down. The heat within Stacie grew. She wouldn't be leaving alone tonight. She hesitated as a spark of the old doubt that had once consumed her tried to slither back. She fought it down with a reminder that no one knew her background. Here she could be anyone she wanted. With a deep breath to steady her pounding heart, she stood.

"I'll catch you later," Stacie said, interrupting Brenda's love chronicle. Without waiting for Brenda's response, she headed for the woman's table. As she made her way across the floor, she had a fleeting thought of the interview with Cheryl Wright the following morning, but it wasn't worth worrying about right now. As she drew even with the table, she flashed her best *you are the center of my universe* smile.

"You always move this fast?" the woman asked in a low voice tinged with a wonderful velvety softness.

A dozen tiny fingers of delight crawled up Stacie's spine as the richness of the voice wrapped around her like a warm blanket on a cold winter's night. All of Stacie's senses went on alert. She was in her zone, doing what she did best: charming women. She braced her arms along the back of the chair opposite the woman and smiled as she set herself a goal, as she did with each new conquest. She predicted she would be stroking this woman to climax in less than an hour and fifteen minutes. Her personal best was fifty-two minutes.

"Won't you join me?" the woman asked.

When she sat, Stacie caught the alluring scent of the woman's perfume. "I'm Stacie," she said as she held out her hand.

"Melody," the woman replied as her thumb caressed the back of Stacie's hand.

Stacie tried to control her pounding heart as Melody slowly released her hand. *Maybe I'll break my own record tonight*, Stacie thought as she said, "It's nice to meet you, Melody Spencer."

A frown of confusion with a mingling of concern crossed the woman's face.

Stacie chuckled and let her fingertips trace the bottom edge of the nametag that rested so seductively above the woman's right breast.

Melody glanced down and nodded. "Ah, the nametag. I always forget."

Stacie arched her eyebrows. "Strange. I couldn't take my eyes off it." She ran her fingers across the tag again before leaning back and picking up her beer. She almost shouted in triumph at the slight flash of disappointment that raced over Melody's face.

In this game, timing was everything. Stacie already knew they would be leaving together. The trick now was to make Melody think it was her idea. There would be less chance of a scene tomorrow morning. She was vaguely aware of Brenda walking past them on her way to one of the pool tables.

"We don't see many women in uniform in here," Stacie said. "In fact, you're my first."

Melody smiled. "I can't believe I'm your first."

16

"Are you stationed around here?" Stacie asked, deliberately ignoring the insinuation.

Melody stared at her for a long second. "Do you really want to waste all our time talking?"

Stacie struggled to keep the surprise from her face. She was normally the one pushing things to the next level, but what the heck. "As a matter of fact, no. Would you like to go somewhere else?"

"Why leave? You aren't opposed to a little . . . adventure, are you?"

Without breaking eye contact, Stacie took a small sip of beer to calm her throbbing heart and to buy her some time to think. She had never been propositioned in such a blatant way. She felt off-balance. How far did she dare go? If Zoey caught them doing anything out of line, she'd toss them both. Considering the bar was her main source of action, Stacie didn't want to be banned. Before she could say anything, Melody's bare foot began to ease its way up her leg and between her thighs.

A thin bead of sweat exploded along Stacie's hairline. A quick glance around reassured her that Zoey was busy stocking the back coolers, Brenda was still playing pool and the few other patrons were occupied talking, playing pool or shooting darts. Everyone seemed too busy to notice what was going on under the table. *It's probably too dark in here for anyone to see what we're doing*, she told herself as Melody's foot continued its probing.

Stacie tried not to squirm, but the boldness of the act and the smoldering look in Melody's eyes were having a profound effect. She drew in several deep breaths to regain control of her body and the situation.

"Maybe we should go somewhere a little more private," she choked out as Melody's toes began a slow rubbing action.

"Or maybe you should just relax and let me do what I want."

"Wh—what do you want to do?" Stacie was on the verge of coming. She mentally began to list the names of all the dead presidents she could remember. Anything to take her mind off the wonderful sensations Melody's toes were creating.

"First, I want you to relax. No one is going to see us, and if they do, they won't say anything. They'll simply watch and wish it were them sitting in your seat. Now, give me some room to show you what I want."

Stacie's heart stuck in her throat. Did she dare?

Melody's foot became more insistent and Stacie felt as though she were looking down on the entire scene from far away. She could almost see Melody's foot nestle deeper between her legs.

"I want to make you come right there in your chair," Melody answered.

Stacie tried her dead presidents trick again, but by now she was having trouble recalling the current president's name. Lust consumed her and to her horror and disbelief, with one last glance around, she obeyed. As she opened her legs, she found her body easing down slightly into the seat, allowing Melody complete access.

"That's better," Melody cooed. "Now relax and enjoy."

Stacie tried to relax, but the knowledge that Zoey could glance over at any moment or that Brenda might decide to join them kept her rigid. Or maybe her tenseness was a result of the pressure from Melody's foot. As the motion grew steadily faster and more insistent, Stacie fought a losing battle with her body's natural urge to move in unison. When the intensity of her desire became unbearable, she reached beneath the table and grabbed Melody's foot, drawing it tighter against her. Stacie felt the first delicious ache of orgasm just out of reach. Melody eased the pressure of her movements. Stacie arched sharply forward, trying to get closer. As she did so, the table slid forward with a loud screech. Stacie was well beyond caring. From a distance, she heard Melody's voice.

"When I turned from the bar and saw you," Melody said in a voice low and teasing, "I knew it was going to be a good evening. I knew you'd spread your legs for me."

"Not here she won't."

Stacie whipped around as one of Zoey's massive hands clamped down on her shoulder. Her lust disappeared faster than a snowfall in August.

"Um, hey, Zoey," she stammered. "What's up?" She suddenly realized that in her desperate chase of Melody's manipulating toes, she had practically scooted herself off the chair. She tried to pull herself back into a normal upright position, but Zoey's hand wasn't going to allow her to move. From across the room, she could see people staring their way and snickering. Sheer mortification quickly replaced the scorching flush of lust.

Zoey leaned forward between them. "I think it's time you left," she said, nodding toward Melody while keeping her hand firmly planted on Stacie's shoulder. "This is your second warning. So don't come back until you can control those toes."

Stacie was certain her face was glowing brighter than the South Padre Lighthouse, but Melody simply shrugged before winking at Stacie and walking away.

"I'll meet you outside," Stacie called after her.

Melody kept walking.

As soon as the door closed behind Melody, Zoey turned to Stacie. "What do you mean, trying to pull that shit in my bar? Do you know what would've happened if Rosie had walked in and caught you two? Or some vice cop? You know how they're always poking around here. They'd love an excuse to shut this place down."

"We weren't doing anything," Stacie squeaked.

Zoey rapped her sharply across the back of her head. "What? You think I'm stupid? The whole place saw you giving her a foot massage with your crotch. Now get on out of here. I don't wanna see you for the next three weeks."

Stacie couldn't stop the whine in her voice. "Come on, Zoey. Not three weeks. That's not fair."

"Go home and take a cold shower." Zoey started walking away and then stopped. "Listen, you're not a bad kid, but you've gotta stop thinkin' with your crotch. I see you in here two, three times a

19

week and you're always leaving with somebody new. There ain't no future in that."

Stacie stood and struggled for a retort that would help salvage what was left of her pride, but for once words failed her.

"Don't come back for three weeks," Zoey reminded her as she walked away.

"Maybe I won't be back at all. You're not the only bar in town."

"Your choice," Zoey said and shrugged.

Stacie could feel the eyes of every woman in the bar following her to the door. She saw Brenda standing by the pool table. For a brief moment she envisioned a wild fantasy of Brenda joining her. They would walk out together and one by one, all of the other women would follow until there was no one left but Zoey.

She squared her shoulders and smirked. Zoey was about to find out that Stacie Gillette was no snot-nosed kid who could be pushed around. She changed her course toward the pool table where Brenda and a small group of women stood staring. As she did so, the women began to turn away from her. Brenda hesitated a moment before shaking her head and turning away.

Memories arrived on black wings with sharp talons poised to shred her confidence. Tears blurred her vision. *To hell with them.* She didn't need the approval of any of those losers. This wasn't the only bar in town. She didn't dwell on the fact that it was the only one she liked. Spinning on her heel, she stormed out the door into a blistering parking lot. She looked around, but Melody hadn't waited for her. *She didn't mean anything to me anyway*, she reminded herself. What a perfect ending for a completely crappy day. *I'm not leaving the house tomorrow*, she told herself as she crossed the parking lot and got into her sweltering car. She inserted the key into the ignition and turned it, only to hear a sickening click. "No," she moaned. She tried cranking the car once more before reaching down and flipping on the radio. Nothing happened. The battery was dead. "This is just fucking great."

She snatched the car keys out of the ignition and threw the car door open before realizing she couldn't go back into the bar. She felt certain Zoey wouldn't be so cold-hearted as not to help her, but she had no intention of going back in and asking. Her apartment wasn't that far from the bar. She'd simply walk home. As she stood by the car, the heat from the parking lot began to seep through the soles of her shoes. She pulled her cell phone off her belt, intending to call Brenda's cell and ask her give her a ride home. Then she remembered how Brenda had turned away from her in the bar.

It's only a few blocks and walking will do me good, she decided. She hadn't been getting enough exercise lately.

Chapter Three

A dagger of sunshine crept through the opened blinds and sliced into Stacie's head. Squeezing her eyes shut, she tried to swallow, but her tongue felt like it had been used to spread asphalt. *Why am I naked?*

She was so dehydrated her salivary glands felt like they had packed up and moved to Nevada. *What did I do last night?* It took a moment for the previous night's events to reassemble themselves into a memory that her diminished brain cells could recognize. She cringed as the previous day and all of its bullshit and humiliation slowly returned. Jack's ultimatum, the way she had allowed a total stranger to manipulate her so completely, not to mention so publicly, then to be tossed out of Rosie's and banished for three weeks as if she were a grounded child, but the worst was Brenda's betrayal. Their friendship was such an integral portion of her life; she took it for granted it would always be there. It was painful enough that Brenda had turned away when Zoey tossed her out, but she hadn't even called afterward to check on her.

The distance from the bar to her apartment had proven much farther than she anticipated. The trek home took over an hour. Her anger grew as the heat from the sidewalk turned her short leather boots into saunas. Buckets of sweat pooled in every crevice on her body. As she stood waiting to cross the street, she spied a familiar yellow sedan. She slapped her head. "You moron, you could have called a cab." With less than two blocks to go, it was pointless to flag it down. She swallowed her frustration and let it drive away.

By the time she finally stumbled into her apartment, she was so hot and exhausted she could barely hobble to the kitchen in search of cool water to ease the ache in her dry throat. Her nearly empty refrigerator revealed a couple of containers of yogurt, an apple that was beginning to hold a strong resemblance to Whistler's Mother, and a nearly full bottle of wine Brenda had left. Surely, there was one miserable bottle of water in the house. She pulled each of the crisper trays open before hobbling to the pantry. Nothing there but a few stale bags of chips and a can of bean dip. She eyed the kitchen faucet and shuddered. Austin city water was notoriously bad, or perhaps it was just the rotten pipes of her forty-year-old apartment building. She was so thirsty maybe it wouldn't matter. She grabbed a cup and filled it with water. The stale stench reached her nose long before she got the cup to her lips. There was no way she could drink that crap. Limping back to the refrigerator, she grabbed the bottle of wine and removed the cork before taking a long gulp. The wine was deliciously cold and went down easily. After a second swig, she made her way to her tiny bathroom and began to fill the tub before stripping down and sliding into the soothing water with the bottle of wine. There she remained until her body took on a prune-like texture and the wine was gone. She retained only the vaguest memory of dragging herself out of the tub and collapsing across her bed, soaking wet.

What a dim-witted thing to do. She had never been a drinker, and now she was paying for her stupidity. Holding her aching head, she eased herself into a semblance of an upright position and squinted at the clock that read twenty minutes past nine. She had forgotten to set the alarm. Jack was sure to give her another lecture on punctuality, but there was no way she could drag herself into the office. She'd have to call in sick. Retrieving the phone by her bed took an exercise in patience. Even the tiniest movement felt like an entire drum corps was marching through her skull. She started gently tapping Jack's phone number in, but stopped and moaned when she remembered the nine-thirty appointment with Cheryl Wright. She hung up the phone and stared forlornly at the clock. The coffee shop was only a few blocks away, but she certainly couldn't rush down there in her current condition.

As she watched the seconds tick off, she realized she wasn't going to make the meeting and Jack would have a stroke when he found out. She sat staring at the phone for several seconds, trying to decide her best course of action. With any luck at all, Cheryl wouldn't call the paper looking for her. The pounding in her head wouldn't allow her to think. *Maybe she never got my message*, she reasoned. *Even if she did, she could have blown it off. Jack said she didn't like the press. I'll call her, maybe she's running late, and I can catch her before she leaves.* Her fingers poised over the phone when she realized she had thrown Cheryl's phone number away.

She put the phone down and clamped both hands over her head. "Think. You can't call Jack and ask him for the number. How can I get the number?"

Through the murky haze numbing her brain, she struggled to recall the number for directory assistance. Slowly her few remaining brain cells converged and transmitted the information to her fingertips. She called and requested Cheryl's number only to discover it was unlisted. Stacie dropped the phone to the bed in frustration. She was going to have to go to the interview.

With the help of the bed and the window frame, she managed to pull herself upright. The room spun and her stomach lurched. She quickly fell back onto the bed. "No way," she mumbled. She couldn't even walk, let alone drive. She groaned. Her car was still at Rosie's with a dead battery. That memory brought back the entire humiliating evening that led up to the predicament she was in now.

I'm not going, she told herself as she dialed Jack's number.

He answered on the second ring and listened quietly as Stacie explained she was sick and wouldn't be able to make the interview with Cheryl Wright. When she finished, she heard him take a deep breath.

"Call and reschedule," he said, "but I meant what I said yesterday. I want that interview on my desk Monday afternoon by four."

The heartless bastard. I'm dying and all he could think about is an interview with a romance writer. "Fine." Stacie considered hanging up, but she really needed the job and she needed Cheryl's number. "Do you have her number? I left the paper you gave me at the office."

He gave her the number. "I hope you feel better," he said as she hung up.

Stacie dialed the number and held the phone slightly away from her ear to case the pounding each ring produced. Cheryl must have already left for the interview. She hung up as soon as the voice mail kicked in. Maybe she could still salvage the interview.

She sat up to set the phone down and the room became a crazed merry-go-round. She grabbed onto the comforter in a desperate attempt to stop the room's whirling. Her stomach gave a sudden sickening roll. Ignoring the heavy metal band practicing inside her head, she ran to the bathroom and threw open the door. A sour wave of stale wine wrapped itself around her. For the first time since moving into her matchbox apartment, Stacie appreciated its compactness as she stepped forward and fell to her knees before the great porcelain throne. Dry heaves bent on ripping her internal organs out left her drenched in sweat and shaking. Several deep breaths finally allowed her to feel confident enough to lean back against the tub. As she did so, her hand bumped something cold. Glancing down, she spied the cause of her misery.

The sight of the empty wine bottle lying alongside the tub threatened to ignite another round of torture. She ripped the hand towel from the rod above her head and used it to cover the vile container, but the stench continued to permeate her nostrils.

With careful deliberation, she picked herself up from the floor and flipped the window latch open. The small shutter-like windows slowly released their grip from the old metal frame before opening and grudgingly allowing a warm breeze to enter. Stacie gulped several deep cleansing breaths before resting her forehead against the middle support of the window frame.

Her life seemed to be spiraling out of control. *You just need to get it together*, she told herself. Her goal of working for a major newspaper was so close she could almost taste it. This was not the time to start screwing around. She forced herself to compose a plan for the day. First, she wanted a cup of coffee, and she needed to buy some basic groceries. She rarely ate at home, but she definitely needed to buy water and coffee. At some point, it occurred to her that she was standing naked in front of an open window and should therefore probably put on her robe, but retrieving it from the back of the door required too much effort.

The doorbell buzzed, causing her to jerk back in surprise. The sudden movement threatened to produce another round of dry heaves. She focused her attention on breathing deeply as the obnoxiously loud buzzer sounded again.

"Go away," she muttered. She didn't feel like talking to anyone today, but her visitor obviously had other ideas as the buzzer droned continuously. Stacie covered her ears in an attempt to block the irritating noise, but her visitor wasn't going away.

She retrieved her robe as quickly as her aching head would allow and stumbled to the door with the intention of using every derogatory adjective and verb in her considerable vocabulary. The sight of the dangling security chain and unlocked deadbolt caused her to pause briefly. She hadn't locked the door the previous evening. Just as she reached for the knob, the door burst open and knocked her backward.

The one time I forget to lock the damn door. Terrified, Stacie scrambled away on her hands and butt.

"Oh. Hi. You should get a dog for protection. I could have been a burglar." Brenda held up her key ring that contained Stacie's spare apartment key. "I didn't even have to use this. Why are you still home?"

Stacie stopped her retreat and collapsed. "Brenda, what in the blue blazes are you doing here?" As her adrenaline rush began to ebb, memories of the previous evening returned. "I don't want a dog or any other animal for that matter. I like living alone. I've told you that a hundred times. Now get out of here. I'm not talking to you," she snapped.

Brenda stepped deeper into the room and eased the door closed. "I know you're mad and you have every right to be. I didn't speak up last night because I didn't think there was any need for both of us to be tossed out. What did you do anyway?"

Stacie sat up and pulled her robe more securely around her. Was Brenda pretending not to know what happened? Had Zoey really kept her mouth shut?

"Zoey didn't tell you?"

Brenda shook her head. "No. I asked her, but she pretty much told me to mind my own business. Were you and that woman you met fighting? I mean, Zoey never tosses anyone out unless they're fighting or she catches them making out big-time in the bathroom." Brenda sat down on the arm of the couch and ran a hand over her chin in concentration.

Stacie held her breath. If Zoey wasn't telling and Brenda hadn't heard anyone else in the bar talking, maybe no one else knew.

"I didn't hear you guys yelling or anything. One minute, everything's fine, and the next Zoey's walking you out the door. What gives? If you guys weren't fighting, then why did Zoey eighty-six you?"

Stacie pulled her exhausted body off the floor and eased it onto a Queen Anne chair that provided more in looks than it did comfort. Brenda really didn't know the reason for Zoey's actions. She tried to think of a logical reason for her expulsion from Rosie's. "You know Zoey never liked me," she started.

"Weird. I always thought she did." Brenda scratched her chin again. "But you weren't fighting and weren't in the bath—" She stopped and stared as if Stacie had suddenly grown an additional head. "Christ in a handbasket. You two were doing it at the table. What were you doing? Man, it had to be plenty for Zoey to toss you." She stood slowly. "That's it, right?" She walked toward Stacie, pointing. "Are you out of your mind? Stacie Marie Gillette, you were making it with a woman you barely knew, in front of Zoey. Are you crazy? You only had a couple of swallows of that beer, so I know you weren't drunk." She rushed on without giving Stacie time to speak. "What possessed you to do something so stupid?" Her voice rose.

Stacie covered her ears, trying to ease the pounding in her head that seemed to be intensifying in equal proportion to Brenda's ranting.

Brenda stopped when she was a couple feet away. "Whew-ee, girl. You stink."

Stacie tried to stare daggers at her, but all she could manage was a grimace. "Why are you here?" she demanded.

Brenda backed up and sat on the couch. "When you didn't return my call from last night, I figured you were really pissed at me."

Stacie glanced at the answering machine and saw the message light blinking. She had been too angry to notice it last night.

"I tried calling you at work a little while ago," Brenda continued. "The woman who answered the phone said you weren't in and no one knew where you were. I thought I'd better come by and check on you. I got scared when you didn't answer the door. My John Wayne act was probably a little bit over the top, but . . ." She shrugged.

Stacie wanted to stay mad. Brenda's desertion the previous night hurt, but if the roles had been reversed, Stacie knew she might have done the same thing. "Thanks for checking on me," she mumbled.

Brenda ducked her head and began to fidget with the hem of

her shorts. "I guess you and your new friend must have had a pretty good time." She smiled as she wiggled her eyebrows.

Stacie sighed before twisting around in a futile attempt to get comfortable. She finally gave up; there was no comfort to be found in the harsh, unyielding chair. "She took off after Zoey tossed us."

"That sucks."

"It gets better. My car battery was dead and I ended up having to walk home."

Brenda's jaw dropped. "You walked home. Why didn't you come back in and tell me? I would have driven you home."

Stacie glared at her. "You weren't exactly at the top of my best-friend list."

Brenda blushed. "Come on, Stacie. If I had caused a scene, Zoey would've tossed me too. You know that. Besides, you didn't think twice about dumping me once Ms. Hot Bod arrived."

"You're supposed to be my friend," Stacie shot back. "And don't tell me you wouldn't have dumped my ass had *Ms. Hot Bod* been looking your way."

"You're right. I'm sorry," Brenda said and shrugged. "I feel horrible you had to walk home."

"Yeah, well, that's not the worst of it. I missed an interview this morning."

"Ouch. Someone important?"

"No, it was just some romance writer, but Jack is riding my butt."

"What a bummer. I'm really sorry."

Stacie let Brenda wallow in her self-condemnation for a few moments before letting her off the hook. "It's okay. I'm over it."

Brenda's head shot up. "Good. You know I don't like it when we're mad at each other."

"Buy me coffee and all's forgiven," Stacie said as she stood. If Brenda drove her, she might still be able to get to the interview with Cheryl Wright.

Brenda hopped up. "I'll run down to the coffee shop on the corner."

Stacie held up her hand. "Give me a minute and I'll go with you. Then you can help me with my car afterward."

"Well . . ."

The hesitation in Brenda's voice made her turn. "Sorry," Stacie said. "I guess you have something else to do on your day off."

Brenda shook her head. "No." She glanced at Stacie and smiled sheepishly. "I'm in no hurry. Go ahead and shower. I'll wait."

Stacie put her hands on her hips. "What are you trying to say?"

Brenda pinched her nose. "You smell like those old whiskey barrels over at Home Depot."

Stacie stuck out her tongue. "It's your fault for buying that nasty cheap wine."

"You drank my wine?"

"I was dying of thirst after having to walk home from the bar. It was either the wine or tap water."

"Oh. Yeah, I see your point." Brenda slipped into a chair to wait.

Chapter Four

The large teacup-shaped clock behind the counter at Hav-A-Java showed six minutes after ten when Stacie and Brenda walked into the crowded shop.

Feeling only slightly better after downing a couple of pain relievers and taking a hot shower, Stacie gave a slow glance around the room before realizing it was useless since she had no idea what Cheryl Wright looked like. A sense of guilt crept over her. She hadn't been very professional in setting up the interview. Then she remembered Cheryl hanging up on her when she called the first time. It was Cheryl's fault, she decided. After all, the paper was doing her a favor by interviewing her. Most authors would've been jumping at the chance of free publicity.

"I'll get the coffee. You grab us a table. The usual?" Brenda asked.

"Yeah."

Stacie spied a vacant table near the back corner and began

weaving her way toward it. With slow deliberation, she worked her way through a treacherous path of briefcases, backpacks and a mass of humanity who all seemed bent on talking too loud. She was only two tables away from her objective when a woman suddenly shot up from her chair. Stacie stepped back to avoid her and as she did, her foot came down on a slippery mass. As if in a dream, she felt her foot lose traction and start to slide from beneath her. Instinctively she grabbed out for the nearest support and caught nothing but air. The back of her hand slapped against something and before she knew it, she was lying on the floor with warm, sticky liquid running in her face.

Her immediate thought was, *I'm bleeding*. A quick swipe of her face with her hand revealed nothing more damaging than the luke-warm remains of a cup of coffee.

"Are you all right?"

Stacie looked up to find a slightly overweight woman staring down at her. Blood rushed to her face so quickly she felt light-headed as she forced herself to sit up. She quickly became the center of attention. Members of the staff hovered over her. A young man kept trying to wipe the mess from her face and shirt with a towel. When she noticed his attempt in helping seemed directed more to the front of her shirt than necessary; she grabbed the towel from him with a glare that sent him scurrying back to the counter. She wiped off her arm and glanced around self-consciously. She saw Brenda standing in line and shrugged in embarrassment.

Brenda rolled her eyes and gave her the old *I don't believe you did that* look.

Before Stacie could respond, someone was at her side.

"Are you okay?"

Stacie glanced around to find the same woman who had asked earlier. "Yes. I'm fine." With a final assurance that there wasn't an impending lawsuit, the rest of the staff returned to work, leaving her with the woman.

"I'm really sorry," the woman said. "It was entirely my fault. I didn't even look before I got up."

Stacie waved it off. "It's all right. No damage done."

"I doubt that," the woman said and pointed to Stacie's shirt.

Seeing the large stain, Stacie shrugged. "It's only a shirt."

The woman smiled so brightly that Stacie found herself doing a double take and staring into eyes the color of cornflowers. The woman appeared to be in her early thirties. Her shoulder-length dark hair framed a pretty face, but she was carrying a few extra pounds. A wedding band gleamed as the woman pushed her hair back.

Nice hands, Stacie thought. *Too bad she's married. Of course, she's a little heavy for my taste, but still she's not bad-looking.*

"It's nice to meet someone who isn't so wrapped up in worldly possessions," the woman said as she held out her hand. "I'm—"

"Stacie, are you okay?"

They both turned to find Brenda hovering behind them with two large cups of coffee.

"I'm fine."

"Girl, are you still drunk or what?" Brenda laughed.

Stacie glanced toward the woman, who was staring at her. *She probably hasn't even been out by herself in ten years*, Stacie thought. "I partied a little too much last night," Stacie couldn't help but brag.

"A little," Brenda crowed. "She was so hung over she couldn't drag her sorry butt to work this morning."

A cloud of disapproval darkened the woman's face. "You must have a very understanding boss."

The statement was clearly a rebuff. Stacie felt a desperate need to defend herself. "My job is fairly flexible. I pretty much set my own hours."

"That's nice," the woman said as she retrieved a large bag from the chair next to her.

The well of frustration building within Stacie over the previous twenty-four hours was beginning to splash over. "I'm a reporter," she insisted.

The woman didn't reply. It was obvious Stacie's credentials didn't impress her.

33

"I work for the *Voice of Texas*," she continued. Why was she wasting her time trying to impress this stranger?

Brenda chose the moment to come to her aid. "Yeah, she missed an interview with a famous writer today."

The woman glanced up.

Stacie almost winked at Brenda. That got the old girl's attention.

"A writer?" the woman asked.

Stacie had her attention now. She decided to play it nonchalant and shrugged. "It was nothing."

"But your friend just said you missed the interview," the woman pointed out.

Stacie leaned forward as if sharing a secret. "It wasn't important. It was only a romance writer. My readers don't really care about that. They're more interested in real writing. I normally wouldn't even bother with something like that. I was only doing the interview as a favor to my editor. My specialty is investigative reporting."

"I'm surprised to hear there wouldn't be any interest for such an interview," the stranger said. "I was under the impression that the romance genre is one of the leading book markets."

"Not really. Sure they may have volume, but look at who's reading that crap. Housewives. Women who are already so bored out of their gourds they wouldn't know real literature if it slapped them upside the head. Face it, if they had any actual skills they would be writing real literature."

The woman's face blazed several different shades of red and her body language had definitely turned hostile. Stacie vaguely noticed Brenda taking a step back from them. At the same instant, an odd heaviness started building in the pit of her stomach. She and the woman continued to stare at each other.

It can't possibly be, she told herself. *There's no way the gods would be so cruel.* She looked into the woman's eyes and knew she was royally screwed. "What did you say your name was?" she asked in a voice that made her sound about seven.

The woman reached into the bag and pulled out a book. She slapped it into Stacie's hand before stalking away.

"Wow. That was weird," Brenda said as she sat down and removed the lid from her coffee.

Stacie took a deep breath and turned the book until she could read the title, *On the Wings of Love*. The author's name slithered across the bottom in what seemed like four-inch type: CHERYL WRIGHT.

"What's wrong?"

Stacie shook her head. "I don't believe it." She tossed the book onto the table and sat down. "Why is my life turning to crap all of a sudden?"

Brenda picked up the book and read the cover. "Why did she give you this book?"

"That was Cheryl Wright. The woman I was supposed to be interviewing this morning. The woman you were kind enough to explain my hangover to."

Brenda eased the book back down on the table. "Oh."

"Oh," Stacie repeated. "That's all you can say?"

Brenda shrugged. "Hey, you're the one who told her she was just a romance writer with no skills, who no one of real consequence wanted to read about. Well, except for those bored housewives, that is."

Stacie dropped her head into her hands. "Tell me that's not what I said."

"Yeah, that's pretty much what you said."

Stacie moaned. "Just shoot me now."

Brenda swatted Stacie's arm. "Come on. It's not that bad. Drink your coffee before it gets cold."

"Jack told me to get the interview or else."

"Or else what?"

"Or else he'd have my library card revoked. What do you think he meant, Brenda?"

Brenda took a long drink from her iced coffee. "He won't do

anything. With all those stories you've been getting. You're their golden child. He wouldn't fire you, would he?"

Stacie pried the lid from her coffee and took a tentative sip. When she was sure her stomach wasn't going to reject the savory brew, she tried another sip. "I don't know. He seemed pretty pissed yesterday morning." She quickly told Brenda about the incident with Congressman Manchester.

"Let me see if I've got this right. Jack was ticked off because he saved space in the paper for your interview, and when you didn't come through, they all had to jump through their butts to fill the space because the paper was about to be printed," Brenda summarized.

Listening to Brenda's recap made Stacie uncomfortable. "Something like that."

"Yeah, I guess I can see his point," Brenda said and nodded. "You probably should watch you Ps and Qs for a while."

"Well, thank you for your encouraging insight," Stacie said.

They sat in silence for several minutes and drank their coffee.

"Do you want to go check on your car?" Brenda asked.

Stacie leaned back in her chair. "I guess I'd better. Then I'm going to have to call Cheryl Wright and see if I can smooth things over."

"I don't know, Stacie. She was pretty mad. Maybe you should give her some time to cool down."

"I have to have the story to Jack by four Monday afternoon," Stacie said.

"That gives you all weekend." Brenda picked up the book. "Hey, I know. Read her book. Then call her up and tell her how much you enjoyed it."

Stacie rolled her eyes. "I'm not wasting my weekend reading a romance novel."

"There's nothing wrong with romance novels," Brenda protested.

"How many have you read?"

Brenda looked around and leaned forward. "I've read a few, but my mom and sister read these things by the dozen. They love them."

"Why? They're ridiculous."

"How would you know if you've never read one?" Brenda challenged.

"I don't have to drop a brick on my toe to know it hurts."

Brenda stood. "I swear, Stacie. Sometimes you are so self-righteous I don't know why I bother talking to you."

"Because someday I'll be famous and you can tell everyone you knew me when," Stacie half-teased as she placed the lid back on her coffee and tucked Cheryl's book under her arm.

"Well, I'm not sure being crazy has ever made anyone famous, but if you say so. Now, let's go get that car of yours. I have things to do. Did I tell you about the new love of my life?"

"No. Please don't. I've suffered enough for one day," Stacie said with a moan as they left the coffee shop.

As they drove to the bar, Stacie tuned Brenda out and tried to think of a way to get back into Cheryl's good graces. *Not that I've ever been in her good graces*, she amended.

Chapter Five

It was after one that afternoon before they finished replacing the battery in Stacie's car. After leaving Brenda, Stacie made a trip to the grocery store to stock up on coffee, water and a few food items. By the time she had returned home and put everything away, she was exhausted. Too tired to cook, she made herself a quick sandwich and dialed Cheryl Wright's number. She was about to hang up when Cheryl finally answered.

"Ms. Wright, this is Stacie Gillette." Silence met her announcement. She shocked herself by rushing to fill the void. "I apologize for this morning. I did try to call you to cancel, but you had already left. Please let me make it up to you. Perhaps you would let me take you to dinner at the Driscoll tonight or tomorrow night. The food there is unbelievable." She wasn't worried about the cost. The newspaper would reimburse her for any meal expense incurred with a client.

"No. Thank you. I have no desire to be stood up again."

Stacie could feel the frost in Cheryl's voice seep through the phone. "I said I'm sorry. I'd like to make it up to you."

"Ms. Gillette—"

"Call me Stacie."

"Ms. Gillette, you should know I've already talked to my publicist about our earlier encounter and requested she contact your editor to inform him that I'm no longer interested in giving an interview."

"Dang," Stacie whined. "Why did you do that?"

"I really need to get back to work. I'm sorry, but I have a deadline."

"Well, I certainly wouldn't want you to miss a deadline. I'm sure there's a horde of anxious readers sitting on the edge of their chairs in anticipation of the next Cheryl Wright romance."

"Good-bye, Ms. Gillette."

The phone went dead before Stacie could respond. "Geez, lady. You're way too impressed with yourself," Stacie growled. The low battery indicator light on the handset distracted her from her impending tirade of Cheryl Wright's faults.

Stacie considered her options as she tapped the phone against her thigh. She felt certain she could eventually convince the woman to give her an interview. The short timeframe was the problem. She didn't have the time necessary to allow Cheryl to cool down. If she was going to have the story on Jack's desk by four Monday afternoon, she would have to have the interview completed by no later than noon Monday. Somehow she needed to find a way to keep Cheryl on the phone long enough to pacify her. Roses might do the trick, but since flowers didn't qualify as a reimbursable expense, she would save them as a last resort. Flattery would probably work. She could read the jacket cover, along with the first and last chapters of Cheryl's book and call her to tell her how much she loved the book. She grimaced at the thought of having to read even the jacket cover. It would be easier to send the flowers. Suddenly it hit her: Cheryl Wright was a lesbian.

Stacie slapped her forehead. "I'm such a ditz." She'd been

thinking of her as a straight woman. "Why did I think she was straight?" She puzzled over the situation as she carried the phone back into the living room to return it to the base. *Wedding band.* Stacie recalled the light catching on the gold band Cheryl had worn. *That's it.* She had associated the band with her being married and had completely forgotten that she was a lesbian.

With that mystery solved, Stacie went back to her original dilemma. How was she going to keep Cheryl on the phone long enough to win her over? As she replaced the handset, she noticed the message light blinking on her answering machine. She punched the replay button, knowing it was Brenda's message. To her surprise, six messages awaited her attention. She cringed as she always did when she heard the voice of the first caller.

"Stacie Lynn, it's your mama. Your daddy and me were wonderin' when you might be plannin' on comin' home to visit. Your sister Junie is havin' another baby in late September. I pray every night that she'll be all right. You know little Tommy, who you ain't never seen, is only a year old, and Doc Kurtz told her she ought not be havin' any more babies. He wants her to stay in bed, but you know your sister. The Good Lord only knows what's goin' on in that girl's head. Her and Bill are still livin' here with your daddy and me."

Stacie punched the erase button and wiped the sudden onslaught of sweat away from her eyes. Her family was her best-kept secret. She let everyone, including Brenda, believe she was from Lubbock, when in fact she had grown up in Wilburn, a town so small it only required one stop sign and Main Street was a gravel road. She didn't consider telling people this too much of a lie since Lubbock was the closest city of any size, even though it was almost two hours away from Wilburn by car.

Her family now owned the house and a small piece of land that produced enough for them to eat and little else. Every year her father would plant the same sad crop of onions and her mom would plant a large garden that would feed them for the next year. At an early age, Stacie discovered education was going to be her key to escaping Wilburn's poverty. When she received a full scholarship to the University of Texas at Austin, she grabbed it and never looked back. Since leaving Wilburn, she had been back twice, once for her grandmother's funeral and a year later for her grandfather's funeral. She entertained no plans of returning anytime soon.

The next message was from Brenda. Since she had already talked to Brenda, she erased it also. The third caller was a hang-up. The fourth and fifth calls were from Jack asking her to call him. She knew she was in deep shit when the sixth call was Jack as well.

"I've been trying to call you all afternoon, so I'm assuming you are either so sick you're at the hospital or else you're not as interested in working as I thought you were. Stacie, I received a very disturbing call from Cheryl Wright's publicist. You and I need to talk. I'll be in the office until six today, so call me if you get this message in time. I'm leaving tonight for a conference in Dallas, so I won't be here this weekend, but I want you in my office at seven sharp Monday morning. I can only hope that you'll use the time between now and then to consider your future with us. It's important to me that my employees are happy, so if you're not, then we need to discuss ways to correct the problem."

"You can correct the problem by getting off my ass and stop giving me these bullshit assignments." Stacie slapped the button to erase all of the messages. She did not intend to call him back today. He would be a lot calmer come Monday. Now, on top of trying to find a way to finesse Cheryl Wright, she was going to have to think of something to appease Jack.

A dull headache began at the base of her skull. She ran a hand across the back of her neck and slowly massaged it. Why couldn't he just let her do her job? She was a great reporter, but he was always trying to sideline her with these goofball assignments. Nobody was interested in reading about the life of a romance writer. "Someday," she muttered.

She focused her attention on the problem of getting an interview with Cheryl Wright. *If I arrive Monday morning with the interview in hand, then Jack will be satisfied and both problems are solved.*

What she needed to do was see Cheryl face-to-face. It was much easier to be persuasive in person than over the phone. Just turn on the Stacie Gillette charm full force and Cheryl would quickly become putty in her hands. In truth, Cheryl wasn't a bad-looking woman. If she would let her hair grow out and lose a few pounds, she'd be cute.

That's the solution. If I can't get Cheryl to come to me, then I'll go to Cheryl. Stacie started flipping through the cards in her Rolodex. Surely she knew someone who could get the address for her. Almost halfway through the file she found the number she needed, a man who worked at the electric company. He had been her contact when she did the piece on the environmental impact of fossil fuels. She rubbed her hands together and smiled. Her luck was about to turn itself around. She dialed the number and silently cheered when he answered on the second ring.

Chapter Six

At ten-thirty that same Friday night, Stacie walked into the Yellow Rose, a predominately country-western club that played a decent variety of music. As soon as she walked in, a wall of noise and cigarette smoke enveloped her. To say it was standing room only would have been a major understatement. As Stacie inched toward the bar, a boot heel came down on her toe. Her yelp of pain was lost in the insulated air of two hundred conversations.

She disliked crowds. Given that there were only two women's bars in town and Rosie's was no longer an option, she couldn't afford to be fussy in her selection. Tonight, she was going to celebrate her latest bout of brilliance. She now possessed the information she needed to get an interview with Cheryl Wright.

Her contact at the electric company had balked slightly when she asked him for Cheryl's address, but the offer of a small monetary donation convinced him to meet her with the information. After meeting him, Stacie drove to the address he gave her. An

Austin street map indicated the house was located in an older, upscale residential area of Austin. In actual miles, the neighborhood was not that far from Stacie's apartment. Economically it was halfway to the moon. She drove along stately streets lined with enormous pecan and oak trees. Despite the recent heat wave, the vegetation was still lush and green here.

These were people with some serious money, she thought as she spied the house number she was searching for. The house, an elegant, single-level traditional country with a covered front porch and side garage, sat on a large lot. Stacie gave the house very little attention. She took her time admiring the red XK8 convertible Jag that sat in the driveway. Stacie gave a low whistle of appreciation before shaking her head. This couldn't be the place.

"That asshole ripped me off." She was about to call the guy from the electric company back and demand he return her money when she noticed the opened garage door. Dozens of packing cartons filled the garage. "Ho, ho." Stacie stared in surprise. "I guess romance novels pay better than I thought," she muttered as she glanced from the sleek Jag to the ripped interior of her own six-year-old Mazda.

A surge of movement snapped Stacie back to the Yellow Rose. The DJ was announcing seventy-five-cent shots for the next ten minutes. Stacie let herself be swept along with the flow of people. It was easier than trying to fight the crowd.

The club consisted of two large rooms separated by a rise of four steps. In the lower room, a split-rail fence surrounded the enormous dance floor. The fence was to protect the whirling dancers from the mass of humanity on the other side, or perhaps it was the other way around. The tables bordering the outside of the fence were made from lengths of wood slabs. Each slab, slathered in enough coats of polyurethane to deter even the most determined penknife, was supported by short sections of tree stumps. Women of all ages, shapes and sizes, wearing everything from blue jeans and western shirts to business suits complete with skirts and heels, packed the dance floor. Stacie spied a small sprinkling of men among the crowd, something she rarely saw at Rosie's.

The bar, constructed of unpainted planks, sat on the upper section and ran the width of the building. Six bartenders worked at a frantic pace trying to keep up with thirsty patrons. Judging from the lines, Stacie decided it was a losing battle. The massive bar could have graced the saloons in any of the old western movies her dad had loved to watch. She remembered her mother's phone message and shuddered. She didn't want to go home. There were too many memories.

A small space appeared on the stairs. Stacie scooted into it and inched her way toward the bar. In her own way, she loved her family and gladly sent money home every month to help them out, but she had no desire to go back, even for a short visit.

Stacie was almost to the bar when someone jostled her, almost knocking her down. She turned to let her annoyance be known and found herself gazing into eyes of liquid jade. *I'm such a sucker for eyes.*

The woman tossed a mane of long chestnut hair over her shoulder before leaning against her and shouting, "I'm sorry."

Stacie smiled and shouted in return, "I'll survive."

The woman looked her up and down. "I should hope so."

It took Stacie a moment to realize that the woman was actually in line for the bar, but the line was so long it was starting to wrap around.

"Can I get you something?" Stacie pointed toward the bar.

"Thanks, but I'm with friends and I have to get their drinks too."

"No problem. What do you need?" Stacie heard the woman behind her start to grumble but couldn't care less. She was on the make and those green eyes were the only thing that interested her now.

"Three Bud Lights." She pressed a bill into Stacie's hand. "We're at a table in the corner. Come and sit with us," she yelled and pointed toward the back.

The line began to move, separating them and making conversation impossible. Stacie watched her disappear in the direction she had pointed. The crowd quickly swallowed her.

Stacie finally made her way to the head of the line and placed her order for four beers. The next challenge came in trying to push her way to the back of the dimly lit room without dropping the bottles. She reached the corner but couldn't find the woman. She turned to make her way across the room when she saw someone waving at her. As she drew nearer, she saw three women at the table, but the only one she paid any attention to was the one with those amazing eyes.

If possible, the music seemed to be even louder back here. Stacie glanced up and saw the large speaker attached to the ceiling directly over the table. She groaned inwardly as she passed out the beers and waved to the three women. She saw one of the other two women shake her head and frown when the green-eyed woman patted the empty chair next to her. Stacie glanced at the disapproving woman, but she had turned away. Her rude behavior was quickly forgotten when a mane of chestnut hair fell across Stacie's arm and warm lips brushed her ear. "I'm Trish and this is Linda and Julie."

"Stacie," she yelled back, trying to control the delicious shudder that raced up and down her spine at the touch of Trish's lips against her ear.

Stacie and Trish attempted to talk, but the music was too loud. Stacie finally smiled and shrugged in resignation. Stacie's back was to the dance floor. The only thing she could see was a large television mounted on the wall. A baseball game was on and every once in a while the group of women sitting next to them would roar. It was difficult to determine if they were roaring in approval or disapproval. Stacie sipped her beer and cursed the deafening noise that was keeping her from talking to the beauty next to her. She began devising a plan to get them out of the bar. Suddenly, the music switched over to a throbbing disco beat. The other two women jumped up and rushed off in the direction of the dance floor.

Trish grabbed Stacie's hand. The manic crush of people racing for the dance floor quickly swallowed them. As the crowd surged forward, Stacie experienced a moment of panic as her foot became entangled with someone else's. She fell against the person in front of her, but the denseness of the crowd kept her upright and she managed to get her feet underneath her.

The dance floor reminded her of the packages of vacuum-packed coffee she purchased while in college. The package would be rock hard until she made a tiny slit in the wrapping, and then the coffee would instantly dissolve into thousands of individual granules. She closed her eyes and envisioned the club's outer shell being ripped away and the mass of dancers spreading out across the surrounding area. She could almost feel the refreshing rush of air encircle her. Rather than the breathing room she was dreaming of, she instead felt the pressure from the crowd increase slightly. She opened her eyes to find Trish staring at her and smiling. Their bodies were molded together.

Stacie saw Trish's mouth moving, but the music was so loud Stacie couldn't hear her. She tried to raise her arms but found the crush of people allowed her limited movement. Her hands settled on Trish's hips.

Trish slid her arms around Stacie's waist and began a slow bump and grind movement against Stacie that seemed to have little to do with the actual tempo of the music.

A quick glance around her revealed nothing but a sea of bopping heads. Stacie relaxed and let herself enjoy the feel of Trish's body grinding against her. The music never stopped but blended smoothly into one composition. At some point, she became aware of a second pair of hands around her waist and a pelvis grinding against her ass. A wave of desire shot through her. As the stranger's movements became more insistent, Stacie slid one hand behind her and encountered the bare flesh of a thigh. A hand grabbed

Stacie's and guided it beneath what she suspected was an extremely short skirt.

She ran her fingers beneath the damp panties and groaned as she encountered the creamy welcome. The dancer began a slow rocking motion against Stacie's fingers.

Stacie's knees grew weak as her need to touch the stranger took control. With her free hand, she pulled Trish's face to her and kissed her. As the kiss grew in intensity, she allowed her hand to drift downward until it found itself between Trish's legs. Her tongue pushed deeper into Trish's devouring mouth as Trish began to move against her hand. The course texture of Trish's jeans grinding against her hand gave an odd counterpoint to the soft flesh of the woman's wetness on her other hand. The dancers around them seemed oblivious to what they were doing. Stacie wondered how many other dancers were involved in the same urgent pursuit. The movements of the woman behind her became more insistent. Stacie pushed a finger into her and slowly withdrew it. The arms around her waist tightened and trapped her hand.

Trish pulled away from Stacie slightly and her hands dropped from her waist. For a moment, Stacie feared she had discovered what was happening behind her, but the thought was quickly erased as Trish grabbed her hand and guided it inside Trish's opened jeans.

Stacie felt as if she had died and gone to heaven as the two women rocked in opposite directions against her hands. She felt a surge of power rip through her as she stroked them both. The woman behind her was about to come, but Stacie refused her the release she was so desperately seeking. Stacie kissed Trish, urging her on. Suddenly the two women's movements synchronized and Stacie found herself between two hot desperate women. To prolong the pleasure she teased them both with a soft, wide circling motion. Slowly she decreased the size of the circle and gently increased the pressure. Both of their bodies moved closer to her. She increased the pressure of her touch. As the two women came simultaneously in a sea of withering bodies, Stacie felt as though she were stroking the entire room to orgasm.

For several seconds, the shaking bodies leaned against Stacie for support. The three of them stood unmindful to the swirling tide of dancers around them. The woman behind Stacie gave her hand a quick squeeze before easing it from her panties and disappearing. At almost the same moment, Trish pulled away. A second later, she took Stacie's hand and began making her way off the dance floor. Stacie glanced eagerly around the dance floor looking for the other woman. To her disappointment, no one made eye contact or waved a greeting of acknowledgment.

As Trish led her across the room, Stacie began to reflect on the last two nights. Was she becoming an exhibitionist? For two nights in a row, she had eagerly participated in public sex acts. She pushed the previous night away. It still left her feeling strangely uneasy. Why didn't tonight leave her feeling the same way? Could it have been because Melody had control last night, while tonight had clearly been in her own hands? She chuckled at the unintended play on words.

Trish led her outside to a large patio. The relief Stacie felt in stepping out of the sweltering mass was so profound it was almost as if a physical weight had been removed from her.

Trish led them to the back of the patio. The farther they went from the door, the more the music receded. Trish gathered her hair and held it up to allow the cool breeze access.

Stacie sensed a sudden shyness in Trish and waited as she rushed on to fill the silence.

"I usually sit out here, but Linda and Julie prefer to sit inside, and since I'm here with them tonight . . ." Trish waved her hands.

"I can't believe how loud the music is?" Stacie said. Her ears were ringing.

Trish seemed to hesitate. "I'm sorry, but I didn't catch your name in there."

"Stacie."

"Hi, Stacie, I'm Trish." She stepped forward and extended her hand. It felt cool against Stacie's.

"I've not seen you around here before," Trish said. "I know I would remember you." She slowly withdrew her hand, but continued to stand at Stacie's side.

Stacie smiled. She was back in her element. "I usually go to Rosie's."

"Ugh."

"What? Rosie's is nice."

Trish shook her head. "The place is fine, but every time I go there, I feel like I'm on display. It's a major meat market. I stopped by there last week and this woman kept hitting on me."

Stacie considered bringing up the incident on the dance floor but decided against it. Trish didn't seem eager to discuss the event. She ran a finger along Trish's arm. "As beautiful as you are, I can't believe you're only hit on when you go to Rosie's." Stacie saw a flicker of irritation in Trish's eyes.

"I don't normally . . . do that. What happened in there wasn't normal for me." She nodded toward the door.

"Nor for me," Stacie admitted. Although she couldn't pinpoint the reason why, Stacie wasn't sure she believed Trish.

Trish looked boldly into Stacie's eyes. "I guess I'm supposed to believe that."

"It's true. Why wouldn't you believe it?"

Trish turned her attention to the plants that were growing along the wall near them. "I can't believe I put your hand in my pants. What if someone had seen us?"

Stacie felt her face glow. So Trish didn't know about the other woman. "It was way too crowded for anyone to see. It just happened. I don't usually do things like that," Stacie said. She thought she sensed tenseness in Trish. Thinking it was shyness she stepped back to give her some space.

Trish took a deep breath and turned to look at Stacie. "That was pretty awesome. If that wasn't normal, what do you usually do?"

Stacie pulled her into her arms and kissed her softly. "I prefer a quieter setting with a lot less people," she whispered into Trish's long chestnut hair.

Trish leaned into her. "I like a woman of action."

Stacie had no intention of letting things get out of her control again. "My car is parked down the street. Why don't we go for a ride?"

Trish hesitated as she gazed at her. "I probably shouldn't. I sort of told someone I'd meet her here tonight."

Stacie stepped back again. "I didn't realize you were seeing someone." She wasn't about to become the third point of a triangle. There were plenty of single women available.

Trish shook her head. "I'm not seeing her. We've never gone out and in truth, I don't really even want to see her tonight. She was kind of insistent and I told her I might be here."

She's fair game, Stacie reasoned. "In that case, let's go for a ride." She kissed Trish again.

"I have to let my friends know I'm leaving," Trish said.

"You go tell them. I'll meet you outside the front door." Stacie kissed her again, but this time she put some steam behind the kiss. She didn't release Trish until their bodies were straining against each other. "Come on," Stacie whispered, leading Trish inside where they separated.

As Stacie pushed and squeezed her way to the front door, she spied Brenda fighting her way through the crowd to the bar. She yelled, trying to catch Brenda's attention, but the deafening noise made her attempt as effective as shouting in a room filled with cotton. She debated the chance of being able to catch up to her. Was Brenda looking for her? Why wasn't she at Rosie's?

Stacie tried to turn toward Brenda but quickly realized it would take her much too long to fight her way across the room. If she kept Trish waiting, the woman Trish was supposed to meet might show up. She gave up her attempted pursuit of Brenda and pushed her way outside where she let her memory drift back to enjoy every aspect of that dance.

Chapter Seven

Ten minutes later, Trish rushed out the door and grabbed Stacie's hand. "Let's go."

Stacie chuckled. This woman was ready to go.

"I live across town," Trish said as they walked to Stacie's car. "And I have a roommate."

Stacie swallowed her groan. She occasionally took women to her apartment, but she preferred not to. It was so much easier to get up and sneak out of someone else's place, if things didn't go well.

Although the streets were well lit and there were other people nearby, Trish kept glancing behind them.

"It's all right," Stacie assured her. "No one's going to bother us."

As they turned the corner, Trish threw one last glance over her shoulder before turning to Stacie and smiling. "You're right. I'm just being silly."

They were barely in the car when Trish began to kiss her. As the kisses became more urgent, Stacie felt the buttons on her shirt being released. "Whoa. Let's save this until we get home. I don't live that far away." She tried to get the key inserted into the ignition.

"No," Trish insisted. "I can't wait. I have to feel you now."

Stacie glanced around. They were parked in the middle of the lot and there were several cars on either side; however, the owners of those cars could appear at any moment. Austin was a liberal city, but being caught in a parking lot doing your lesbian girlfriend probably wasn't the smartest idea.

"Trish. Come on. Hold up."

Trish stopped suddenly and leaned back to glare at her. "What's the matter with you? I thought you were hot. Why are you suddenly going Prudeville on me?"

"Prudeville?" Stacie stared at her. "What are you talking about? Come home with me and I'll show you who's a prude."

Trish laughed harshly. "But I'll have to go home with you to find out. What happened to the awesome chick who screwed two women at once on the dance floor?"

Stacie frowned. "How did you know about . . . ?"

Trish laughed again. "Oh, please. Do you think someone just walked up to you and stuck their pussy on your hand?"

Stacie leaned farther back from Trish. She didn't like where this was going.

"It was Linda," Trish cried and threw up her hands. "We decided you would be cool enough to handle it. We do it all the time."

Stacie rubbed her forehead in confusion. "But how did you know I would be here?" Her confusion grew. "I've never met you before."

Trish rolled her eyes and fell back against the seat. "You don't get it. We saw you come in and you looked cool. So we chose you."

"You chose me?"

"Yeah. You don't think I just happened to bump into you, did you?"

Stacie shook her head. "I'm not sure what's going on here, and I'm not sure I even want to know." She pushed the key into the ignition. Suddenly she didn't want to do anything but go home. Alone. She pulled the key from the ignition. "Maybe we should just forget about tonight. Come on. I'll walk you back to the bar and you can go home with your friends."

"Geez Louise, I don't believe you," Trish huffed. "And I thought you were so cool."

Rather than getting out, as Stacie had anticipated, Trish leaned across the console and kissed her again.

"Don't be mad at me," Trish said. "If you want to go back to your place, fine. Let's go. I'll be good." She trailed a line of kisses along Stacie's jaw. "I'm just so hot for you I can't wait. You really turned me on in there."

Stacie tried to regain the passion she had felt earlier on the dance floor, but all she could think about was that they had set her up. The entire act had been planned. *But you enjoyed it*, a small voice nagged. *Don't blow a good thing*. Trish would probably be explosive in bed. Stacie forced herself to return the kiss.

"Umm. That's better, baby. Kiss me again," Trish whispered. "Kiss me the way you did while we were dancing."

As she turned sideways for a better position, Stacie's hand accidentally brushed across Trish's breast. The nipple instantly hardened, causing Stacie to groan with desire.

Trish moaned. "Harder, baby." She placed Stacie's hand over her breast and squeezed.

Stacie's thumb and forefinger took on a life of their own and gently began to manipulate the swollen nipple.

"Yes," Trish whispered in a voice thick with desire. She kissed Stacie again.

Stacie's better judgment told her to drive home, but she was already well beyond the point of stopping. She slid the seat back to its farthest position from the steering wheel, pulled Trish into her lap and kissed her passionately.

Trish pulled away just long enough to yank her shirt off over her head. As Stacie watched in eager anticipation, Trish released her bra and flung it away.

The glow from the nearby streetlights presented Stacie with a fabulous view of Trish's full breasts. Stacie's mouth found first one then the other. When Trish rose to her knees and leaned over her, Stacie almost came by herself.

Trish began to wiggle and Stacie realized she was coming out of her jeans. Stacie thought she should protest, but the musky scent of Trish's desire reached her nostrils and her lips ached to taste her.

The car rocked wildly as Trish struggled to free herself from the confining jeans. They both jumped when a horn blew.

Stacie gave a nervous laugh when she realized that one of them had bumped the horn. Probably Trish, since she was practically sitting on the steering wheel. By some miracle, the jeans finally came off and still Stacie's lips couldn't reach their destination. "I've got to taste you," she said with a moan. *Damn console.*

"Put the seat back," Trish instructed.

Stacie fumbled for the tiny lever next to her door that would drop the seat back, but her arm was trapped between Trish's legs. "I can't reach it," she cried in frustration.

Trish was balanced precariously over Stacie. "Let me sit up a little and then you'll be able to pull your arm out."

Stacie waited until Trish pulled her legs up and planted a foot on either side of Stacie's legs. With room to free her arm, she reached down and tilted the seat back. Already savoring what was to come, she scooted down in the seat to give them both more space. As she did so, she saw something that caused her to freeze. Silhouetted against the streetlights was a figure standing in front of the car watching them. She had a fleeing image of what the individual must be seeing—her scooting down between Trish's legs and Trish's bare bottom up over the steering wheel.

"Hurry up. What's taking so long?" Trish hissed.

"Someone's out there," Stacie whispered.

"Where?"

"Standing in front of the car."

"Man or woman?"

"I can't tell. It's too dark."

"What should we do?" Trish asked, a tinge of fear creeping into her voice.

Stacie glanced at the keys still dangling in the ignition. She had a vision of speeding out of the parking lot with Trish's butt glued to the windshield. A nervous giggle escaped.

"What the hell are you laughing about?" Trish demanded as she began struggling to get into the passenger seat.

Before Stacie could answer, the person in front of the car turned to walk away and Stacie's knees went weak with relief as the streetlight illuminated the person's features. It was Brenda. Stacie opened the door. "I know who it is." She stepped halfway out of the car. "Brenda."

She didn't stop.

Why didn't she stop? She must have heard me.

"Geez Louise." Trish gasped as she struggled to get her clothes back on.

Stacie got out of the car. "Brenda, wait up. It's me—Stacie," she yelled.

"Get back in here," Trish hissed.

Stacie leaned down to peer inside the car. "It's okay. It's a friend of mine. I'll be right back." As she walked away, Trish was still calling her name.

Brenda was practically running. Stacie called out to her again and started jogging after her when Brenda didn't slow down. *What is going on?* Stacie wondered as she took off after Brenda. *Maybe she's embarrassed to have caught us.* But that wasn't like Brenda. She was more the type to walk up, rap on the car window and, with that silly grin of hers, ask if they were busy.

"Brenda," Stacie yelled again. As she ran after Brenda, she realized that Trish was running after her. *We must look like idiots.*

Although she had a head start, Brenda couldn't match Stacie's speed. When Stacie finally caught up to her and grabbed her arm, she was shocked when Brenda suddenly whirled on her.

"Why?" Brenda demanded. Her voice shook with anger.

Stacie stepped back in surprise.

"Why?" she shouted again.

Stacie could see people across the street turning to stare at them. "What are you so angry about?" she asked. "Lower your voice before someone calls the cops."

Brenda took a step toward her, fists clenched at her sides. Standing over Stacie, she glared down at her.

Stacie held her breath. She had never realized Brenda was so tall.

"Brenda," Trish said from somewhere behind Stacie. "I thought you were working tonight."

"Well, surprise. I'm not," Brenda snapped as she continued to glower at Stacie.

A queasy sensation ran through Stacie's stomach. She tried to speak, but the hatred in Brenda's eyes tied a huge knot in her tongue.

"Let's go somewhere and talk about this," Trish urged as she came alongside Brenda. Her movement switched Brenda's fury away from Stacie.

Taking advantage of the diversion, Stacie eased back several steps before speaking. "Do you two know each other?"

"Don't play stupid with me," Brenda snarled at her.

Stacie held up her hands. "Look, I don't know what's going on here."

"You just couldn't stand it, could you?" Brenda asked. "You couldn't stand that I had found someone."

Stacie frowned and turned to stare at Trish. *What the hell was Brenda talking about?*

"Brenda, we need to talk," Trish said, stepping forward and taking Brenda's arm.

Brenda yanked her arm away, nearly knocking Trish down in the process.

"Hey," Stacie yelled as she reached out to steady Trish. "What's wrong with you?"

"You," Brenda snapped. "You're what's wrong."

Stacie's patience was wearing thin. "Listen, I don't know what's going on here, but it seems you two were . . . are . . . involved. I knew nothing about that, Brenda." She looked Brenda in the eye, hoping she could see her sincerity.

"You lying asshole," Brenda said.

Stacie's blood began to boil. She stepped forward until she and Brenda were practically toe-to-toe. "I'm telling you I didn't know you were dating Trish or anyone else for that matter."

"I told you."

Stacie opened her mouth to deny the accusation but suddenly remembered the night before at Rosie's. Before Melody came in, Brenda had been raving about some woman and she hadn't been listening. "The woman you were talking about last night?"

Brenda nodded.

"How was I supposed to know it was her?" Stacie asked.

"I told you all about her."

Trish stepped closer. Even in the low light, Stacie could sense her anger. "Brenda, I told you I'm not interested in dating anyone full-time."

The tears that sprang to Brenda's eyes washed away Stacie's anger. In all the years they had known each other, she had never seen Brenda cry. "I'm sorry," Stacie said and reached for Brenda's arm.

Brenda shook her off. "I don't need your phony sympathy or your friendship." She turned and walked away.

Stacie started to follow, but Trish put out an arm and stopped her. "Give her time to cool down. She'll be okay."

"I'm not so sure of that," Stacie mumbled as Brenda disappeared into the darkness.

Chapter Eight

Stacie swung her feet over the edge of the bed and squinted at the clock. It was a little after eight. Her eyelids felt as though someone had lined them with sandpaper. The events of the previous evening had kept her up most of the night. She had finally dozed off just before sunup but disjointed and disturbing dreams prevented her from resting.

After an awkward departure from Trish, Stacie had gone home alone and called Brenda. When there was no answer, she left a message on Brenda's machine apologizing and swearing that she hadn't known who Trish was. She asked Brenda to call her when she got home, no matter what time it was. Stacie's phone hadn't rung.

A jaw-cracking yawn escaped as she grabbed the phone and dialed Brenda's number. She needed to make Brenda understand about what happened last night. She held her breath as Brenda's phone rang. She knew Brenda would be home now; she liked to sleep in on Saturday mornings. On the third ring, just before the answering machine would have kicked in, Stacie heard the welcoming click of the receiver being picked up. She exhaled loudly and smiled. Brenda was talking to her again. To her astonishment, the phone went dead. *There must be something wrong with her phone.* She called back. This time Brenda answered the first ring, but again the line disconnected. *She's hanging up on me.* Angry, Stacie disconnected and hit the redial button. *Why is she being such an ass?* The phone rang five, ten, fifteen times, but no voice mail kicked in. Brenda had disconnected it. *What a whining baby!* Stacie tossed the handset onto the rumpled bed and sat down on the edge. She couldn't remember ever feeling so wrung out. The previous thirty-six hours had taken their toll. She scrubbed her face with her hands before falling back onto the bed.

"I'm so tired," she moaned. She vowed to stay home that night and turn in early. She didn't want to dwell too closely on the fact that she really didn't have anywhere to go. If Brenda stopped talking to her . . . She refused to let the thought take hold. Things between her and Brenda would be fine as soon as she was able to explain what really happened. She forced herself off the bed. It was time to get started. She needed to settle this thing with Brenda and then charm Cheryl Wright into giving her an interview.

Stacie started a pot of coffee brewing before showering. She didn't intend to let this silliness with Brenda continue. She would drive to Brenda's and make her listen to reason. Besides, if Brenda and Trish were such a hot item, why had Trish come on to her, first on the dance floor and then later in the car? Apparently, Brenda was a lot more committed to this new relationship than Trish was.

An hour later, Stacie left the house with her second cup of coffee, a notepad and a plan. After squaring things with Brenda, she would swing by Cheryl Wright's and sweet-talk her into a quick interview. Then she would go into the office and knock out the story this afternoon. Jack would find the story on his desk when he walked in Monday morning and forget about her playing hooky yesterday. She was tired of getting her butt chewed for every little thing. Someday when she was a famous journalist, she would set her own hours, choose her own assignments and tell everyone she didn't like to go fuck themselves.

Her mood didn't improve when she pulled into Brenda's empty driveway. She had made the trip for nothing. She shoved the car into reverse and roared out into the street. If Brenda wanted to continue this friendship, then she could dang well make the next move. Determined to put the events of the previous night behind her, she drove across town to Cheryl Wright's address. The sight of the Jag in the driveway gave her a new surge of hope. Finally, something was going right. She parked on the street in front and grabbed her notepad. Jack would be pissed that she'd gone to the interview without a camera. *I'll tell him Cheryl didn't want her photo taken.*

She walked to the front door and rang the doorbell. Several long seconds passed before she rang again. "This woman is so rude," she muttered as she tapped the notepad against her leg. "If you're going to pretend not to be home, you could at least put the car in the garage." Finally, in exasperation, she rang the bell a third time.

The door opened so quickly, Stacie stepped back in surprise.

"What do you want?" Cheryl demanded as she pushed open the storm door.

Stacie forced herself to smile. Someday, she would put people like Cheryl Wright in their place. She extended her hand. "Stacie Gillette. I'm from the *Voice of Texas*. You agreed to do an interview with us."

Cheryl stared at her for a long moment. "How did you get my address?"

Stacie lied without missing a beat. "My editor gave it to me."

Cheryl's face grew dark with anger. "Ms. Gillette, my appointment with you was yesterday morning. Perhaps your hangover prevents you from remembering. Now your editor sends you to my house, after I expressly stated I didn't do interviews in my home. This is my home, Ms. Gillette. Can you understand that? My home."

Stacie swallowed her anger. The woman did have a point, but she needed this interview. "I apologize for yesterday morning. You're absolutely right. I was an ass. What I did was completely unprofessional and inexcusable, but in my defense, there were mitigating circumstances. Please, I would really appreciate it if we could just do the interview."

Cheryl Wright hesitated.

Stacie almost danced with glee when she saw the tension in Cheryl's shoulders relax. She had her, and then Stacie made the stupidest comment of her career. She looked Cheryl in the eye and said, "After all, we lesbians have to stick together." The crowning glory was a sly wink. Before she could comprehend what was happening, Cheryl closed the door in her face.

Stacie stood staring at the closed door for several seconds, unable or unwilling to believe that she had said something so incredibly stupid. *What's wrong with me?* What had ever possessed her to say such a thing? She reached out to ring the doorbell again but stopped. If she wasn't careful, Cheryl could file a harassment charge against her.

Stacie made her way back to her car and sat there for several seconds. How was she going to tell Jack she didn't get the interview? He had sounded pissed in his last message. Would he really fire her?

"Stop it," she chided herself. "You're giving yourself an ulcer." He wouldn't fire her. She was a great reporter and Jack knew it. He wouldn't be dumb enough to fire her.

She cranked the car. *I'll go get Brenda. The two of us can* . . . The thought died away. For a moment, she had forgotten that Brenda was no longer speaking to her. It hit her suddenly that she had nowhere to go. It was too early to go to Rosie's or the Yellow Rose. Not that she could go to either of those places anyway. Zoey would just kick her out again, and she didn't want to take a chance of running into Trish at the Yellow Rose. Besides Brenda, she didn't have any friends. Any friendships that might have developed had been ruined by sex. She never bothered to get close to any of her coworkers. Her family was several hundred miles away, and that was actually too close as far as she was concerned. With nowhere else to go, Stacie pulled away from the curb and drove home.

When she walked into her living room and saw the red light blinking on the answering machine, she smiled, knowing it would be Brenda. She hurried over to the machine and pressed the play button. When the message began, a cold finger of dread started in the pit of her stomach. As the words pounded into her, the dread expanded and consumed her. By the time the machine clicked off, Stacie was sitting on the floor shaking and crying.

Chapter Nine

Long shadows from the setting sun crept across the glossy hardwood floor. Stacie watched without comprehending as the dark images fell across her legs. A tangle of wires from the answering machine and phone cascaded around her. She pushed the rewind button and replayed the message.

"This is Jack. I'm sorry to have to do this over an answering machine, but I can't seem to catch you at home and as usual, your cell phone seems to be turned off."

Stacie checked her cell phone and found that it was off. She tossed the nuisance aside. It was an added expense that she didn't need. She'd only gotten it at Jack's insistence. She didn't like the feeling of always being available to anyone. Other than Danny and Brenda, she had never given the number to anyone, so the only person who ever called her on it was Jack. That was why it was off most of the time.

"Cheryl Wright's publicist called me again," Jack's voice droned on. "You can imagine my surprise when she lit into me for giving you her home address. I can't think of any reason why you would tell her such a lie. Did you forget that I specifically told you Cheryl Wright did *not* want reporters in her home?" The sound of him taking a deep breath filled the tape. "You know my stance on ethics. I'm sorry, Stacie. I have no choice but to fire you. Someone from HR will contact you next week to make arrangements for whatever pay or benefits you have coming." He paused. "I'm truly sorry it came to this, but—" The machine had shut off at that point, swallowing whatever else he might have said.

Stacie's mind refused to accept his words. How could he fire her? Writing was all she had ever wanted to do. When she was ten, she read *To Kill a Mockingbird*. She took the book to her favorite teacher, Mrs. Hawthorne, the next day and told her she wanted to write a book just like it someday. Mrs. Hawthorne told her, to become a great writer she would have to read many different kinds of books and fill her mind with as much knowledge as she possibly could, and then she told Stacie about the University of Texas at Austin and the excellent journalism courses offered there. She listened carefully as Mrs. Hawthorne explained that only students with excellent grades were allowed to enter the program.

Later that night after the supper dishes were cleared and washed, Stacie sat on the small back porch making plans for her future. She didn't intend to spend her entire life living from one paycheck to the next. Someday she'd be able to walk down the street and people would point and say, "There goes Stacie Gillette, the famous writer." She'd buy herself a shiny car and a house in the city. It would be a big city like New York. Looking through the torn screen, she could see Junie, her eight-year-old sister, sitting at the kitchen table playing with an old doll whose head was speckled with tufts of coarse, frizzy hair. The doll had originally been Stacie's, but when she turned ten, she decided she was too old to be playing with toys. In a grand show of indifference, she tossed the doll into the corner behind her bed, far enough away to show she no longer needed it, but still near enough to grab after the lights were all off.

Junie had found it, and Stacie was too proud to admit she still slept with the doll. She still missed the comfort it gave on the nights when her parents' low angry voices crawled through the large crack beneath the door.

She watched as Junie carefully wrapped the doll in an old baby blanket and tucked it into the doll cradle their father had made from a wooden produce crate.

Her brother, Danny, who was five, sat under the table, pushing a beat-up plastic car around the table legs. One of the back wheels was missing from the car, and it wouldn't roll on its own.

Watching her siblings, she experienced a sense of sadness. Maybe she would move to Dallas instead of New York, and then she could still see Junie and Danny whenever she wanted.

Glancing beyond the kitchen, she could see part of the living room. The scarred toes of her father's work boots were visible beside his chair. Although she couldn't see him, she knew he would be asleep by now. Exhausted from a long day in the fields, Carl Daniel Gillette always fell asleep in his chair after supper. He worked for A. J. Garrison, one of the largest farmers in the county. Her father drove a tractor in the spring and summer, and with the arrival of fall, he would drive either a combine or a cotton picker. It didn't matter which one he drove, he was always tired.

Her mom, Lorene, worked at the poultry-processing plant at the edge of town. She came home every day and took a long shower. She always swore that when she was dead and buried, she'd still be able to smell those dead chickens.

Stacie had been to the plant a few times and it was really gross. Dead chickens were everywhere, with the smell of chicken guts stinking up half the town. Even before talking to Mrs. Hawthorne that day, Stacie had already made up her mind. She'd rather be a farmer than work in the processing plant. Driving a tractor couldn't be nearly as bad as pulling chicken guts out with your hands.

She understood her family was poor. Most families around Wilburn were. If you didn't work on one of the three large farms nearby, you worked at the poultry plant. According to her father, neither job paid enough for a gnat to live on. Even with her parents' combined salaries they barely got by. There was never money left over for luxuries like those she saw on television at her friend Tammy Robbin's house.

Stacie's father wouldn't buy a television. He called them idiot boxes and swore they were the ruination of the world. She was always careful not to mention the fact that she watched television whenever she spent the night with Tammy. She enjoyed seeing the things people on the shows owned. They all had shiny new toasters, televisions in practically every room of the house and couches that didn't have holes in the cushions.

Stacie didn't spend the night with Tammy very often because Tammy's father had spells. The spells started after he came back from Vietnam, long before Tammy or Stacie were born.

Stacie had never seen him have a spell, but hearing Tammy talk about how he would fall down and thrash about was enough to keep her from saying more than hi and bye to him. Sometimes during dinner, he would tell funny stories about what it had been like when he was in the Army before he went to Vietnam. He was always saying that Wilburn was stuck in a time warp.

She didn't know what a time warp was. She only knew that she needed to find a way out. She considered the Army and leaving the way Tammy's father had, but she didn't want to take a chance of getting spells, and besides, he came right back to Wilburn afterward, and she wanted to move away forever.

Although she was only ten, she knew her parents couldn't afford to send her to college. If she wanted to go, she would have to pay for it herself. Wilburn didn't offer many opportunities for employment, but she was determined to find a job. After making a mental list of places where she might find work, she had stretched out on the porch and watched the stars.

The following day after school, she began her search. It took her three weeks, but she finally convinced Mr. Hicks at the grocery store that he needed someone to help him with the store. He hired her and agreed to pay her the amazing fortune of three dollars a week. The job required that she dust all the shelves twice a week, clean the glass on the dairy and meat coolers and sweep the floors every weekday morning before the store opened.

Her parents were reluctant to let her take the job, but anticipating their objections, she was prepared with solutions. "I can ride with Mom," she said. Her mom carpooled with Mrs. Anderson, who lived down the road from them, and paid five dollars a week to help with gas. Stacie's dad complained it was highway robbery, but since they only had one car, and he needed it to get to work, her mom continued carpooling. "I'll have time to sweep out the store before school and then I can go back to do the rest after school and still meet Mom at five."

"Go ahead. You won't last two weeks," her father said, his voice heavy with exhaustion.

Stacie wanted to protest, but she knew better than to argue. She looked to her mom for support, but her mom kept her head bent over the shirt she was mending for Danny. Stacie walked back into the kitchen, dropped into a chair and folded her arms. She knew she would last more than two weeks. She intended to go to college. She would do whatever it took if it meant she didn't have to marry some smelly boy and get a job in that stinking chicken plant.

The following morning she was up early and had her chores completed by the time her mom was ready to leave for work. One of Stacie's responsibilities was to ensure Danny was up and dressed for school. He started crying when she made him get up early, but a good whack across his butt with a hairbrush convinced him to stop whining.

The job proved much harder than Stacie had anticipated. The actual work wasn't difficult, but getting Danny up early was a chore, and then the dash from the plant over three blocks to the store left her exactly thirty-seven minutes to sweep the entire store and run the six blocks over to the school. In the afternoon, the process reversed. Mr. Hicks would hand her a list of things to do each day when she came in. She had to have the things on the list completed by no later than 4:55 p.m. That gave her ten minutes to gather her books and run back to the plant where her mom and Mrs. Anderson always walked out at five minutes after five.

All of the effort paid off when Mr. Hicks handed her three crisp one-dollar bills on Friday afternoon. They were so perfect; she carefully tucked the bills between the pages of her history book to keep them from getting creased or wrinkled. She wanted them to remain in pristine condition so she could show them to her parents.

It took all her willpower not to whip the bills out as soon as she saw her mom, but she forced herself to wait. She had planned the entire scenario. The family would have dinner, and then she would do the dishes. After the kitchen was in order, she would casually stroll into the living room and hold up the three immaculate bills. Her parents would be so impressed and her sister and brother would stare at her with wide-eyed awe. Maybe her father would even apologize for doubting her grit.

The plan started perfectly. Supper went well. Her father even talked some. That meant he wasn't too tired. He was always in a better mood when he wasn't completely exhausted. As soon as the dishes were finished, she dashed to her room and gently removed the three beautiful bills. She placed each bill side by side and studied them. This was the beginning of her dream. Someday a shiny book cover would boldly display her name across the bottom. Gathering the bills, she made her way back to the living room where everyone would soon be staring at her in awe. Not only would she show them the money, but also tonight she would tell them about her plan to attend college and the book she intended to write someday.

Junie and Danny were in the kitchen playing when Stacie came in. She decided she would show her parents first and then her siblings. She walked on into the living room. Her father's eyes were closed, but she could tell by his breathing that he wasn't asleep.

"Look, Dad," she said, proudly holding up the money.

"Yeah," he replied, never opening his eyes.

"Dad," Stacie said, "look at what I have."

"Stacie, take that on back to your room. Your dad's tired," her mom said.

Stacie turned to her mother, who was shaking her head and motioning for Stacie to leave. Before she could do so, Danny came in from the kitchen. "Where'd you get all that money?" he yelped.

At the mention of money, her father's eyes opened. "Where'd you get that money, girl?"

"I got paid today," she replied, happily waving the bills.

"Paid?" His eyes narrowed. "For what?" he demanded.

"Carl, she's been workin' for Jim Hicks at the store all week," her mom reminded him. "Stacie, go on back to your room."

He shook his head and leaned back. "Three dollars? That's all you made for a whole week's work."

"Yeah," Danny mimicked. "Three dumb dollars."

Stacie stood, uncertain what to do. Things weren't going as she planned. Everyone was supposed to be proud of her. Junie hadn't even stopped playing with that stupid old doll to come look at her money.

Maybe they didn't realize how important it was to her. "I'm going to college," Stacie announced.

Her father looked at her and frowned. "College? Who's been puttin' that silliness into your head?"

"Nobody. And it's not silly," Stacie said. Her body was starting to tremble.

"Don't get sassy, little girl." He leaned forward and pointed a finger.

Stacie stepped back beyond his reach.

"We ain't got no use for college girls around here," he continued. "Girls don't do nothin' but get married and have a houseful of younguns that a man spends the rest of his life payin' for. You won't be needin' college for that."

"I need college to write my book," Stacie said, trying to explain.

"Book," her father said and started laughing. "Well, ain't you just full of big ideas."

Stacie looked to her mother, hoping she would understand, but her mother was concentrating on her sewing. "I want to write a book someday. But first I have to go to college, and I know you don't make enough money to send me." Stacie wasn't sure exactly what happened first. She heard her mother scream at her father, but she wasn't sure if her mother screamed before or after he erupted out of his chair. The only thing Stacie was sure of was the stars that exploded before her eyes when he slapped her. The force of his slap had lifted her from her feet and sent her sliding butt-first across the kitchen floor.

Chapter Ten

Stacie staggered up from the floor, struggling to remember that she was no longer ten years old and her father was several hundred miles away. She leaned against the wall for support. How had everything gone so wrong, so quickly? It all started when Congressman Manchester wimped out on her questions and walked away. That was when Jack decided to punish her by sending her out on that dead-end interview with Cheryl Wright.

"That's it," Stacie whispered. Everything that had happened to her in the last few hours was caused by that crazy woman. Stacie quietly built her case. If Wright hadn't hung up on her the first time she called, they could have done the interview Thursday evening and she wouldn't have gone to Rosie's. She ignored the fact that she went to Rosie's every Thursday night to meet Brenda. If she hadn't gone to Rosie's, she wouldn't have gotten caught playing footsie with Melody, and she wouldn't have been banned from Rosie's. The evidence continued to fall neatly into place. If she hadn't been tossed out of Rosie's, she wouldn't have gone to the Yellow Rose and met Trish, and Brenda would still be talking to her. For Stacie, it all boiled down to one thing. *If that damn romance writer had given me the interview as she agreed to, I wouldn't have lost my job.* All of her problems stemmed from the interview with Cheryl Wright.

Afterward, Stacie couldn't recall driving through darkened streets to Cheryl Wright's house. She did remember the porch light popping on as she stepped up to ring the doorbell. When Cheryl didn't answer the doorbell, Stacie began pounding on the door with her fists.

"Open this door," she yelled. "I know you're in there." She tried peeking through the windows, but the inside of the house was too dark to distinguish anything. She stepped back into the yard and the glowing lamp in the upstairs window taunted her. Stacie raced back to the door. She had come here to get the damn interview, and she wasn't leaving without it. She pounded on the door with her fists again, her anger growing. Cheryl Wright was refusing to acknowledge Stacie's need for this interview. Just as Stacie's parents never acknowledged her first job, her graduating summa cum laude from UT or her stories that were picked up by the AP.

She turned to go back into the yard and it was then that she noticed the decorative stone rabbit tucked beneath a small table sitting at the end of the porch. Without thinking, Stacie grabbed the rabbit and tossed it through the front window. An alarm began shrieking. "That should get you out here," Stacie said as she swayed slightly.

Suddenly it struck her what she had just done. She grabbed her head and backed away from the door. "What in God's name am I doing?" She looked around desperately for a switch that would silence the ear-numbing shriek of the alarm, but of course it was not to be found. Stacie put her hands over her ears. Why didn't Cheryl turn the alarm off? *Because, you crazy fool, you've probably scared her to within a inch of her life*, she screamed at herself.

As she continue to stand there waiting for Cheryl to come out, she became aware of another siren. Unfortunately, this one wasn't coming from within the house. *I'm going to jail*, she realized. It occurred to her that she might run, but her car was brightly illuminated by the streetlights. By now, one of the neighbors would surely have taken down her license plate number. Besides, Cheryl Wright could easily identify her. Stacie dropped down onto the front step. She was still sitting there when the police car arrived.

Losing one's temper was apparently not a valid reason for tossing a stone rabbit through a window, because Stacie was handcuffed and quickly hustled off to jail. As the car pulled away from the curb, Stacie glanced up at the still glowing lamp and closed her eyes in defeat. She had made a complete fool of herself, and Cheryl Wright hadn't even been home.

The next several hours were beyond humiliating. Stacie was searched, fingerprinted and placed in a cell with ten or twelve other women. She had been offered a phone call, but there was no one for her to call. Brenda wasn't speaking to her and she had no intention of calling her and asking her for anything. Calling Jack was out of the question. She considered calling her brother, Danny, but he was so far away that it would take him hours to get there. He could probably wire the money to bail her out, but he would need every penny he had. With the loss of her job, finances were going to get tighter for both of them.

Inside the cell, she was careful not to make eye contact or offend any of the other women. She found herself a small empty space near the front and sat on the floor. Hoping it would discourage any of the other prisoners from talking to her, she folded her arms over her knees and rested her forehead against her arms.

She refused to give in to the tears burning the back of her eyes. After this stupid stunt, she would be lucky to get a job flipping burgers. There was no chance that Jack would rehire her now. Why had she gone to Cheryl's? That had to be the dumbest impulse of her entire life. What would she do now? How would she continue to send money home to her family?

Someone tapped Stacie's shoulder. She raised her head and blinked slowly.

"Are you Gillette?" the heavy woman who woke her asked.

Stacie nodded.

"They're calling you," the woman said and nodded toward the jail door.

"Thanks," Stacie said, unable to believe she had fallen asleep. The female guard standing at the door called her name again. Stacie stood and winced. Her entire body ached from sitting on the concrete floor. She hobbled to the door. "I'm Stacie Gillette," she said.

"Took you long enough to speak up." The guard, a tall, stocky redhead, studied her as she opened the jail door. "Hey, aren't you that reporter that snuck in here and got Hinson to talk?"

Stacie nodded.

"Wow, you sure took a nosedive," she said and chuckled.

Stacie failed to see the humor in the situation but thought it best to keep quiet. "Where are we going?" she asked instead.

"Charges have been dropped."

Stacie stopped and stared. "What do you mean?"

"I mean you caught a lucky break. The woman who owned the house you busted up isn't going to press charges. Come on. Follow me."

Stacie walked behind the guard.

"Must be nice to have such an understanding girlfriend," the guard said as they walked out into the outer area of the police station.

Before Stacie could respond, someone called her name. She turned toward the voice and a flash exploded in her face. She threw her arm up to ward off the blinding light and another flash detonated. "What's a photographer doing back here?" Stacie asked.

The guard shrugged. "I don't know. I guess he found a way to sneak in." She glanced back at Stacie. "You know, kind of like you did with that interview with Hinson. I'd sure like to find out what asswipe let you in. We all got a butt-chewing over that one."

"There's not supposed to be photographers in here," Stacie protested, deliberately ignoring the guard's comment about her interview with Hinson.

"Do you want to hang around arguing jailhouse policy or do you want to get out of here?" the guard asked with her fists planted firmly on her ample hips.

Stacie glanced back to where the photographer had been, but he was no longer in sight. She forgot about him and followed the guard.

It was almost a half-hour later when Stacie walked out into the early morning light. After she'd spent the night in jail, even the suffocating humidity didn't seem so oppressive. She took a deep breath and tried to ignore the sick sense of loss that shot spasms of pain through her gut. *What am I going to do?* she wondered, running a shaky hand across her face. How was she going to get home? She had exactly three dollars and twenty-seven cents in cash on her and her car was sitting in front of Cheryl's house. She had probably had it towed away by now, she thought miserably.

"Hello."

Stacie turned and found herself face-to-face with Cheryl Wright. She hung her head in shame. "Ms. Wright, I don't know what got into me. Thank you for not pressing charges against me. You had every right to. I'm so sorry about last night. I'll pay for the damage and I swear I'll never bother you again."

Cheryl cleared her throat. "I'm sorry I got you fired."

Stacie's humiliation deepened. "How did you know about that?"

"It's a long story."

They stood in silence.

"Did they feed you?" Cheryl asked, as she traced a line in the sidewalk with the toe of her sandal. "We could go for breakfast or something."

Stacie shook her head. She wanted nothing more than to go

home and stand under a hot shower for an hour. She had never felt so dirty. She wondered if this was how her mom felt after working at the chicken processing plant all day.

An awkward silence ensued. Stacie finally broke it. "Is my car still at your house?"

"Yes. If you like you can ride with me," Cheryl offered. "It'll save you the cab fare."

"Aren't you afraid to be in a car with me?"

Cheryl exhaled a small breath. "Naw. I removed the stone bunny before I drove over."

Stacie looked at her and saw the slight smile. "I'm really sorry," she said again.

Cheryl studied her for a long second before speaking. "I think we got off on the wrong foot. Not that it's an excuse, but I'm under an incredibly short deadline for my next novel. I chose a really bad time to move halfway across the country and . . ." She hesitated. "Let's just say nothing seems to be going right. When I agreed to do the interview, I was under the impression it was going to be later in the month."

Stacie shrugged. "I had a deadline of Monday at four."

Cheryl nodded. "Too many cooks in the kitchen, I guess." Seeing Stacie's puzzled look, she added, "Just something my grandmother used to say."

Stacie nodded.

"Why don't we continue this conversation in the car? This sun is starting to boil my brain."

They walked to Cheryl's car in silence. As they approached the gleaming new Jag, Stacie took in its sleek lines and sexy cast alloy wheels. The door locks disengaged with a discreet click, unlike the loud clunk of her Mazda. Stacie opened the door and slid into a world of luxury unlike anything she had ever experienced. She was practically green with envy as she devoured the rich burl walnut and supple leather trim. She held her breath as she ran her hands over leather seats that were as soft as a woman's inner thigh. "What color is this?" she asked in a voice softened with awe.

"The dealer called it cashmere. The exterior is salsa."

"And the top?" Stacie asked, anticipating another exotic tint.

Cheryl chuckled. "Dark beige." She glanced at Stacie. "Isn't that a letdown?"

"Nothing about a car like this is a letdown. Drive my Mazda for a couple of days and you'll really appreciate this beauty."

Cheryl seemed to study her for a moment. "This is an XK8 convertible. It has a two hundred and ninety-four horsepower V-eight engine, with a six-speed ZF electronic automatic transmission. There is a trunk full of other bells and whistles, but to be brutally honest, I bought it because driving it makes me feel hotter than a firecracker on the Fourth of July. And just so you'll know how much I appreciate this beauty, I drove a sixteen-year-old Ford pickup before."

Stacie stared at her in disbelief before issuing a small whistle. "I can't believe those cheesy romances—" She caught herself and stopped. "Sorry. I just don't get it."

Cheryl sighed and shook her head. "No one ever does." She cranked the car and eased out of the parking spot. "The only disadvantage to owning my Jag is that the police seem to take a special notice. I've owned the car less than six months, and I've gotten three tickets. I received zero tickets while driving my pickup."

"That was probably because the truck couldn't reach the speed limit, much less break it," Stacie said as she continued to stroke the seats in appreciation.

"Point taken," Cheryl replied as she stopped for a red light.

"Can we put the top down?" Stacie asked.

"Sure, if you don't mind the heat."

Stacie shook her head quickly. "Not after the last few hours. I can't image how anyone survives being locked away for years on end." The top glided smoothly back, letting the full force of the morning sun pour over them. "That feels so good," she murmured as she closed her eyes and turned her face toward the warmth. Just a couple of days ago, she had been sitting in her dungeon office trying to think of a way to skip out of work early. Now, she had no job, very little in savings and a family who depended on her to make their life easier.

When Stacie was sixteen, her father lost his job on the Garrison farm. Before leaving, he convinced Mr. Garrison to sell him the small house that they had been renting since Stacie was eight months old, along with the three acres behind it. Her father used their life savings as a down payment. He was determined to farm for himself, and of all things to grow, he chose onions. With nothing but an old tractor with a rusty plow, he started his farming dynasty. Come planting season, he commandeered the entire family to hand-plant thousands of onion sets. Stacie's back still ached every time she looked at an onion. He tended the fields like a mother hen would her chicks and the onions flourished. When it was time to harvest, once more he turned to his family. With no tools, they were forced to harvest the three-acre field by hand. Afterward the onions were allowed to dry before being bagged and loaded onto her father's old truck. Everything was great until he went to sell them and discovered he wasn't the only farmer who'd experienced a fantastic production year. In fact, onion crops had done so well that there was a surplus and the price bottomed out. Many farmers simply plowed their crops under. It was cheaper than harvesting them. Others left the onions lying in the field, free for whoever wished to pick them up.

Then four years ago, the chicken processing plant in Wilburn closed and pretty much succeeded in killing the small town. Stacie's mom drove the twenty-five miles to Clifton to put in an application with the small-engines manufacturer where her son-in-law, Bill Walker, worked, but she couldn't pass the speed and dexterity test. Arthritis was her only lasting reward for twenty-odd years of plucking chickens. Even with the financial help Stacie sent each month, her parents struggled to make the modest house payment. Their situation improved slightly after their grandson, Tommy, was born.

Junie and her husband, Bill, found themselves struggling to meet the rent, hospital bills and the cost of a babysitter, so they moved in with Stacie's parents to combine their resources until times were better. Now, the five of them were living in the small house.

At least Danny had escaped. He was currently in his final year at Texas A&M. Stacie sent him a monthly check that allowed him the luxury of not working two jobs while going to school as she had done.

A hand on her arm woke her.

"I think you fell asleep," Cheryl said.

Stacie glanced around and realized they were in Cheryl's garage. "I'm sorry. The sun felt so good. I only meant to close my eyes for a minute." She quickly stepped out of the car. "Thanks for giving me a lift, and again I'm sorry about your window. I'll give you my address and you can send me the bill." Even as she made the offer, she wondered how she would be able to pay for it.

"Why did you toss the rabbit through my window?" Cheryl asked, getting out of the car.

The sudden rush of heat in Stacie's face had nothing to do with the sun she had so recently enjoyed. "I honestly don't know. I thought you were home."

Cheryl blinked and stepped back. "Is the fact that you thought you were throwing it at me supposed to make me feel better?"

Stacie's head felt as though someone had removed the top of her skull and filled it with molasses. "I wasn't throwing the rabbit at you. I thought . . . that . . . I thought you were inside and ignoring me."

"Is this how you normally respond when someone ignores you?"

"No. But the last few days haven't been normal." Stacie's words came out much whinier than she intended. Cheryl wasn't responsible for Stacie's problems.

Yes, she is, a petulant voice cried. *If she had just given you the interview, none of this would have happened.*

That still didn't give you the right to throw something through her window, her conscience nagged.

Stacie tried to push the argument from her head as she reached into her pocket for a pad and pencil. "Here's my address, so you can send me the bill." She quickly scribbled down the information and handed it to Cheryl. She started to walk away but stopped. She had a question of her own. "Why didn't you press charges?"

Cheryl stood gazing at her for a long second. "You may not like my answer."

Stacie waited.

"You remind me of someone I once knew. You're young, too smart for your own good, ambitious to a fault, cocky, but I'll bet you the royalties of my next book that deep inside, you're scared shitless."

Stacie's response was automatic. She slipped her hand into her pocket for her car keys. "See. You don't know everything. What have I got to be scared of?"

"You don't have a job, for one thing."

Stacie waved her hand in a dismissive manner. "Jack Conrad did me a favor by firing me. I'll have a better job by the end of the week."

Cheryl absently rubbed her earlobe as she gazed at Stacie. "Then I guess I was wrong. Take care of yourself." She turned and walked away.

The following morning Stacie was pouring her first cup of coffee when her phone rang.

Brenda, she thought as she raced for the phone. Rather than Brenda's name, INCOMING CALL flashed on the caller identification screen. Her heart pounded as her palms began to sweat. This could be it, her big chance. She envisioned someone at the *Austin American Statesman* discovering she was in the job market and already calling her. She took a deep breath and picked up the phone. Her greeting was barely out of her mouth when a grating voice seeped through the line.

"Ms. Gillette, this is Ron Bauer from the *Juice* and I was wondering if you'd like to make a statement."

Stacie frowned. Why would they want a statement? Shouldn't he be asking for clips and a résumé? Did he say the *Juice*? The *Juice* was a weekly tabloid that claimed to have the latest and hottest "juice" on what was happening in Austin.

"Ms. Gillette, is it true you threw a brick through Cheryl Wright's window? Why did you do it? Was it a lover's spat?"

Stacie hung up the phone. Before she could step away, it rang again. She glared at the screen. Bauer was calling back. She snatched the phone up. "I have no comment," she said before he could respond.

"So it's true. You and Cheryl Wright are lovers."

"No!" Stacie yelled. "It's not true. I barely know Cheryl Wright."

"Then why did you toss a brick through her window?"

"It wasn't a brick. It was a rabbit."

"You threw a rabbit through her window."

Before Stacie could explain that it was a stone rabbit, the phone went dead. "Of all the lowdown, despicable, scum-sucking excuses for a reporter," she growled.

A few days later, a large brown envelope arrived in Stacie's mail. Inside was a single sheet torn from the *Juice*. A photo clearly showed her being escorted by the jail guard. The story was topped with a headline announcing, LOCAL REPORTER THROWS RABBIT THROUGH LESBIAN NOVELIST'S WINDOW.

Shame filled her as she stared at the photo. Her hair was sticking out in several different angles and her clothes looked as though she had slept in them. *You did sleep in them*, she reminded herself. Someone, the sender presumably, had used a red felt-tip pen to draw a large question mark over the text of the article. Although there was no return address, she suspected Brenda had mailed her the article. Brenda loved the *Juice*. Stacie took the article to the kitchen and rummaged around until she found a match. After placing the article in the sink, she set it afire, praying Cheryl would never see the disgusting article. *No wonder Cheryl hates reporters.*

Chapter Eleven

Stacie sat on her couch staring into space. The Sunday paper lay scattered in hopeless disarray around her. After tediously reviewing the classified section every day for the past two weeks, she had found nothing for which she was qualified. Even the position for a cook with one of the major fast-food chains was asking for a minimum of two years of experience. How hard could it be to flip a burger and drop frozen french fries into a pan of hot grease?

During her first week of being unemployed, she e-mailed her résumé and her best clips to every daily newspaper in Austin, San Antonio, Dallas and Houston. Then she waited, alternately pacing or cleaning her small apartment. For the first few days, she checked her e-mail every fifteen minutes, certain one of the newspapers would be overjoyed to snap her up. She even fantasized about the possibility of a small bidding war developing between potential employers.

When the responses did start pouring in, they carried the same message. "We are not hiring at this time. Your résumé will be placed on file for future consideration."

By the end of the first week, she grew desperate enough to send her résumé and clips to the smaller weekly papers within these cities, but she received the same tired line. She refused to let herself believe that the ridiculous article in the *Juice* had anything to do with these rejections. With each rejection, she reinforced her self-esteem by telling herself it was nothing more than a slow economy. As soon as the economy picked up, so would hiring and she'd be at the top of their lists.

At night, she paced her tiny bedroom worrying about her rapidly dwindling savings account. Her rent was due in a week. Then there were her car payment, utility bills, a credit card bill for the new tires she had needed last month, and her family. Her final paycheck and the tiny savings account would barely cover one month, but afterward she would be broke.

She stared into space and thought about trying to call Brenda again, but she didn't want to hear the sound of the phone disconnecting in her ear. She hated whoever invented caller identification technology. Without it, Brenda would have to answer the phone eventually. Maybe she should drive over to Brenda's apartment. *Yeah, right, and get the door slammed in your face.* She slumped over onto the couch, ignoring the crackling and tearing of the newspaper beneath her.

Stacie squeezed her eyes shut against the dim light seeping through the closed blinds. With the previous night's insomnia and the steady rain beating down outside, sleep should have come easily, but she felt restless. It had been raining for three days, and the weather forecasters were predicting still more during the day. She wanted to go out, or just talk to someone, but there was no one to call. Making friends had never come easy for her as child and the situation hadn't improved as she got older.

She knew she possessed the ability to communicate effectively with others. After all, she had aced a face-to-face interview with a serial killer and picked up more women than she cared to remember. The problem occurred when she tried to interact with someone on a personal level, not when she was Stacie Gillette the reporter or Stacie Gillette on the prowl. If she had encountered any of those women at a party and been limited to participating in social chitchat, she would have sounded like a bumbling idiot. The prospect of conversing one-on-one left her tongue-tied. Her brain shut down, leaving her unable to think.

As soon as the person walked away, as they always did after a few minutes of watching her stare into her drink and stutter, brilliant lines of witty dialogue would come to her.

During her long nights of sleeplessness, she had come to realize that her friendship with Brenda survived because Brenda refused to let it die. It was Brenda who looked Stacie up after moving to Austin, and it was Brenda who insisted they get together weekly to catch up. Stacie missed her more than she could ever have imagined. She simply couldn't get beyond the shame that kept her from camping on Brenda's doorstep until Brenda forgave her. In her heart, Stacie knew she had let her best friend down. Brenda tried to tell her about Trish, but Stacie had been too busy scoping out her next conquest to listen.

A heavy weight settled in her chest, forcing her to sit up to breathe. As she fought to pull air into her lungs, she experienced a moment of fear. Could she be having a heart attack? She jumped up from the couch and began talking to herself.

"I'm not having a heart attack. I'm twenty-seven years old. The only thing wrong with me is that I'm going stir-crazy from being in this apartment so long."

Stacie tried to think of someplace she could go. She couldn't go back to Rosie's for another week, not that she ever intended to return there. The Yellow Rose was an option, but her stomach tightened at the thought of running into either Trish or Brenda.

Unable to keep still, she went to stare out her front windows. The rain was little more than a sprinkle. As the walls continued to close in on her, she grabbed her keys and cell phone. She had used it as one of the contact numbers on her résumé and for the first time, she was glad to have the annoying thing. She would drive over to Zilker Park, which was located on Barton Springs Road. The park was enormous. She remembered reading somewhere that the greenbelt alone covered over eight hundred acres. The park was also home to the Barton Springs Pool, a spring-fed pool that maintained a year-round temperature of sixty-eight degrees and was nearly a thousand feet long. It was a popular destination for many during the long hot days of summer. Since Stacie's swimming skills had never progressed beyond a crude dog paddle, she found exploring other sections of the park to be much more enjoyable.

As she drove through the park, the amount of accumulated water in the low-lying areas surprised her. She decided to go to the botanical garden. She enjoyed hiking the shaded trails. At this time of year, the ponds would be dotted with pink, purple, white and yellow water lilies.

By the time she arrived at the center, the rain had stopped. She struck off on a trail behind the visitor center. She was happy to see that the rain had discouraged all but the hardiest tourists.

After crossing the small footbridge, she came across a narrow side trail that disappeared into the thick woods and decided to follow it. As she walked, she considered ways to get her foot in the door of one the dailies. Talent wasn't the issue. She knew she possessed the necessary talent. Her problem was contacts. She needed to reconsider her strategy and remember that who she knew would be nearly as important as what she knew. Stacie Gillette the reporter was going to have to rectify that situation. She needed to go through her Rolodex and start making calls. As she made her way through the rain-soaked woods, the problem became clear. Her résumé wasn't making it beyond the personnel department. The people who knew her byline obviously didn't know she was seeking a position.

She was so pleased with her new strategy that she almost missed the faint mewling sound. If the noise hadn't seemed to echo, she might have ignored it. The whimpering seemed to be coming

86

from behind her. Stacie backtracked, peering through the nearly impenetrable brush on either side of the trail, but all she could hear was rushing water. As she turned to continue on her way, she heard it again, a slight mewling. Suddenly all of the terrifying headlines of abandoned babies came back to her. *Could someone have dumped a baby out here?*

Limbs tore at her as she fought her way into the thick brush. After a few feet, the tangle of vegetation gave way to a small swift-flowing stream. The stream was normally a dry creek bed, but the heavy rainfall of the last few days had transformed it. Stacie strained to hear above the noise of the rushing water. There it was. It sounded as though it was on the other side of the creek. *No, to the left*. Confused, she moved closer to the creek and stopped short at the sight of two kittens in the middle of the stream, huddled on a branch no bigger than her arm. Both were soaking wet and shivering. Relief that it wasn't an abandoned child gradually gave way to concern for the small castaways.

The creek was only about eight feet wide, but the water was swift and she couldn't be sure how deep it was. She searched the ground around her until she found a limb that was about four feet long. Standing as close as she dared to the edge of the bank, she used the limb to determine the creek's depth at various locations until she felt certain it was only slightly above knee level. Stacie stared at the kittens. The thought of stepping off into the rushing water made her stomach cramp. Swimming was not her strong suit. She tried not to think about what would happen if she slipped and fell. She looked around trying to find a way to get them out without drowning herself.

A possible answer presented itself in the form of a low-hanging limb. She grabbed onto it and tugged. It felt strong enough to hold her. By holding onto the limb, she might be able to reach out far enough to grab the kittens without having to get into the water.

After giving the branch one final test, she leaned out, intending to grab the kitten closest to her. As she reached out, one of the kittens shocked her by issuing a loud hiss and slapping at her. The tiny nails scratched the back of her fingers. The wound was nothing, but the unexpected attack was enough to make Stacie jerk her hand back and yelp. The sudden movement of the kitten caused the branch they were sitting on to shift and the second kitten toppled off into the water.

It frantically beat the raging water with its sadly inadequate paws. Forgetting about her own safety, Stacie made a wild grab for it. Her grip on the wet branch slipped, causing her to fall facedown into the angry stream. She panicked and slapped at the water in a desperate search for something solid to grab. After several futile attempts, her hand managed to grab hold of a stone that was firmly embedded in the creek bottom. She managed to get her feet beneath her and was almost up when her foot slipped on the slippery stone bottom and sent her crashing back into the stream. It seemed to take forever before her grasping hands located a firm handhold on another rock. This time she forced herself to relax and stop fighting the water. With careful deliberation, she pulled her knees beneath her body. It took her a moment to pull herself upright and regain her footing. Terrified she would fall if she moved, Stacie looked around for the kittens. They were both floating in the water now. Her attempts to save them had only made matters worse. As she watched their helpless bodies being swept away, she felt a streak of anger burn through her. This might be the only thing over which she could still exert some control. She hadn't been able to make Congressman Manchester answer her questions, or wrest an interview from Cheryl Wright. She couldn't go back to Rosie's and Brenda wouldn't return her calls. She had lost her job and people who wouldn't know a good story if it rose up and bit them on the ass were tossing her résumé in trash cans. Damn them all, she was going to save those kittens!

Scrambling out of the creek, she raced alongside the rushing water until she was even with one of the kittens. She jumped into the water to grab it, but the churning water was too fast and she missed. Screaming in frustration, she made her way back to the bank and started running, but this time she ran passed the tiny spinning creatures before wading back into the stream. As the water swept them to her, she hauled first one and then the second one from the torrent before carefully extracting herself.

On the safety of the muddy bank, she tried to examine the kittens. Both were drenched and shivering. With nothing to dry them with, she cuddled them against her body and started back to the visitor center. As she struggled through the brush to the trail, she could feel the tiny bodies trembling against her. "You'll be dry in no time," she promised them. Once on the path, she jogged back to the visitor center. By the time she arrived, her lungs burned and a stitch in her side had her gasping in pain.

The parking lot was now full of people taking advantage of the rain stopping. Several of them cast a wary eye toward Stacie as she stood beside the center trying to decide what she should do with the kittens. She couldn't afford to keep them. If she left them here, someone would surely give them a good home.

One of the kittens mewled and burrowed deeper into her arms. Stacie smiled for the first time in days. Finally, something had gone right for her. She continued to watch them. Why shouldn't she be the one to find them a good home? If she left them here, she couldn't be sure they would be cared for properly or kept together. She felt certain they were littermates, and after what they had gone through, it would be wrong to separate them. How much could it cost to take care of two kittens for a couple of weeks, anyway? Finding them a home would give her something to do. With her mind made up, Stacie went to her car and found an old beach towel in her trunk. She dried the kittens as well as possible. They were still shaking, but she suspected it was more from fright than cold. How could anything be cold in this humidity?

It was at that point that she noticed how drenched she was. She grimaced when she examined herself. Her favorite white shorts were covered in mud stains that no amount of detergent would ever remove. Her arms and legs were covered with scratches from pushing through the dense brush. There was blood on her right knee. A closer look revealed a nasty scrape that started stinging the minute she noticed its presence. She shrugged; a shower and a Band-Aid would repair most of the damages. Too bad the rest of her life couldn't be as easily repaired.

With the kittens wrapped in the beach towel on the passenger's seat, she vaguely recalled someone telling her cats didn't like to ride in cars.

"You guys don't get crazy on me, okay? We'll be home in no time."

Stacie cranked the car and headed for her apartment. As she left the park, the rain struck again in earnest, making it almost impossible to see. She glanced at the kittens huddled together inside the towel and tried not to think about what might have happened to them with this new deluge.

The pounding rain extended the trip home to more than twice its normal time. Stacie parked in the closest available slot to her apartment. A quick search of the car's interior revealed there was no umbrella. She had been in such a rush to get out of the confining apartment, she hadn't thought to bring one. "Like I'm not already soaked," she mumbled as she stared out at the pouring rain. She picked up the kittens. "We'll wait a couple of minutes," she said, rubbing them with the edges of the towel.

Fifteen minutes later, it was still pouring and she was about to roast in the hot car. Tired of waiting, she cradled the towel with the kittens as closely to her chest as possible before making a wild dash across the parking lot.

Her apartment was on the second floor. As she made her way up the stairs, she reminded herself to slow down to avoid slipping on the wet metal stairs. It suddenly occurred to her that it had been raining when she moved in. Dragging her hodgepodge of personal belongings up the slippery stairs had been a maneuver in caution. "When I buy a house, it will not have stairs," she grumbled.

The kittens were still shivering when she got them inside. She ran to the bathroom, grabbed a large bath towel and set it on the floor. With both kittens in her lap, she gently began toweling them off. She knew next to nothing about cats or any other animal for that matter. Her father hadn't allowed them to have pets, because he claimed they served no seeable purpose. He kept a couple of hunting dogs around, but he sold or traded them so often that she learned early not to become attached.

Both kittens were dark brown with streaks of tan. One had a small patch of white on its nose. She picked it up. "Come on, girl or boy, whichever you are." As she rubbed the towel over the kitten, it began to cry and squirm. "What's wrong? Don't you want to get dry? I thought cats hated water."

Tiny claws snagged her finger.

"Okay. You win. I'll leave you alone." She placed the kitten back on her lap. As she reached for the second one, it hissed and arched its back. "Yeah, I know you're bad." She chuckled. "You'll feel much better once you're dry and warm." As she turned the towel to use the dry end, a dark crimson streak caught her attention. Upon closer examination, she identified the streak as blood.

Stacie picked up the first kitten and carefully examined it. She found the wound on the inside of one of its back legs. Because of the blood-matted fur, she was unable to determine how deep it was. She stared at the wound, uncertain what she should do. The other kitten meowed loudly. Was it hurt also? A careful examination didn't reveal any visible damage.

Suddenly both kittens began to whimper. The sound escalated into a throaty howl. She tried picking them up, but they only cried louder. What if they had internal injuries? What did you do with sick kittens? A vet. She needed to call a veterinarian. Which one? Brenda would know. She wrapped the towel around her new charges and started for the living room before remembering Brenda wasn't talking to her.

Maybe she'll call me back if I tell her about the kittens. She's a pushover for any animal. She stopped. She wasn't going to go whining to her. She would take care of it herself. It wasn't as though she was completely helpless, she reminded herself. With the bundle tucked under one arm, she dialed directory assistance and requested the number to the nearest animal emergency center that would be open on a Sunday.

Upon contacting the center, she quickly explained how she came by the kittens. The minute she mentioned the cut, she was urged to bring them in to be examined.

Stacie changed into clean clothes. After grabbing an umbrella, she wrapped the kittens in a dry towel before heading back out into the pouring rain. As she raced across the parking lot, she couldn't help but wonder if the sun would ever shine again.

Chapter Twelve

The veterinarian, Dr. Talley, was a jovial, white-haired man in his sixties. As he led Stacie to an examining room, he informed her he had been practicing for forty-two years. He carefully examined each of the kittens, while Stacie related the details of their rescue. With the exception of the minor leg wound, he announced both patients to be healthy.

After Stacie repeatedly referred to the kittens as *her*, the vet pointed out that in fact the injured one with the white patch on its nose was a male. She tried to hide the embarrassment caused by her ignorance of animal anatomy when he held each kitten up and gave her a quick lesson on how to determine the gender of felines.

After laying out a half-dozen shiny instruments, he told Stacie to hold the injured kitten still while he gently trimmed the fur away from the wound. She closed her eyes when he gave the kitten a shot to prevent infection. When he was finished, he gave her a tube of salve with instructions to apply it twice daily. As he picked up the kittens, he stopped and looked at her. "Are you a reporter?"

Stacie nodded. She couldn't bring herself to tell him she had been fired.

"I thought I recognized you. I read your coverage on Hinson. That was quite a stunt you pulled to get that interview."

"Thanks."

He cleared his throat. "You didn't really throw a rabbit through your girlfriend's window, did you?" he asked. "I mean, how could anyone who went to as much trouble as you have for these kittens possibly do something so atrocious?"

Stacie closed her eyes and exhaled slowly. "She's not my girl-friend. I did throw a *stone* rabbit through the window." She opened her eyes. He was watching her, clearly waiting for the rest of the story. When it became obvious she didn't intend to elaborate, he sighed before he whisked the kittens away and shooed Stacie off to the front office to tend to the paperwork.

At the front desk, a week's supply of kitten food and a bill for two hundred dollars awaited her. Stacie tried not to flinch as she handed over her credit card. *What am I doing? I have no prospect of a job. I don't have enough money to cover my bills beyond this month and I just dropped two hundred dollars on kittens I don't intend to keep.*

It was almost dark when she stepped out of the vet's office, but the rain had stopped. She glanced at the little fur balls in her arms. Dr. Talley had fed them and their little tummies were round and firm.

After reaching her car, she placed the kittens in the passenger seat. They immediately wound themselves around each other and went to sleep. Stacie sat in the car watching them sleep. They were so tiny. The vet assured her they were old enough to eat by them-selves and encouraged her to consider keeping them.

They are cute, she admitted, but she couldn't afford to take on any additional expenses. She wasn't even sure how she was going to pay the vet bill and the cost of the broken window. Cheryl had for-warded the invoice for the window as Stacie requested. The cost for the materials and labor was staggering, leaving Stacie no choice but to call the number on the invoice and place the charge on her credit card.

After graduating from college, Stacie thought the financial hard times were behind her. She didn't consider herself materialistic. She liked nice things, but she was willing to drive an older car until Danny was out of college and settled. Once he went to work and started helping their parents, she would be able to afford a few minor luxuries. Someday, after she settled into a job she loved, she wanted to buy a house. Until then, her small apartment would do. *You won't have the car or apartment much longer if you don't find work*, she reminded herself.

The full weight of her predicament hit her. A tornado seemed to erupt inside her skull, forcing her to grab the steering wheel to maintain her balance. She could end up homeless. This was how it happened. One minute you're a productive member of society and the next you're picking up cigarette butts off the street. The fact that she didn't smoke seemed beside the point.

As she mulled over the possibilities, she realized there was something worse than being homeless. The horrifying thought of having to move back in with her parents germinated and grew as she recalled her father's anger. A slight tremor slithered down her back at the memory of the large obscenely colorful bruises he had inflicted on his wife and children. No one was immune from his thunderous explosions. His anger started the vicious cycle that still plagued her family.

As the tentacles spread deeper into her memory, dredging up the past, Stacie's body began to tremble. Everyone around her father quickly learned to be ever vigilant of his moods. You could never be certain what would set him off. Sometimes it was nothing more than the tone of your voice with which he took issue. Other times, it could be that his coffee was cold. It might be some plate or utensil set before him that wasn't as clean as he thought it should be. As children, they would occasionally become so engrossed in playing that their vigilance slipped and they would make too much noise. Those times kept a bone-chilling fear hovering just below the surface of Stacie's childhood. Never knowing when his anger would explode became more terrifying than the actual anger. When he finally erupted there would be hours of total silence within the house. Those were the times when Stacie felt the safest. The volcano had erupted. It would take time for the pressure to rebuild.

Although the physical violence was horrible, for Stacie the most devastating harm was his verbal abuse. Maybe it was because she was the oldest that the brunt of his cutting words generally fell on her. Or perhaps it was because she couldn't hide her dream of becoming a writer. He always twisted her words and made them sound as if her ambition only served to highlight his weaknesses.

As she grew older, Stacie came to realize her drive was too powerful. There were times when it filled their small house to the point of bursting. In a household where dreams had long since died, buried beneath layers of poverty, Stacie's unshakable determination became ground zero for her father's wrath and cutting remarks.

Her siblings found their own ways to avoid his cruel words and blows. Junie gave in and adopted her father's opinion that women were meant to get married and have children. Stacie had been in her freshman year at UT when Junie dropped out of high school six months before graduation and married Bill Walker. The arrival of children took longer than anticipated. Nearly seven years would pass before their son, Tommy, was born, and now she was pregnant with their second child.

Danny survived by keeping his dream of going to college to himself until the last possible moment. Only Stacie knew that he had forged his parents' signatures on his secret scholarship applications. He forged their signatures on his report cards too, not because of bad grades, but because he didn't want them to know he received straight As. The weekend after graduating from high school, Danny told his parents he and a buddy were going to spend a few days fishing and camping out by the lake. He left the house with his tackle box, fishing pole and a brown paper bag containing some clothes. Rather than going fishing, he hitchhiked all the way to College Station where he had been accepted at Texas A&M. A week later, he mailed his parents a letter with an address if they wanted to contact him. To Stacie's knowledge, they never had.

When Stacie heard about Danny's "slinking out," as her father still referred to it, she drove to College Station and found Danny working more part-time jobs than she could keep track of. She finally convinced him to let her help. With his scholarship and her monthly contribution, he was able to quit all the jobs except for the one where he worked as a waiter. He insisted the tips were too good to give up. Stacie suspected it wasn't only the tips but the free meals that kept him working there.

She shook her head to clear away the memories. Nothing could ever make her go back to Wilburn and live with her parents. She would rather starve to death on the streets.

Chapter Thirteen

After a quick stop to pick up kitty litter and a brush that the sales clerk insisted she would need, Stacie returned to her apartment and got the kittens settled in the bathroom. She sat on the side of the tub and watched them explore their new surroundings. They quickly located the litter box she had set up in the corner. It didn't take them long to curl up on the old blanket she had stuffed in a cut-down cardboard box. Just when she thought they were falling asleep, the female kitten suddenly batted her brother's shoulder and they became cavorting acrobats. Stacie smiled at their antics and even joined in by teasing them with a piece of the loose blanket trim. The female attacked Stacie's shoestring, holding it in her teeth and front paws as her back paws began vigorously kicking Stacie's shoe. Laughing, Stacie reached down to disengage the tiny claws. As she did, the kitten grabbed her hand. Suddenly they didn't feel so harmless.

"Ouch. You're a feisty little girl." She scooped both kittens up and held them at eye level. "That's it. I'm going to name you after my favorite brother-and-sister team, Jem and Scout Finch." The newly named Jem tilted his head to one side. "You don't know who Jem and Scout are, do you?" She returned the kittens to their box and absently scratched behind their ears as she told them all about her favorite book, *To Kill a Mockingbird*.

She lost track of time as she rambled on with her story. By the time she finished it was almost ten and the kittens were asleep. As she gazed down at them, she felt a strange tenderness toward them. *I can't afford to keep them*, she reminded herself. Tomorrow she would call the newspaper and run an ad. She would find a good home for them. Whoever took the kittens would have to agree to take both and promise to keep them together.

Staring at them, she told herself it would be the best thing for everyone. After she went back to work she wouldn't be able to spend time with them. With a resigned sigh, she tiptoed back to the living room and flipped on the television. As she surfed through channel after channel of news, sports, infomercials, reruns of reruns and movies with descriptions that practically bored her to tears, she tried to pinpoint the strange hollow feeling gnawing at her, but she couldn't identify it. She finally gave up, flipped the television off and went to the refrigerator to make herself a sandwich.

Ten minutes later, she was still standing in front of the open refrigerator unable to make up her mind what kind of sandwich she wanted. Why was she even looking for a sandwich? She wasn't hungry. She paced around the apartment looking for something to do. The place didn't need cleaning. There was no laundry to do. She stopped to check on the kittens and found them still fast asleep.

As she made her way back through the living room, she spied her Rolodex. Grabbing it, she sat on the couch and began to flip through the cards looking for someone she could call. There had to be someone she was still on speaking terms with. Most of the entries were names she had collected while working at the paper. A few names she didn't even recognize. She deliberately skipped over the card with her family's information. Danny was the only one she might call, but she wasn't yet prepared to tell him about losing her job. With the turning of each card, her discontent grew. She finally pushed the Rolodex aside. There was no one to call. She had been too good at keeping everyone at arm's length. Besides it was late Sunday night; no one liked to be called then anyway.

She walked to the window and pushed the curtain aside. Security lights gave her an excellent view of the parking lot. Her Mazda sat at the end of the lot all alone. How had her life gotten so out of control? *Stop feeling sorry for yourself.* She whirled blindly away from the window and stumbled against the entertainment center. Something fell. On the floor lay the book Cheryl Wright had shoved into her arms at the coffee shop. Stacie slowly picked it up and stared at it. *It's all her fault*, she told herself. *If she hadn't been such an ass, I could have gotten the interview. You blew your chance at the interview. You were too hungover to go.*

Stacie jumped back. The thought had been so strong it took her a minute to realize it had only existed within her own mind.

"Great. Not only am I talking to myself, but now I'm hearing voices."

Tired of pacing, Stacie sat on the couch with the book and read the jacket cover. The plot revolved around a young woman who leads a rescue team into the Florida Everglades to find a plane crash. She glanced at the title again, *On the Wings of Love*, and found herself wondering if the heroine had found love with a member of the rescue team or if her lover was someone on the ill-fated plane.

She shrugged; the story line actually sounded interesting, if you read that sort of stuff, which of course she didn't.

She read the acknowledgments and the dedication page. The book was dedicated to Cheryl's parents, Cletus Ray and Sarah Jean Wright. Stacie grimaced. The names brought to mind too many people she grew up with. She flipped to the back of the book, looking for a blurb about the author, but she couldn't find one. Jack Conrad had mentioned the lack of information available on

Cheryl. Was that why he decided to assign an article on her? She pushed the thought away and turned to the first paragraph. As she continued reading, she told herself she was doing so out of curiosity. If she intended to be a novelist someday, she needed to know what the public was reading, and according to Brenda, readers devoured thousands of romance novels each year.

The sun was up when Stacie closed the book, having read it straight through. She sat on the couch holding the book. Her rash decision to judge the literary value of the work before reading it had cost her. The book was good. If she had only read it when Jack asked her to, rather than getting drunk the night before the interview, she wouldn't be sitting here now wondering what was going to become of her.

As she sat there reflecting on Cheryl's creation of a strong, intelligent heroine rather than the weak, simpering victim Stacie associated with romance novels, the kittens came trotting across the floor. Spying her, they both began meowing.

She remembered her intention to place an ad to find them a home. As she stood watching them, she decided it was too early to call the paper. She would do it later. She scooped the kittens up and rubbed her face against their soft fur. "Are you guys as hungry as I am?"

After putting the salve on Jem's leg, she fed them, then made herself a western omelet. As she ate, she kept thinking about Cheryl's book and realized she owed her an apology. Gathering up her breakfast dishes, she debated whether she should call or write a letter. A letter seemed too formal. A phone call would be better. She would wait until after nine before calling. Afterward she could call and place an ad in the newspaper for the kittens.

Satisfied she had a plan for her day, she went back to the living room and turned on the television to catch the morning news.

Chapter Fourteen

The clanging alarm from a fire engine jarred Stacie awake. She opened her eyes to find the television still on and tuned to an afternoon talk show. It took her a minute to pull herself upright from her twisted position on the couch where she had fallen asleep watching the morning news.

A high-pitched yowl tore her from the couch, certain that one of the kittens was hurt. She found them wrestling under her bed. "Jem. Scout. Come here." She tapped her hand on the floor and they stopped playing and raced toward her. Stacie reached for them and Scout promptly attacked her hand. She played with the kittens until they curled up, exhausted.

The clock on the bedside table reminded her it was after two already. She needed to call Cheryl and the ad-sales department at the newspaper. As she sat watching the kittens, she decided she should wait until Jem's leg was healed. People might be less inclined to take a kitten that needed medical attention. *That's the best thing to do*, she decided. She had already purchased the food and medicine to take care of them for a week, so it wasn't as if it was going to cost her any more than it already had. With that decision made, she went to call Cheryl.

As she held the receiver to her ear, waiting for Cheryl to answer, Stacie realized her palms were sweating. When Cheryl answered Stacie momentarily forgot why she had called.

"Hi. It's Stacie Gillette. I was the reporter who . . ." She stopped, not wanting to remind Cheryl of their last meeting.

"Yes. I remember you, Stacie. How are things going?"

"Good," Stacie lied.

"I'm glad to hear it. I've been feeling horribly guilty about all that mess."

Stacie thought about telling her she should, but she held her tongue. "I called to tell you I read your book, and I enjoyed it."

Cheryl hesitated a moment. "I suppose I should be ecstatic that you lowered yourself to reading a mere romance novel. You must have been truly bored."

There was no mistaking the edge in her voice. Stacie tried to ignore it. "Hey, I didn't call to make you mad. I just wanted to let you know I liked your book."

"Have you found a job?"

Cheryl's sudden change of topic caught her by surprise. "No." Cringing at having admitted to still not having a job, she raced on. "I'm in no hurry. I may take some time to write a book of my own."

"Really. I'm impressed you can afford to do so. I worked full-time while I wrote my first three novels. It was hard. It's wonderful that you won't have to. What's your novel going to be about?"

Stacie froze, at once horrified that the comment about writing a book had popped out of her mouth and the fact that she didn't have the vaguest idea what it would be about. Writing a book was something she hadn't thought about since she was a kid. Sure, she wanted to write a book someday. Like, after she retired.

Cheryl chuckled. "Don't tell me you're worried I'll steal your idea. After all, I'm only a romance writer."

Stacie couldn't think of anything to say and was relieved when Cheryl went on.

"Thanks for letting me know you enjoyed my book, and good luck with your manuscript. I look forward to reading it someday." She hung up before Stacie could respond.

Dejected, Stacie walked down to check her mail and pick up her newspaper, thinking about the conversation with Cheryl. It hadn't gone exactly as she had hoped, although she couldn't pinpoint what she had hoped the call would achieve. Where had that goofy idea of writing a book come from? Cheryl probably thought she was another writer-wannabe. The kind that tells everyone she's writing a book but never seems to put a single word on paper.

After picking up her mail and newspaper, she sat at her kitchen table and read the job listings. She no longer ignored the less desirable jobs. Washing dishes was better than being hungry. She circled an ad for a construction company seeking a receptionist and one for a telemarketing firm seeking people with excellent verbal skills.

She called the construction company first and was told the position had already been filled. Before she could dial the number to the telemarketing firm, her phone rang. The sudden noise startled her. It had been days since her phone rang. She glanced at the caller identification screen and recoiled in disgust. What did the *Travis County Reporter* want?

After a gruff greeting, the caller, Estelle Vargas, got right to the point. "Ms. Gillette, I understand you're currently seeking employment. As you may know, I'm the owner and senior editor of the *Travis County Reporter*. I would like to offer you a position. It's nothing fancy, but if you work hard there's room for advancement."

Stacie couldn't believe her ears. She had submitted dozens of applications, but the *Reporter*, as it was known locally, was definitely not among them. In Stacie's opinion, the *Reporter* was little more than a glorified weekly newsletter. It was a free paper distributed to every restaurant, bar, convenience store and anywhere else a news-stand existed.

Stacie shook her head. She'd rather wash dishes than write for a rag. "Ms. Vargas, I appreciate being considered, but I'm really not interested."

"I thought you needed a job." Her rough smoker's voice grated on Stacie's nerves.

"I am looking for employment. I'm just not interested in working for the *Reporter*."

"Well, excuse me, Ms. Gillette. I didn't realize our little paper would offend your sensibilities. I only called because someone I have a very high regard for told me you had the potential of becoming a decent reporter."

"Who?" Stacie asked before she could stop herself.

"It doesn't matter. After talking to you, I think they made a mistake. You couldn't handle the job."

Stacie stood taller. "I graduated summa cum laude from UT Austin. From the little I've seen of your newspaper, and I use that term loosely, a high-school freshman would be qualified."

The flick of a cigarette lighter hissed through the phone. "Talk's cheap, sweetheart. I have a fifty-dollar bill that says you won't last a month with us. Do you want to know why?"

"I'm sure you'll tell me whether I want to know or not," Stacie replied. Why didn't this woman take the hint and hang up?

"There are two reasons. First, you're lacking people skills and that's the kiss of death for a reporter. You've got to make people like you, or they'll never trust you enough to give you the story."

"There's nothing wrong with my people skills. If you read anything except your own drivel you'd know that several of my articles were picked up by the wire."

Vargas snorted. "Three stories don't deserve the adjective 'several.' Besides, Hinson used you. He played hard to get in order to drive the media into a feeding frenzy. He knew someone would eventually get to him, and once one reporter had the story, all the others would go nuts. He was looking for a book and movie deal. But he screwed up when he gave you the story."

"What do you mean, he screwed up?"

"You blew the story. Oh, you gave all the facts, all right, but you were too green behind the ears to milk the story for all it was worth. You wrote the story as if it were a book report. You were so clinical, the story lost its pizzazz."

"If it was that bad, why was it picked up by the wire?"

Vargas moaned. "You're not really that dumb. Kid, you had the only live interview. My six-year-old nephew could have written the story and the wire would have picked it up."

Stacie didn't want to believe that was the reason, but she kept hearing Peter James, the senior staff reporter from the *Voice*, complaining about how she blew the story with Hinson. Could she have done a better job? "What's the second reason?" Stacie asked, not wanting to dwell on the fact that Vargas might be right.

"You're lazy."

"I am not lazy!" Stacie wanted to reach through the phone and throttle this woman. What did she know about how hard Stacie had worked to put herself through college?

"For the last thirty-four years, I've been at my desk by six every morning except Sunday and an occasional week of vacation. I rarely leave before six each night. Do you know why?" Vargas asked.

"Because you don't have a life," Stacie replied.

Vargas laughed a loud booming laugh, the kind Stacie's grandmother referred to as a belly laugh. "I heard you were a smart-ass, but they forgot to mention you have a sense of humor. I like that in a person. So how about it? You want this job or not?"

Stacie wanted to tell her to shove the job, but after her initial revulsion she was beginning to feel compelled to take it, if for no other reason than to prove Vargas wrong. "Yeah, I'll take the job, and your fifty-dollar bet."

"Good. Have your butt in my office by seven tomorrow morning. And remember, the first time you're late, you owe me fifty bucks." She hung up.

Stacie glared at the phone. The obnoxious woman had deliberately hung up without giving her an address or directions. "That's fine." She smirked as she headed for her bedroom where her laptop sat. She was a reporter. Finding the *Travis County Reporter* wouldn't take ten minutes.

After locating the address, Stacie called the main exchange to verify the address. She wasn't taking any chances.

The young woman who answered the phone confirmed that the address was the correct one for subscriptions. Stacie thanked her, but hesitated. "The correct address for subscriptions," she repeated.

"Yes."

"Do you have offices elsewhere?" Stacie asked.

"The production offices aren't located here."

"Where is Estelle Vargas's office located?"

"Well, she has an office here, but her main office is over at the production building."

"I see," Stacie said and couldn't keep from smiling. Estelle Vargas was a sly old dog. "Where can I find her tomorrow morning at, say, seven?"

"She will definitely be at the production building. Tomorrow is Tuesday. That's when the initial layout begins."

Stacie talked to the receptionist a few minutes longer and learned some basic information about the paper. Afterward, she grabbed the kittens.

"Come on, guys. Let's go for a ride."

She stopped long enough to pick up the most current copy of the *Reporter* from a convenience store before driving to Zilker Park. Since it was a weekday, the park was quiet. She found a shady spot on which to spread her blanket and spent the next several hours playing with the kittens and reading the paper from cover to cover.

Chapter Fifteen

At six-thirty the following morning, Stacie sat in her car staring at the address she'd written on her notepad. The building looked like an old brick-fronted warehouse. There was nothing but a small sign over the door to indicate it was the home of the *Travis County Reporter*. Several cars were already in the parking lot and others were straggling in. The high number of employees entering the building surprised her. How could the *Reporter* possibly support that kind of payroll? They must depend a lot on volunteers and interns, she decided.

Bored with people-watching, she let her thoughts drift back to the issue she had read yesterday. She grudgingly admitted that the articles were well-crafted and even interesting sometimes. Two in-depth articles on local musicians were excellent. *What a shame to waste all that talent on trivia.*

A glance at her watch told her it was time to go in. A cold knot settled in her stomach. *I'm Stacie Gillette the reporter*, she told herself over and over as she locked her car and walked across the parking lot. *I'm a brilliant reporter and they're lucky to have me working for them. Estelle Vargas called me. I didn't come to them for a job.* By the time she reached the door most of her nervousness was gone.

She stepped into a small but tastefully furnished sitting room. Three blue and green plaid armchairs sat in front of the windows on the entrance wall, and two matching ones sat before the sharp modern matte black desk. Behind the desk sat an older woman reading the morning paper. She continued to read even after Stacie approached her desk. A nameplate on the corner of the desk identified the woman as Gretchen Mora.

So much for Estelle Vargas's iron hand, Stacie mused. "Good morning."

"You're early. Have a seat," the woman said without looking up from the paper.

Stacie started to object but stopped as she recognized the raspy smoke-charred voice. She hid her smile as she took a chair near the main door. Estelle Vargas was sitting at the receptionist's desk. Behind the desk was a wide floor-to-ceiling bookshelf stuffed with books. On either side of the bookcases were closed doors.

She tried not to let her irritation show as Vargas continued to ignore her. *She's pissed because I'm here. She thought I'd show up at the main office.*

Stacie made herself relax. She wasn't going to let this crazy woman get to her. She forced her attention from Vargas to the numerous pieces of art scattered throughout the room. There was a pleasing selection of oils, watercolors and a couple of mixed-media sculptures, along with a few breathtaking photographs. Each piece reflected some landscape or image of Texas. A large oil painting hanging on the wall to her right depicted a lanky cowboy with heels dug into the dirt, trying to bulldog a young longhorn. His face was a study of effort and determination. The longhorn looked just as determined.

Across the room, one of the sculptures caught her attention. She walked over for a closer look. It too was a Texas longhorn, made entirely from tiny buttons and seashells. She became so engrossed with the intriguing details of the piece she forgot where she was.

"That's the work of Dolores Maldonado. Do you know of her?"

"No." Stacie felt her brain threatening to shut down. She prayed Vargas wasn't going to spend a lot of time on chitchat. *I'm Stacie Gillette the reporter. I'm Stacie Gillette the reporter.*

Vargas nodded. "She's truly amazing. A car accident left her blind when she was fifteen, yet she creates these magnificent pieces. She once told me she has all of these images stored in her head and they flow out of her fingertips and into her work."

Stacie tried to think of something to say about the beautiful piece, but everything she thought seemed either silly or too gushy.

"I'm Estelle Vargas."

A sense of power seemed to radiate from the woman as Stacie stepped to the desk and introduced herself.

The woman behind the desk was not the brick-wall drill sergeant Stacie had anticipated. Estelle Vargas could better be described as the poster child for Mrs. Santa Claus. Her cap of short gray hair jutted from her head like silver springs.

It wasn't until Vargas stepped from behind the desk that Stacie realized the woman was standing, at five-two. Stacie towered over her as they shook hands. The only hint that she might not be your usual cookie-baking grandmother type was her dark brown eyes. Stacie had read the tired cliché about "piercing eyes" a hundred times, but in looking at Estelle Vargas, she discovered the true meaning of the term. Dressed in dark slacks and a navy blouse with a round lace collar, Vargas didn't give the appearance of being as ferocious as she sounded.

Vargas motioned to the chair closest to the desk. "Have a seat." She started back behind the desk but stopped. "Would you like some coffee or something?"

"No, thank you," Stacie replied as her body began to relax. The interview was starting and she now truly was Stacie Gillette the reporter.

Vargas came back and took the chair next to Stacie. She didn't seem to notice that her feet dangled above the floor. "So, you found me," Vargas said and chuckled.

"Do you play these games with all new employees, or was I special?" Stacie asked, relieved that her brain and tongue were once more working together.

Vargas looked at her and rolled her eyes. "Trust me, sweetheart, you're not special. You're just another half-baked junior reporter who's still way too big for her britches."

Stacie frowned. "What the heck does that mean?"

"It means you show your ass more than you show your talent."

"You don't know anything about me. I've—"

"I know you have a short fuse," Vargas interrupted. "That's an undesirable trait for a reporter."

Stacie glared at the woman. She was deliberately baiting her, and Stacie fell for it. "I do fine as a reporter."

Vargas folded her hands in her lap and looked so much like an impish child, Stacie would have smiled had the imp not been busting her chops.

"That's not what I heard. The rumor mill says you tried to play hardball with Congressman Manchester, but you couldn't even find first base."

"Bull," Stacie snapped. "Manchester didn't want to answer the questions I was asking, so he ran." Stacie didn't like the turn the conversation had taken. Vargas was staring at her and shaking her head. "Tell me about the job," Stacie prompted.

"I need a copyeditor."

Stacie's head flew up. Vargas couldn't be serious. Stacie stood. "You're joking, right? I'm a reporter."

"The best copyeditors were once reporters."

"Why do you even need a copyeditor? Software can handle most of those duties now. That's assuming you have modern software, of course."

"I think you'll be impressed with how modern our process is," Vargas said. "I like to think of our copyeditors as the last line of defense."

Stacie stared at her. "Are you afraid some handcrafter is going to sue you because you revealed her secret technique for gluing Popsicle sticks?"

"No," Vargas said as she took a slow deep breath. "Look. This was a bad idea. I'm sorry, but I don't think you're suitable for the position. Like I told you before, I called you on a whim and I made a mistake. I'm sorry you drove out here for nothing." Vargas hopped off the chair and walked behind the desk.

A cold knot formed in the pit of Stacie's stomach. She was being turned down for a position with the *Reporter*. If she couldn't secure a position here, how could she ever expect to acquire one with a real newspaper? She stood, but her feet welded themselves to the floor. Suddenly she had to have this job. Nothing in the world seemed as important as getting this position. She felt certain that if she didn't get this job, she would never again work in the newspaper business. She tried to speak, but old fear returned to lock her tongue securely to the roof of her mouth. Sweat began to form along her hairline. She closed her eyes and mentally began her mantra. *I'm Stacie Gillette the reporter*. After several tries, she was finally able to say, "I'd like the job." Merely uttering the words helped boost her confidence. She continued her chanting.

"It wouldn't work," Vargas said. "You have no respect for the paper and your work would reflect that."

"I'm a professional. I can do what needs to be done."

Estelle Vargas came out from behind the desk. "That's my point, Stacie. You would do what *needed* to be done, but the fire would be missing."

Stacie Gillette, the reporter, was back. "You're not covering world events here. How much fire does a copyeditor need?" she demanded.

Vargas pointed to the longhorn sculpture that Stacie had been studying earlier. "Do you know what you said when I told you Dolores Maldonado was blinded at the age of fifteen, yet she's still able to create these amazing works of art?"

112

Stacie remembered the conversation but didn't know where Vargas was headed with her question.

"You can't remember," Vargas said, without waiting for her to answer, "because you didn't say anything."

"What did you want me to say?" Stacie asked.

"I can't help but think you didn't say anything because nothing about the work involves you. Ms. Gillette, you are one of the most self-centered individuals I've ever had the displeasure of meeting."

Stacie started to protest, but Vargas held up her hand and stopped her.

"You didn't think about your paper's deadline when you pissed off Congressman Manchester. As I hear it, you didn't even go back to help with the void your little temper tantrum created. You were fired because you didn't complete an assignment, and since walking in here, you've done nothing to convince me you've changed."

"How do you know that?" Stacie demanded.

Vargas rolled her eyes again. "Surely you know by now that newspaper people are notorious gossips."

An awkward silence fell between them.

Vargas finally broke it. "I want people around me who want to work and who love the business. I'm sorry, but I don't think you fit that bill."

"I've wanted to be a writer since I was ten years old," Stacie said.

"Where are you from originally?"

"Wilburn," Stacie replied before thinking and instantly regretted her slip.

"Where the heck is that?"

"Two hundred miles from nowhere," Stacie answered as she headed for the door. Estelle Vargas certainly wasn't going to be interested in hiring a hayseed from Wilburn. After leaving for college, she quickly discovered it was better to tell people she was from Lubbock or even Dallas. The minute she said Wilburn, most people treated her as if her IQ had just dropped a hundred points.

"Why should I give you this job?"

Stacie stopped and turned back to face her. "Because I'm a good reporter and you need my youth and my talent."

Vargas chuckled as she shook her head and said, "You shouldn't be so hard on yourself."

"I'm not bragging. It's the truth. I really am a good reporter."

"Your actions on your previous job indicate you aren't."

"Maybe I'm a bad employee, but that doesn't make me a bad reporter."

"Maybe?" Vargas asked incredulously.

Stacie gave in. "Okay, I'm a bad employee. I'm not very good at playing with others, but I really want this job." She hesitated. "I need this job," she said honestly.

Vargas studied her closely for several seconds before nodding. "All right, I'll give you a chance to prove yourself, but my original bet stands. I don't think you'll last a month."

Stacie stepped forward and extended her hand. "I'm a very stubborn person," she said as they shook.

"And I'm the boss from hell," Vargas replied as she went behind the desk, pulled a sheet of paper from a drawer and wrote something.

Vargas motioned for Stacie to follow her but stopped when she reached the closed door to the right of the bookshelf. She glanced back at Stacie. "Let's hope your talent is at least half as big as your ego." Without waiting for an answer, she turned and said, "Come on. I'll show you around."

Stacie clamped her tongue tightly between her teeth. She needed the money this position would provide, but she intended to keep looking for a real job. As soon as she secured one, she intended to tell Estelle Vargas exactly where she could stick her second-rate outhouse liner.

Oblivious to Stacie's inner turmoil, Vargas was explaining the reason for the paper's two offices. "All of the work on the paper is done here at this building. The office downtown is strictly for show. Our advertisers and subscribers seem to prefer the glass and flash of a new building, but I love this old place and wouldn't dream of moving."

Although rough-looking on the outside, the high, steel-beamed ceilings, brightly painted concrete floors and seemingly endless hallways did possess a certain charm. As they walked down the hallway, people called out greetings to them from beyond the open doorways. Vargas returned their greetings but never stopped.

Small brass plates in the shape of Texas adorned the wall beside each door they passed. Stacie read some of them: Arts Editor, Music Editor, Calendar Editor, Retail Advertising, Classified Advertising, Circulation.

Even with her back to Stacie, Vargas seemed to sense what Stacie was doing. "The presses are located in the far back corner of the building."

"How many people do you employ?" Stacie asked.

"Thirty-four full time, seventeen part time and four interns. The part-timers are mostly in distribution. As you know, we distribute thousands of free copies to hundreds of locations here in Austin. What you may not realize is that we also have a large subscriber base, both here and around the state, and a small percentage is mailed nationwide."

"Why do you give the paper away here in Austin? Wouldn't more people subscribe if it weren't available for free at every corner?" Stacie asked.

Vargas looked at her watch and cupped her hands into the shape of a megaphone. "Boys and girls, we have a new champion. The esteemed Stacie Gillette asked the million-dollar question in less than fifteen minutes."

A muffled chorus of cheers echoed all around them.

"The answer to your question is: We depend mainly on advertising revenue."

Stacie gritted her teeth. Why hadn't Vargas simply answered the questions to begin with? There was no need to announce Stacie's ignorance to the entire building. She wanted nothing more than to tell Estelle Vargas where she could stick her crummy paper, but she suspected Vargas would find a way to turn the comment back on her.

115

"Here we are," Vargas announced as she walked through a side door into a large break room. Vending machines, microwaves and two refrigerators lined most of the two side walls, while the center of the room held a number of old mismatched Formica dining tables, many of which were surrounded by employees drinking coffee.

Stacie followed as Vargas made her way through the dinette colony. As they neared the back of the room, one of the tables sent Stacie spiraling back in time. She had been seven when her parents bought a dinette set from a neighbor, Mrs. Mercer. The set was identical to the one in front of her. The set her parents bought was old but looked brand new. On each corner of the table was a wide strip of rich turquoise blue. The remainder of the top was white with tiny gold flecks that sparkled like real gold when the light caught them just right. It rested on four gleaming chrome legs, and a chrome border ran around the edge of the table. The chrome was so glossy Stacie could see her reflection in it. The backs and seats of the four matching plastic-covered chairs were exact replicas of the table's design. On the top of each chair's back was a silver handle. Mrs. Mercer told them it was there so you wouldn't get fingerprints on the shiny plastic when you pulled the chair away from the table.

On the night they brought the set home, Stacie's mom prepared a special supper. The table was prettier than some of those fancy ones she'd seen in the magazines at the drugstore. Her mom filled the table with a plate of fried porkchops, bowls of fried potatoes and fresh mustard greens, and a large skillet of corn bread made with all milk rather than the combination of mostly water and a little milk she normally used in order to make the milk last longer. She carefully placed the skillet on the old wooden cutting board, so as not to burn the table. Just before they sat down to eat, a cool breeze began to blow through the back screen, chasing away the suffocating heat from the oven. A storm was blowing in.

After using the special silver handle to pull her chair out, Stacie twisted around in her seat and used the skirt of her dress to polish away any fingerprints she might have left on it. Everything was going so well. Her mom lovingly caressed away any tiny spill from the new table and her dad began teasing her about loving the table more than she did him. Stacie held her breath until he started laughing his good laugh that told them everything was okay, not the scary one that made Stacie's stomach quake.

A clash of thunder sounded as though the sky had exploded. Junie screamed and threw her arms over her head. In the process, she knocked over her glass of milk. Suddenly, the peaceful dinner turned ugly.

"Stop that damned screaming," her father shouted at Junie as he jumped up, hitting the table with his leg.

At his unexpected outburst, Stacie flinched and threw herself to the side to dodge the fist she thought was coming. Two-year-old Danny began to bellow at the top of his lungs.

In the middle of the bedlam, her mom was desperately trying to mop up the spilled milk with a threadbare kitchen towel.

"Stop wiping the goddamn table and make that kid quit screaming," her father yelled.

Stacie tried to get out of her chair to escape to her room, but the beautiful chrome legs entrapped her foot. Off balance, she reached out to keep herself from falling and accidentally hit the edge of her father's plate. It went crashing to the floor.

His face turned purple with rage. "Why is it we can't sit down and have a decent meal like regular folks?" he yelled.

Danny began to cry harder.

Junie's screams stopped, but she began to sniffle.

Her father pointed a finger at Junie. "So help me, girl, if you start that bawling, I'm going to give you something to bawl for." He whirled to her mom, who was trying to calm Danny. "Can't you shut that kid up?"

"He's scared," her mother whispered. "You're scaring them all."

Her dad suddenly grabbed the skillet of corn bread and slammed it against the beautiful Formica top. Heedless of the raging storm, he stomped out of the house, leaving behind a deathly silence that was more painful to Stacie than any beating he could have given her.

No one else moved for several seconds. They all stared at the obscene wound the cast iron skillet had inflected on the magnificent table. A large section of Formica had shattered and split. One long crack seemed to be pointing directly at Stacie. She held her breath as her mom's trembling hand reached out and attempted to cover the wound, as though she could heal it, but it was too late. The magic was dead. The gold flecks, Stacie realized, were mere fragments of some obscure material scattered haphazardly over a sheet of white Formica. The chairs were nothing more than cheap plastic that would split over the next few months, leaving sharp edges that bit angrily at Stacie's legs.

"Are you all right?"

A hand on Stacie's arm snapped her back. She blinked and nodded. "My parents used to have a dinette set just like this one," she said. "I was just remembering the day they bought it."

Estelle peered at her, then nodded. "I was twenty-seven when my first husband and I purchased one almost identical to the yellow one over there." She pointed to a table a few feet away. "We thought we were such hot shit."

"What happened to it?" Stacie asked.

"I don't really know. When I walked out the only things I took were my kids and a few clothes. He probably gave it to one of his girlfriends."

"Sorry, I didn't mean to bring up bad memories," Stacie said.

Estelle shook her head. "Leaving him was one of the smartest things I ever did."

"*Hola, mi* boss woman."

Stacie looked up to find a tall young man wearing a baby blue button-down shirt and dark slacks. His ebony hair, styled in a complicated mass of swirls and curls, screamed "gay man."

Estelle rolled her eyes. "Jaime, please, either learn enough Spanish to complete a sentence or else speak English."

Jaime clutched his chest. "You wound me. My culture has been stolen by imperialistic capitalists and you mock my valiant attempt to recover a portion of my heritage."

"Please, you were born in Pennsylvania and your parents are Quakers," Estelle said.

"Thou art so right, my friend, but those funny hats kept messing up my hair and I've lost the buckles off my pilgrim shoes." He waved his hands in the flamboyant manner of a flaming queen. "Besides, my hot Latin persona gets me a lot more dates than my chaste Quaker friendship ever did." He pointed to Stacie. "Who's your new friend? She's cute."

"Jaime Bradley, meet Stacie Gillette, the new copyeditor and my next challenge. Jaime is the arts editor."

He took Stacie's hand. "Oh, you'll enjoy working here. Despite Estelle's attempt to sound like an ogre, she's really an old softie."

"Watch who you're calling old," Estelle growled as she stood on tiptoes to reach a pushpin on the bulletin board and used it to post the paper she had brought from her office.

Jaime stepped in and placed a resounding kiss on top of Estelle's head.

"Stop that, you crazy thing, before I file a sexual harassment suit against you." Estelle playfully pushed him away.

"Oh, please," he said. "If anyone ever sexually harassed you, you'd give them a raise and move their desk in with yours. Now move your hand and let me see what you're posting. It's probably just another one of your pitiful attempts at pretending to be a tyrant."

As they bantered back and forth, Stacie took the opportunity to study Jaime's dreamy hazel eyes framed by impossibly long lashes. Why were gay guys always so gorgeous?

Jaime gave a loud shriek and began laughing before shocking Stacie by giving her a quick hug. "Oh, sweetie, you have my sympathy. If there's anything you need, you just come to me." He started across the room and shouted, "Staff meeting in five minutes."

The scraping of chairs filled the room as the employees began leaving the break room.

"What was that all about?" Stacie asked as she pointed to the paper Estelle had posted.

Estelle smiled and tapped the paper.

Blood raced to Stacie's face as she read:

STACIE GILLETTE

$50

ONE MONTH

"What do you think you're doing?" Stacie asked, mortified.

"It's my way of making you angry enough to stick with me for a month," Estelle explained.

Stacie lowered her voice so that the few remaining people in the break room could not hear. "That's demeaning. What makes you so sure I won't simply walk out the door now?"

"Just a hunch. Besides, you need the job, remember? And it's not demeaning. I'm offering you a challenge."

"Was it this same hunch that prompted you to offer me this job?"

"No. I've already told you why I offered you a job. After meeting you, my gut feeling is that you have potential." She held up her hand. "Let me qualify that by saying, I think you have a lot to learn, and you need to get over yourself."

Stacie bristled.

"Don't get your feathers all ruffled up like an old rooster." Without waiting for Stacie to reply, she walked away. "Come on. We have a staff meeting and we're going to be late."

When they stepped into the conference room a loud chorus of applause and whistles met them. Estelle raised her arms to silence the group, and to Stacie's dismay the noise rose to a deafening level. She glanced at Vargas, who was standing with her arms folded, gazing at the group with a tolerant smile. As soon as the noise level dropped, Estelle motioned for everyone to sit down. Stacie took a chair that Jaime held for her.

"Well, I can see now that everyone is looking forward to my losing fifty bucks," Estelle said.

120

Jaime patted Stacie's arm. "I'm going to see to it personally," he shouted. The room erupted into chaos again.

Stacie realized Jaime had evidently told everyone about the bet. Her face burned but she forced herself to smile. She would show them all. Unlike these losers, her career was not going to end in this hole.

Again, Estelle waited for them to settle down before she spoke. "Okay, Jaime, you can be Stacie's coach." She glanced at Stacie. "Do you speak Spanish?"

"No."

"Good. Then let's pray he'll spare you and, in turn, the rest of us, his pitiful attempts at bilingual communication."

Jaime clutched his chest.

Before he could speak, Estelle rolled her eyes. "Yes, we know."

"You wound me," the entire room chorused.

Stacie smiled at the look of mock indignity on Jaime's face.

He turned to her. "Do you see what I have to put up with? No one appreciates my true talents here."

For once her brain didn't freeze. "It appears we're kindred spirits," she said as she eyed Estelle Vargas. "I suppose we'll just have to show everyone how wrong they can be."

Chapter Sixteen

After work that day, Stacie parked in the lot at Hav-A-Java, already imagining the first sip of her favorite brew, café mocha with whipped cream and an extra shot of chocolate syrup. With the new job, she could afford to splurge a little and celebrate. The fragrant aroma of coffee pulled her through the doorway. She smiled when she saw there were only two people in line ahead of her. Today was proving to be a great day all around.

By the time she reached her table with her steaming cup of liquid paradise, she was practically foaming at the mouth. She closed her eyes and sipped the coffee through the whipped cream. Nothing had ever tasted better. "God, I've missed this," she murmured.

"If that tastes half as good as you make it look, then I'm buying a gallon."

Startled, Stacie's eyes flew open. It took her a moment to recognize the woman standing by her table. She took in the white sleeveless blouse and khaki shorts that displayed long tanned limbs, and a rush of heat swept over her. She attributed the sudden flush of embarrassment to how silly she must have looked swooning over the coffee.

"Don't start blushing on me," Cheryl Wright said. "Let's pretend we've never met and start over." She extended her hand. "Hello, I'm Cheryl Wright."

The reminder of their previous encounters only made Stacie blush worse.

"May I sit down?"

Stacie nodded and pointed dumbly toward the chair across from her.

"I'm treating myself," Cheryl said. "I mailed my manuscript to my editor this morning and I've given myself the rest of the week off." She took a sip of her iced coffee and sighed with deep contentment.

Say something, moron. "Congratulations," Stacie stuttered.

"When I mail a manuscript, I always feel like someone has lifted this enormous burden from my shoulders. My moving cross-country while writing this one didn't help, but with everything going on, it couldn't be helped." She hugged herself and warmed the room with a huge smile.

Cheryl's relief was so contagious Stacie relaxed enough to ask, "If it's so hard, why do it?"

Cheryl tilted her head to one side. "I love writing. I can't imagine what I would do if I couldn't write. As you know, approaching deadlines are stressful and, of course, when I'm stressed I can't write because I'm too busy counting the days until the deadline. I end up trapping myself in this vicious cycle."

She continued to talk about stress and deadlines, but Stacie missed most of the conversation. There was something different about Cheryl that she couldn't pinpoint. Had she cut her hair? Or lost weight? Something was different. "Did you cut your hair?" Stacie asked, as surprised by the question as Cheryl seemed to be.

Cheryl's hand went to her hair. "No."

"Sorry. You look different."

"It's probably because I've slept. After going to the post office this morning, I went home and slept for six glorious hours."

"Why haven't you been sleeping well?" Stacie asked, remembering the stone rabbit she had tossed through her window. She prayed Cheryl hadn't been staying awake dreading a repeat performance.

Cheryl's exuberance diminished slightly. She took a sip of coffee before answering. "It's nothing. I'm just having a little trouble convincing myself everything is all right." When Stacie didn't say anything, Cheryl began to elaborate. "I lived with a woman for almost eight years. When my last two books did really well, I started being noticed as a writer. I had a few book signings with the first one. When the next one started selling well, my publisher set up a book tour. Lea, my ex, didn't like me traveling so much. In truth, I didn't like it much either. I'm a homebody. Our relationship was never very stable and the tour just pushed us further apart. I didn't take much of a break before starting the next manuscript." She shrugged. "We split up. I guess it would be more accurate to say I left, and she had a few problems accepting that the relationship was over." Cheryl took a long swig of her coffee and then another.

Stacie sensed she was struggling with something.

Cheryl laughed suddenly. "Anyway, I'm ecstatic to finally have some free time. I can't wait to start my first sightseeing excursion in Austin. Where should I go? What should I see first?"

Stacie thought for a moment. "Go to the state capitol first and take a tour. It's such a beautiful building. Then walk down Sixth Street."

"What's on Sixth Street?"

"Just the hottest music, greatest food and coldest beer to be found in all of Texas."

Cheryl rubbed her hands together. "I'm going to start tonight." She stopped suddenly. "I'm sorry. I've been rambling so, I've not even asked about you. How are things going?"

124

"Good. In fact I started a new job today." Stacie turned her attention to the cup of coffee in front of her, but not before she saw Cheryl's face light up.

"How wonderful. There's another reason to celebrate. What's the new job?"

Stacie wrinkled her nose. "I'm a copyeditor for the *Travis County Reporter*."

"I don't think I've heard of it. What is it?" Cheryl asked.

"It's a weekly rag on the cultural events going on in South Texas." Stacie shrugged. "It's not my dream job, but it'll pay the bills until something better comes along."

Cheryl nodded in agreement as they both drank their coffee. "What does your partner do?"

"Partner?"

"Yes." Cheryl stopped and a slight blush tickled her cheeks. "Oh, I'm sorry. I assumed the woman who I saw you with here was your partner."

A cold emptiness settled in Stacie's stomach as it always did when she remembered Brenda. It had been two weeks and Brenda still hadn't tried to contact her. "No. That was Brenda. She was an old friend."

"Was?" Cheryl asked, eyeing Stacie closely.

The air around Stacie seemed to grow heavier. Cheryl Wright was not only perceptive but curious as well. She tried to think of a quick generic reason for using the past tense, but nothing came. She was either going to have to tell the truth or sit there like a petrified tree. She was sure Cheryl already thought she was beyond weird. "Yeah." At the last moment, a half-truth came to her. "We haven't been seeing much of each other during the last few weeks. I guess there's too much going on."

"That's too bad. Why is it we always put the ones we love last on our list of things to do?"

To Stacie's horror, tears began to stream down her face.

"Oh. I'm sorry." Cheryl grabbed several napkins and pressed them into Stacie's hand. "I didn't mean to upset you."

125

Stacie shook her head and wiped her eyes. "We had an argument and I guess it's bothering me more than I realized." *Where did that come from?*

"Would it help to talk?"

Stacie wadded the napkins into a tight ball, determined to get her roller-coaster emotions under control. "You should be celebrating. You don't need me crying on your shoulder." She glanced at her watch, suddenly desperate to get away from Cheryl. Every time she was around her, she ended up making a complete fool of herself. "I really should be getting on home. I need to check on the kittens."

Again Cheryl's face lit up. "You have kittens. How many?"

"Two." Stacie gave her the short version of finding the kittens in the park. When she finished Cheryl had tears in her eyes. Stacie got up to get more napkins from the counter. "I grabbed extra in case we decided to stay and talk a while longer," she teased.

"I love cats," Cheryl said. "What do you suppose happened to the mother?"

"The vet suspected someone took them to the park and abandoned them."

"That is so cruel." Anger caused Cheryl's voice to quiver. "Anyone that insensitive should be taken out and . . . and . . . oh, it just makes me so angry."

Stacie blinked, taken aback by the passion in Cheryl's voice. *This woman would care deeply for anything she loved.* The thought surprised her more than Cheryl's declaration.

"What breed are they?" Cheryl asked.

"I'm not sure. They're sort of dark brown with yellowish-gold markings," Stacie said before quickly adding, "Jem has a white blaze on his face."

"Jim?"

Stacie ducked her head, suddenly self-conscious. "I named them Jem and Scout, after the kids in *To Kill a Mockingbird*."

"That's my favorite book," Cheryl exclaimed. "When I read the book, I felt like I knew everyone in it. The characters were so similar to people I grew up with."

"I can't imagine characters like that living in Los Angeles."

Cheryl waved her off. "Good grief, woman. I didn't grow up there. I was born and raised on a dirt farm in the hills of Tennessee. The town was so tiny we barely got a dot on the map. Heck, we were so small we had to borrow a sidewalk from Greensboro just so we'd have one to roll up at sundown."

Stacie stared, amazed that Cheryl could so easily discuss her past.

"You look surprised."

Stacie shrugged. "I guess I'm surprised you talk about it."

"Why wouldn't I talk about where I'm from? It's my home and someday I fully intend to move back there."

"So why did you leave?"

"Ambition, greed, curiosity, and did I mention greed?" Cheryl ran a hand over her face. "From the time I was fourteen all I could think about was escaping those mountains. I wanted to go someplace where no one knew who I was, who my parents were, and all the way back to my great-grandparents."

Although her family didn't go back that far in Wilburn's history, Stacie understood Cheryl's need to escape. She wanted to tell her she empathized with her, but to do so she would have to explain her own childhood, and she wasn't ready to release that demon. "I thought knowing who you were, that whole back-to-your roots thing, was supposed to be great," she said. "People spend hours researching their family history and even pay out big bucks in order to know who their great-grandfather was."

Cheryl chuckled. "Oh, there wasn't much chance of us ever forgetting our ancestors." She glanced at Stacie. "You know, I almost forgot I'm talking to a reporter."

"Not hardly," Stacie said and slumped back into her seat. "I'm a copyeditor."

"Today was really your first day?"

Stacie nodded.

Cheryl leaned in. "Tell me about your day." She gave a conspiratorial wink. "I'm always looking for professions for my characters."

Stacie turned her cup in a slow circle. "The senior editor, who also happens to be the owner, is certifiable." She told Cheryl how Estelle Vargas deliberately concealed the fact that there were two locations for the *Travis County Reporter* and about the fifty-dollar bet she made and posted.

"She posted it on a bulletin board," Cheryl said, her eyes round with surprise.

Stacie nodded. "I'm telling you, she's a weird bird. I spent the rest of the morning filling out paperwork and meeting everyone. Then, after lunch, Vargas brings in a stack of copy and dumps it on my desk. For the rest of the day, I read and edited music reviews, articles on upcoming art and craft shows that seem to pop up in every little podunk town in South Texas, and lists of which bands are playing where. But the high point of my day was an in-depth report on Uncle Clem's Brown Jug Band."

Cheryl's eyes sparkled with suppressed laughter. "I guess romance writers don't look so bad anymore."

Stacie tensed. She didn't want things to get ugly between them again. Talking to Cheryl was enjoyable and surprisingly easy.

"I'm teasing you," Cheryl assured her as she reached across the table and patted Stacie's hand. "Try doing what I do. When I start feeling sorry for myself, I think about other jobs I could be doing."

"What do you mean?" Stacie asked, frowning.

"Well, for example, I could be a garbage collector. Can you imagine having to ride around all day long hanging on to the back of a garbage truck? Or I could have been a CEO imprisoned in an office day in and day out." She leaned forward. "I have the greatest job on earth." She held up her hands to stop any protest from Stacie. "I know. I was complaining earlier about deadlines, but everyone has deadlines of some sort. I set my own hours. If I want to go outside, I grab my laptop or a pad and pencil and go sit under a tree. I can do my job almost anywhere." She folded her hands and leaned still closer. "But the best part is when someone comes up to me and tells me my book made a difference. That's the ultimate rush. Whenever I start thinking about burning all my pencils and paper or dumping my laptop into the nearest lake, I pull out a folder where I keep those wonderful letters that I occasionally get from readers and I read them."

Stacie couldn't stand it any longer. "How can a romance novel make a difference?"

"You know the answer to that already," Cheryl said as she settled back into her chair.

Stacie frowned. "No, I don't."

Cheryl studied her for a moment and slowly ran a finger over the corner of her mouth. "We were poor and there weren't a lot of options available to us for entertainment. We were too far back into the mountains to be able to pick up regular television reception and we couldn't afford one of those gigantic satellite dishes. On our fifth birthday, we each got our own library card. Twice a month, we would walk into town to the tiny library." She smiled and stared beyond Stacie's shoulder as she continued. "The library probably contained less than two hundred books, but the librarian, Mrs. Jenkins, was a wonderful woman. She left the mountains when she was a young girl, only to move back after her husband died. One of the things she introduced me to was a wonderful program known as interlibrary loan. Suddenly, thousands of books were at our fingertips." Cheryl sipped her coffee that was melting into muddy goop and gazed at Stacie. "My mother never physically left the mountains, but through books, she traveled the world. When the world could no longer contain her energy, she flew to the outer galaxies of the universe. My father didn't know salad forks existed, but he dined with kings and led their armies to stunning victories." She stopped and took a deep breath.

Stacie waited, sensing Cheryl had more to say.

When Cheryl began to speak her voice was softer. "I was fifteen," Cheryl began. "I knew I was somehow different from the other girls. There were days when it felt as though a herd of wild mustangs were galloping loose inside me. Then, I stumbled across a book that literally changed my life." She gazed at Stacie. "It was a lesbian romance novel. After reading it, I started to understand myself. That herd of wild mustangs slowly disappeared and I accepted who and what I was." She started to take another sip of her coffee, but wrinkled her nose in disgust and pushed it aside.

They sat in silence for several long seconds before Stacie said, "I live a few blocks from here. Since we're both celebrating, why don't I run by the market and grab a couple of steaks to grill? Or if you don't eat meat, I can prepare something else."

"I wish I had the discipline to only eat vegetables," Cheryl said. "Unfortunately, I have to admit, I'm a carnivore through and through. There's nothing like a tender medium-rare steak. Since you're cooking, you have to let me do the grocery run."

Stacie started to protest but realized she would have to charge the food to her credit card, and its balance was already sorely inflated from the kittens' vet bill and Cheryl's window. Besides, it was primarily Cheryl's fault that she had been fired. She finally nodded in agreement.

Chapter Seventeen

After giving Cheryl directions to both the nearest grocery store and her apartment, Stacie rushed home to feed the kittens. When she entered her tidy apartment, she was glad she had worked so hard cleaning it while unemployed. Her apartment normally ranged in the clean but messy stage.

The kittens were ready to play and kept her laughing while she fed them and quickly changed their litter. "We're going to have company, and I want you guys to be on your best behavior," she warned them. In answer, Scout batted Stacie's foot with her paw. "I'll take that as a yes," she said, grabbing the garbage and running down the stairs to drop it in the dumpster.

When her doorbell rang several minutes later, she was sitting on the floor playing with the kittens. "Remember, be nice," she whispered as she gathered them into her arms. So far, they hadn't attempted to dart out the door, but she wasn't taking any chances with them.

She opened the door to find Cheryl with several grocery bags. "Dang, you've got a week's worth of groceries," she exclaimed. She reached to help, but her hands were full with the kittens.

"I forgot to ask which wine you prefer."

Stacie tried not to shudder. She hadn't touched anything alcoholic since that horrible night. Before she could comment, Cheryl rushed on.

"I couldn't make my mind up on which wine you would like best and then there was the salad issue. Should I be suave and urbane and make you an elegant three lettuce concoction or would a simple green salad from a bag do? I won't even embarrass myself by telling you about the ten-minute poll I took of which salad dressing most people preferred." A bead of sweat trickled down the side of Cheryl's face.

Stacie laughed and motioned her into the apartment. After closing the door, she set the kittens down and took some of the bags from Cheryl. "The kitchen is in here," she said, indicating that Cheryl should follow her. By the time the bags were settled onto the counter, the kittens were in the doorway demanding attention.

"Oh," Cheryl exclaimed as she scooped them up. "They're adorable."

Stacie stepped to her side. "This is Jem and this is Scout."

"I would like to get a kitten, but Shakespeare would have a stroke and tear the house apart."

"Shakespeare?"

"My cat. He's one hundred percent alley cat, but he's very handsome and such a snob." She shook her head. "I can't believe a cat is in such control of my life." She scratched Scout beneath the chin.

Scout's head dropped back as her eyes closed and she purred a symphony of perfect ecstasy.

Prompted by jealousy, Jem chomped down on Scout's tail. Scout responded by opening her eyes just long enough to give Jem a swift paw to the head.

"Hey, you two." Cheryl held them aloft, one in each hand.

"If they get to bothering you, I can put them back in the bathroom," Stacie offered.

"No. I adore kittens," Cheryl assured her.

Stacie was glad. She felt guilty enough that they had been in the apartment alone all day. She didn't want to compound the abuse by locking them away in the bathroom. "Why don't you have a seat? I'll get started on dinner."

"Can I help with anything?" Cheryl asked.

"No, I can handle it. Besides, the kitchen is so small, we'll just get in each other's way. Have a seat at the table and I'll pour us some wine." She removed the two bottles and studied the label. One was a cabernet, the other a shiraz. "Which do you want?" She held up the bottles.

Cheryl studied them. "Let's try the shiraz and save the cabernet for dinner."

"Tell me about Los Angeles," Stacie said as she uncorked the wine and poured them each a glass.

"I was only there for three years. Before that, I lived in San Francisco." Cheryl took a sip of her wine. "In L.A., everything seemed to be running full tilt twenty-four seven, but there are places so beautiful it'll bring tears to your eyes." She continued on about the beauty and differences in the two cities.

"They sound like wonderful places to live," Stacie said, refilling Cheryl's glass. Stacie had barely touched her wine, but she pretended to top it off to make it look like she was drinking.

"I enjoyed living in San Francisco," Cheryl said. "I'm still not sure how I feel about L.A. It's a city of so many contrasts. It's horribly crowded. It's just this unbelievable mass of humanity, but at the same time there's this sense . . ." She paused. "I'm not sure I can explain how I felt. The city is colossal, but there were times when I would feel completely alone. Not the nice kind of solitude we sometimes need, but a different type of loneliness that I can't really explain." She shrugged. "Maybe it was from growing up in such a small community, where everyone knows everyone else. Then there was the economic disparity. Sections of L.A. are so poor you'd think you were in a Third World country, but you drive a few miles and there are areas where the wealth is so prevalent that a million dollars means next to nothing."

"Can you imagine having that kind of money?" Stacie said with a sigh. She topped off Cheryl's wine again before taking her own glass to the kitchen counter.

"You know what they say. Money can't buy love," Cheryl said.

Stacie snorted. "You just haven't been to the right part of town."

Cheryl gasped. "Stacie, I can't believe you said that."

Stacie glanced up from the steaks she was marinating. The shocked look on Cheryl's face made her laugh. "I'm joking. Well, not about the right part of town, but I know what you meant."

The kittens were falling asleep in Cheryl's lap. "You know, right after I moved to L.A. a woman I was kind of dating took me to one of those places." She hesitated.

"What kind of place?" Stacie prompted before sipping her wine.

Cheryl cleared her throat.

Stacie glanced back at her and saw her face was beet red. "Omigosh. You went to a whorehouse."

"It wasn't called that," Cheryl insisted.

Stacie forgot about the food and gaped at her. "You really went and you . . ." It was Stacie's turn to stutter.

"No. I didn't actually . . . you know. It wasn't like that exactly."

"What was it exactly?"

"Well, I only went the one time and I didn't stay for the entire . . . um . . . um . . . session."

"You left in the middle of it!" Stacie walked back to the table. This was too good to miss.

"No. I mean, yes." Cheryl waved her away. "Go back over there and work. I can't tell you if you're standing here watching me."

Stacie went back to the counter and slowly opened the bag of salad. "Okay, I'm not watching, so you can start anytime."

"Why did I bring this up?" Cheryl muttered.

Stacie glanced at Cheryl's empty wineglass and refilled it as discreetly as possible, so as not to discourage Cheryl from finishing her story.

"This is what happened," Cheryl said. "I was dating a woman who was a little, well, I guess you could say different."

"Different how?"

"You know. She was into kinky stuff."

Stacie peeked over her shoulder. With her vibrant healthy glow and farm-fresh looks, Cheryl appeared too *average* to be into kinky sex. *As if I'd know what kinky sex was if it hit me upside the head.* She waited for Cheryl to begin her story again.

"Anyway, she took me to this place. I guess she had made . . . arrangements earlier because when we walked in we were escorted back to this large bedroom."

"What did it look like?" Stacie couldn't keep her questions to herself.

"From the street the house looked like one of those old movie star mansions. The room we came into, I guess you'd call it a parlor, was very elegant. I remember there was a beautiful crystal chandelier, and an enormous ornate fireplace filled most of the end wall. The other room, the one with the bed, was very nice also. There was a much smaller chandelier not nearly as elaborate. The bed was one of those monstrosities with a headboard that went half way up to the ceiling." She sipped her wine. "We were told to have a seat. The armchairs where they told us to sit were placed in front of what I first thought was a large window because of the floor-to-ceiling drapes. As soon as we were seated, the lights dimmed and the curtains slid open." She stopped and took a much larger sip of wine.

Stacie worked on the salad. She was beginning to regret she had encouraged this story. It had been almost a month since she'd had sex. She didn't consider the episode at Rosie's or the Yellow Rose as sex. That had simply been playing around before the real fun started.

"There was another room beyond the curtains and there were

135

these two women," Cheryl said. "They started having sex with each other. I swear I was so scared I almost peed my pants. I expected the vice squad to pop in any minute and haul us away to jail."

Her sigh made Stacie look back at her. Cheryl was holding her head in her hands.

"Stacie, I was so pea green I didn't have any idea what was about to happen."

Stacie kept her ignorance to herself and waited.

"After watching them for a while, the woman I was with started to get undressed and they came over to help. I freaked when one of them started unbuttoning my shirt and tried to kiss me."

"What did you do?" Stacie asked, unable to believe how aroused Cheryl's story was getting her.

"I shoved her away, bolted over the chair and ran like a scared rabbit. I didn't stop running until I got to my car." She groaned and shook her head. "I was so inexperienced." She looked up at Stacie. "You must think I'm a bumbling hayseed."

"Who knows? Had I been in that situation, I might have done the same thing." The words were meant to be comforting, but Stacie didn't think she would have left. She thought back to the situations in the bars. Before then she had never participated in public displays, but there was something faintly exciting about the chance of being caught.

"You wouldn't have left, would you?" Cheryl asked.

The question caused a wave of heat to tiptoe up Stacie's neck and over her scalp. "No. I probably wouldn't have."

Cheryl let out a long sigh as the blush ran across Stacie's face.

Stacie turned and found Cheryl staring at her with a resigned look. She tried to interpret the expression, but Cheryl turned her attention to the sleeping kittens.

"You're much too easy to talk to," Cheryl said. "Give me something to do that will keep my mouth shut." She stood and gently placed the napping fur balls on the chair.

"The steaks are ready to take down to the grill. If you want, you can walk down with me. I don't like to leave the food unattended after I put it on the grill. Or, you can stay here if you'd rather not go back out into the heat." Stacie felt slightly off kilter, as though she had missed something very important.

Cheryl hesitated a moment before saying, "Why don't I stay and get the salad ready?"

Stacie nodded in agreement, grabbed the steaks and rushed away. Something had happened between her and Cheryl and she couldn't pinpoint what it was or even the exact moment it happened. One minute they were laughing and talking, much like she and Brenda once had, *only better*, she decided. Then something happened.

As she slowly made her way down the steps, part of the answer came to her. Cheryl withdrew. *After I admitted I might not have left, things between us changed. She probably thinks I'm as weird as her kinky ex-girlfriend.* A small pang of hurt settled in her chest. She enjoyed talking to Cheryl. A part of her was hoping they could become friends, but she'd probably screwed it up with that stupid comment about sex. *Maybe I should totally give up sex.* She stopped short. It had been a month since anyone touched her. *I already have.*

Chapter Eighteen

"You survived your first week," Estelle Vargas said as she handed Stacie a cup of coffee.

Stacie pushed away the article she was editing and stood. "Yeah, but thank God it's Friday."

Estelle laughed. "Big weekend plans."

"Always," Stacie bluffed. She wasn't about to admit that aside from laundry and taking the kittens out to the park, she had no plans for the rest of her life. "What about you? Which of these fascinating events are you planning to attend?" She tapped the latest copy of the *Travis County Reporter* that had been sitting on her desk when she came in that morning.

"None," Estelle replied.

"None! How can you bear to miss even one single moment of these—?"

Estelle held up her hand. "Okay, enough. Sit down and drink your coffee before it gets cold. It's not like I plan on bringing you a cup every day, you know." She took the chair beside Stacie's desk as Stacie sat.

"So why did you bring me coffee?" Stacie asked.

"I wanted to see how your first week went. I guess I'm hoping you're a little happier with the job than you were on Monday morning."

"Why is that so important to you?" Stacie asked.

Estelle looked at her in surprise. "I want my employees to be happy. I've worked in jobs where I was miserable, and don't want people to feel that way here."

Stacie sipped her coffee. *Was Estelle serious? Or was this just one of those fake bonding moments that management seemed to thrive on.* She decided to avoid the conversation. "If you're not joining the multitude of crafters, roadies and critics, what are you doing?"

Estelle crossed her legs and leaned back. "I'm going to the valley."

Stacie grimaced. "It's a hundred and twenty in the shade down there."

"I like the heat. After being away nearly fifty years, I still miss it."

"Were you born there?" Stacie guessed Estelle to be in her early sixties.

Estelle sipped her coffee. "No, I was born in Mexico. My father died when I was six. There weren't many jobs for men and even fewer for women in our small villages. My mother's brother lived in Brownsville and helped us with the arrangements to emigrate. We lived with his family for almost a year. Mom couldn't speak English when we first came over, but she managed to get a job cleaning in one of the hotels." A smile teased Estelle's lips. "My mother is shorter than I am and has this enormous energy level." She glanced at Stacie. "Mom is eighty-six now and can still work circles around me. She reminds me of that cartoon character of the Tasmanian devil."

Stacie stared into her coffee cup. Estelle's mom left her homeland for an opportunity to better her family's life, while Stacie's

139

mother stood by and watched her children being used as punching bags. Stacie shook off the memories as Estelle continued with her story.

"Mrs. Reilly, the woman who managed the housekeeping department, was fond of Mom. One Christmas Mom gave her one of her *pinturitas*."

"*Pinturitas*?" Stacie asked.

"It means little pictures. My mother loved to paint and she was very good. Anyway, long story short, Mrs. Reilly showed the painting to her brother-in-law who owned a gallery in Houston. Shortly thereafter, Mom was able to stop working at the hotel and paint full-time. Her little pictures put her three kids through college."

"Wow. It must have been terrifying for her in the beginning," Stacie said before nodding toward the copy of the *Reporter*. "That's why you do this. Your mother's an artist."

Estelle gazed at the paper and a look of sadness crossed her face. "No," she said. "That's an entirely different story." She hopped up. "It'll have to wait for another day. I have a meeting." She rushed off before Stacie could say anything.

For several moments after she left, Stacie continued to stare at the empty doorway, lost in thought. Even though it was something she dreamed of doing for years, leaving Wilburn, and the security that familiarity breeds, had been scary. She tried to imagine how terrifying it must have been for Estelle's mom to leave everything familiar to move to a foreign country where she couldn't even speak the language. Why hadn't her own mother been braver? She felt certain Estelle's mother wouldn't have stood by and watched as her children were whipped until blood seeped from angry red welts.

"Hey, you."

Stacie jumped backward, almost flipping over her chair.

"Whoa, girl. What's wrong with you?" Jaime stood in the doorway.

Stacie's heart pounded as a light sheen of sweat broke over her body.

Jaime stepped into her office. "I'm sorry I startled you. I thought you saw me. You were looking right at me." He placed a hand on her shoulder.

Stacie prayed he couldn't feel her trembling. She had been so lost in thought she hadn't even noticed him. He peered at her.

"Stacie, are you all right?"

"Yes, I'm fine," she said and shrugged his hand off her shoulder. "I was thinking about an article and I guess I zoned out."

He took the seat Estelle had vacated only moments before. "You jumped like a king cobra was suddenly dropped in your lap, although a certain anatomical area of my body is often cited as being very similar to that majestic serpent."

"You mean quick and smelly?"

"Well, someone's in a snit today. I do hope you plan on getting laid this weekend," he snipped back.

Stacie smiled. Jaime could be a bit over the top sometimes, but she appreciated his sense of humor. In fact, he was well-liked and respected by everyone she had spoken to at the paper. He was a hard worker and always there to lend a hand to anyone who needed help.

"What brought you slithering to my desk?" she asked.

"A group of us are going to Angelino's for lunch and I thought you might like to join us."

Stacie's mouth watered. She loved Angelino's four-cheese lasagna. "I can't. I've already made plans." That wasn't exactly true, but she was too ashamed to tell him she couldn't afford to go to lunch. This position paid quite a bit less than her former job. She was going to have to be extremely thrifty in order to meet her own obligations and still be able to send money home.

Jaime waved his hand. "All right, but if you're not there, we're going to talk about you."

Stacie laughed. "You don't know enough about me to talk about me."

"We're newspaper people. Since when is knowledge so important? What we don't know, we'll simply make up."

141

Stacie picked up the article she had been working on before Estelle stopped by. "Make up something exotic."

"I was thinking more of erotic, *chica*," he teased.

"Can I ask you a personal question?" she said.

Jaime smiled slightly and wiggled his eyebrows. "*Sí*. But if you do, then I get to ask you one."

Stacie hesitated. She didn't particularly like answering personal questions. "It's no big deal. I was just curious about your last name."

"Shame on you. Trying to renege on a deal before it's even made." He made a clucking sound with his tongue before launching into his story. "My father, Allen Bradley, descended from a long line of devout Quakers. But alas, the life was too confining for poor Dad. He left Pennsylvania and made his way across country on foot. He worked odd jobs whenever he needed to earn a few dollars. He arrived in Albuquerque broke and went to work for my grandfather, Ignacio Moreno, harvesting apples. That's how he met my mother, Guadalupe Moreno. They were married six months later and raised four children. The youngest being the gorgeous specimen in front of you."

"I thought Estelle said you were born in Pennsylvania."

"That's because in a moment of weakness, Dad heeded his mother's pleas to come back and raise his family as proper Quakers. Needless to say, the experiment didn't work and soon after I was born our little tribe journeyed back to New Mexico and stayed." He made a production of examining his nails. "I like to think I got the best of both their worlds. My calm serene outer shell is totally Dad, but just below the surface waiting to explode is the smoldering Latin blood of *mi madre*."

Stacie couldn't help but laugh.

He pretended to scowl at her. "Laugh, you infidel, but you leave me with no choice but to extract justice. You owe me one question," he reminded her with a mock scowl.

Stacie's laughter turned into a groan. She didn't intend to make a production of it, but there were plenty of questions she had no intention of answering. "Okay," she agreed. "One question."

"Tell me your entire life story." Jaime looked extremely pleased with himself.

"I would, but that's not a question, and you only get one question."

He frowned. "I see I'm faced with a sly mind. I'm going to have to be much more devious around you." He thought for a moment. "What are the details of your life story?"

She shook her head. "Sorry, but that question would take too long to answer. You're going to have to wait for the movie. I've got a load of work to do and considering today is Friday, I have absolutely no desire to stay late."

"Ah-ha. A hot date is it? I'm demanding full details." He stood up. "I will let you off the hook until Monday, only because by then I'm sure the details will be even juicier." With a quick wave, he left.

Chapter Nineteen

The phone rang as Stacie struggled through her front door with bags of cat food and kitty litter under each arm. She set them by the door and took time to check the caller identification screen to make sure it wasn't her mother. The monthly check she sent home was going to be a little late, and while she didn't think they would ever question her not sending it, she didn't want to take any chances. Her father would never let up if he discovered she had been fired.

She grabbed the phone when she saw Cheryl's name flashing. They hadn't spoken since Tuesday evening when Cheryl called and again thanked her for dinner.

"Did I catch you at a bad time?" Cheryl asked when Stacie answered.

"No, I just got home." Jem and Scout came tearing out from her bedroom.

"I'm sorry. I can call back after you've had time to catch your breath."

"No. I'm fine, really. What's up?" Scout was trying to climb Stacie's pant leg. *That won't be cute in a few more weeks*, Stacie thought as she reached down and extracted the kitten's claws from the material of her slacks. Jem instantly howled his jealousy. Tucking the phone against her shoulder, Stacie scooped him up and he immediately began to chew on her thumb.

It seemed to Stacie that Cheryl hesitated slightly before saying, "I'm calling to see if you'd like to come over. I made spaghetti sauce today, and as usual I got a bit carried away and made enough for a small family."

Stacie swallowed her impulse to accept right away. She didn't want Cheryl to think she was a dork with no life.

"If you're busy, I understand. I know it's short notice," Cheryl said.

"No. I'd love to come over. I love spaghetti." Stacie grabbed her head and grimaced. *I am a dork!*

"Great. Since you just got home, I'm sure you'll want to rest for a while, so we can eat whenever you get here."

Stacie ran her hand through her hair and did a quick estimate on how much time she needed. "Would seven be too late?"

Cheryl chuckled. "No. That would be perfect. It'll give me time to finish the garlic bread."

"It sounds wonderful. Can I bring anything?"

"Do you like homemade peach ice cream?" Cheryl asked.

Stacie's mouth watered. "My grandmother used to make peach ice cream when we were kids and I loved it." *Stop saying you love everything. She'll think you're an idiot.*

"Then you don't need to bring anything but an appetite."

After saying good-bye, Stacie put both kittens on the floor and hung up the phone. She rubbed her thumb that Jem had used as a chew toy.

Both kittens were staring up at her, crying at the top of their lungs.

"You guys are getting spoiled." She gathered them up and nuzzled her face in their fur. "Don't even try to pretend you're hungry," she scolded. She kept food out for them all the time.

She carried the kittens into the bedroom and placed them on the bed. She grabbed a stuffed teddy bear and attacked them with it until they were distracted enough to play alone. With them temporarily occupied, she quickly sorted through her closet in search of something to wear. She pulled out a white shirt but immediately ruled it out. A white shirt and spaghetti would be begging for disaster. She finally selected blue shorts and a brightly hued Hawaiian print top. Holding them up, she turned to the kittens. "What do you think, guys?"

At the sound of her voice, they paused briefly in their play to look at her. The pause was short-lived as Scout bit Jem's tail and the chase was on.

"Some help you guys are," she called out as Jem zipped out the bedroom door with Scout on his heels.

Stacie took extra care in shaving her legs to avoid razor nicks. She showered with her favorite lavender-scented soap, whistling happily the entire time. Afterward, as she stood before the bathroom mirror combing her hair, she suddenly laughed aloud. "Why are you in such a great mood?" she asked the grinning face in the mirror. "Because it's Friday, I have a job, and I'm going to have dinner with Cheryl."

She stopped in mid-stroke. *Why would having dinner with Cheryl make me so happy?* She puzzled over the thought for a minute before the answer came. *She's a friend and I enjoy talking to her.* Satisfied with the answer, she applied a mist of cologne before going back to her bedroom to dress.

Jem and Scout were sitting up on the slacks she had taken off and placed on the foot of the bed. She rubbed their heads, already feeling bad about leaving them alone again. "I'll make it up to you guys tomorrow," she promised. "We'll play all day."

After slipping into her sexiest black lace underwear, she pulled on her shorts and shirt.

Stacie rang the doorbell at precisely seven. She studied the label on the bottle of wine she had brought and tried not to concentrate on what had occurred the last time she rang Cheryl's doorbell, but she couldn't stop herself from glancing beneath the table in the corner to see if the stone rabbit was there. It wasn't. Before she could fully explore what its absence meant, the door opened.

"Hi, come on in," Cheryl said.

Stacie handed her the wine. "I thought you might like this. The guy at the liquor store said it was a great dessert wine." Her feet seemed to be glued to the porch.

"Thank you." Cheryl took the bottle and gently ushered Stacie into a living room filled with color, from the warm burgundy walls to the rich glow of the cherry wood floor. A long sofa the color of sandstone ran the length of an interior wall. Across the room from it sat a matching chair and one of dark burgundy with an exquisitely embroidered headrest. A large round, low table filled the center of the room. As Stacie stepped closer, she could see the intricately carved details beneath its glass top.

"My uncle carved that," Cheryl said when she noticed Stacie studying the table.

"It's beautiful. What kind of wood is it?" *What a stupid question. Who cares what kind of wood it is?*

Cheryl moved to stand beside her. "It's walnut. This is my most prized possession. My Uncle Sonny is my favorite uncle. He never learned to read and the only thing he could write was his name. Hand the man a penknife and he could turn a broken tree limb into the most amazing pieces of art."

"I've never understood this kind of talent," Stacie said as she leaned over the table for a better view. "Can you imagine what it must feel like to look at something like this and know you created it from nothing?" She stood and looked at Cheryl. "I guess you do. You must feel the same way each time you finish a book."

Cheryl smiled and said, "By the time I finish a manuscript, all I feel is relief. I enjoy that for about a week and then it's time to start thinking about a new story line."

Before Stacie could respond, a cat almost twice the size of a normal cat strolled majestically into the living room.

"Say hello to Shakespeare, the true ruler of this household."

147

Stacie could only stare as the cat walked to a large ottoman in the corner of the room and hopped up on it with incredible grace. "I can honestly say I've never seen a cat that big."

"He is amazing," Cheryl said as she walked over and patted his head. Her efforts were met by a yawn of indifference as the enormous feline regally draped himself across the ottoman. His green eyes narrowed as he dismissed the insignificant humans. "As you can see, he lives for my attention." Cheryl rolled her eyes.

Shakespeare looked away from them. His head tilted in lofty disregard.

"I think we've been dismissed," Stacie said.

"Indeed. Come on into the kitchen. The spaghetti is almost ready. What would you like to drink?" She rattled off a selection of beverages.

Stacie opted for a beer as she followed Cheryl into a large formal dining room with a dining table large enough to seat eight. A matching walnut china cabinet sat on one side and an antique sideboard filled the other. A quick left brought them into a spacious modern kitchen of stainless steel and Italian marble. "Wow," Stacie said without meaning to.

Cheryl blushed. "I know. It's too much room for one person, but I saw the house and fell in love." She pulled a cold beer from the refrigerator and poured it into a tall pilsner glass.

"Who would have ever believed that romance novels were so popular?" It was Stacie's turn to be embarrassed. "I'm sorry, that was rude. Your finances are none of my business." Even as she apologized, her brain was doing the math for the house and the car.

"I'll tell you a secret, but you can't tell anyone," Cheryl said as she handed the glass of beer to Stacie and motioned her to a barstool at the marble-topped island. "I was one of those lucky people who got into and out of the dot-com market at exactly the right time." A wicked smile teased the corner of her lips. "My entire life doesn't revolve around romance novels."

"I guess I do seem a little overly obsessed. I'm sorry."

Cheryl removed a bowl of salad from the refrigerator and placed it on a table in the corner. "I hope you don't mind eating in here. I thought it would be more comfortable than the dining room."

"Hey, you're talking to someone who usually has a sandwich in front of the television. Eating at a table is a treat for me."

Cheryl laughed. "My dinner is usually a bowl of cereal. I hate cold cereal for breakfast, but I like having it for dinner. Weird, huh?"

"My favorite food for breakfast is Oreos and coffee. Whenever I get depressed or I want to celebrate something big, I stay in bed and stuff myself with Oreos."

Cheryl looked her over and sighed. "I bet you're one of those disgusting people who can eat everything they want and never gain an ounce."

It struck Stacie then that the first time she had seen Cheryl she thought she was overweight. Looking at her now, she no longer thought so. *She must have lost weight*, she reasoned.

"You don't look like you have a weight problem," Stacie said.

Cheryl waved her off. "Please. I've been trying to lose the same ten pounds for the last five years. I swear the day I turned thirty, everything on me turned south."

Stacie laughed aloud. "Come on. You make it sound like thirty is ancient."

Cheryl eyed her closely. "Just as I suspected. You haven't been subjected to that milestone yet, have you?"

"No. But I don't think it will be a big deal."

"Oh, I do hope I will be around to see you celebrate the big three-oh because I want to be there to remind you of those very words."

As Cheryl removed a large pot and dumped the steaming spaghetti into an oversized silver colander, Stacie found herself hoping that her friendship with Cheryl would continue to grow and that they would be friends for many years to come.

Chapter Twenty

The tension in Stacie's muscles slowly drained away as she sat on Cheryl's patio listening to water ripple over a slab ledge before spilling into the pool of the water garden. Accent lighting revealed an aquatic paradise complete with water lilies and a beautiful copper dolphin softened by a velvety patina.

Toward the back of the yard was a separate building. Stacie thought the units were referred to as mother-in-law suites. She wondered if that was where Cheryl wrote.

Cheryl appeared with a fresh beer for Stacie and a glass of wine for herself. "I love sitting out here," she said as she handed Stacie the beer.

"I can't believe it's so quiet. It's almost like living in the country," Stacie said.

"Did you grow up in the country?"

"No. I grew up in Lubbock." The old wariness crept back into Stacie. Cheryl freely admitted the poverty of her background, so why couldn't she? Memories of her father crept in and sent a shiver down her spine.

"Is it too cool out here?" Cheryl asked, apparently seeing Stacie shiver and misunderstanding.

"No. It's nice out."

"What's Lubbock like?" Cheryl asked.

Stacie suppressed the sigh. She hadn't intended to let the conversation turn to her. "It's a lot of nothing set smack in the middle of nothing."

"Is your family still there?"

"My parents and sister are. My brother is at A&M." Stacie decided to stick to the truth as much as possible without revealing too much.

"I've heard of A&M. It specializes in agriculture doesn't it? Is your father a farmer?"

The old tightness clamped down on Stacie's brain. She didn't want to talk about her family. She could sense Cheryl waiting for her to respond. "The college is known for its agriculture program, but it also has a great engineering department. That's why Danny chose A&M. My dad works for the newspaper."

"Oh, so you're following in the family footsteps. How wonderful. He must be extremely proud of you."

"Yeah, he is. What about you? Why did you decide to move to Austin?"

"I came here about five years ago to do a writer's workshop. It was in April and there were wildflowers everywhere. I fell in love with the city. When I realized I really didn't want to live in L.A., I remembered Austin and how beautiful it was."

Stacie asked another question without giving Cheryl a chance to turn the conversation back to her. "You mentioned your family loved to read, but you never said if you had siblings."

"I have three brothers, two older, one younger, and I have a younger sister. I'm the middle child."

"What did your dad do for a living?" Stacie asked, determined to keep the conversation away from herself.

Cheryl was slow enough in answering that Stacie turned to see if she was paying attention. She found herself under observation. "Is this Stacie Gillette the reporter or Stacie my friend asking?"

Stacie leaned back in surprise. Cheryl thought of her as a friend. She wished she could take back the lies she had told Cheryl about her family, but it was too late. Cheryl was waiting for her to answer. "I'm not a reporter anymore. You know that."

"Yes, I know, but I also know there's a little thing known as free-lance."

Stacie grunted. "Trust me. The only thing I'm writing anymore is an occasional grocery list."

Cheryl gave a short wave of her free hand. "I'm sorry, I'm being silly. I've never been ashamed of how my father earned a living. He did what he knew how."

"Talk about a lead-in," Stacie teased. "I can't wait to hear the story."

"Until about six years ago, my father ran moonshine."

It took Stacie a moment to process the term. "Moonshine. I thought that was something that happened during Prohibition."

"Americans have been making moonshine from practically the moment they landed in North America." Cheryl chuckled. "You don't want to get me started on this. I'll talk your ear off."

"Please tell me."

Cheryl looked at her. "Are you sure? I'm serious when I tell you this is a subject that can keep me going all night."

"I'm really interested," Stacie assured her. *I'm interested in any-thing that keeps the conversation off me.*

"All right, just tell me to hush whenever you get tired of listening." She took a sip of her wine. "Let me give a little history first. In the seventeen nineties Alexander Hamilton, the Secretary of the Treasury, came up with an excise tax. Some say he advocated a central government under a monarch, but that's another story." Cheryl waved her hand back and forth as though erasing that line of thought. "Hamilton's act required that all stills be registered. Tax collectors were appointed and granted the power not only of search and seizure, but to tax all whiskey at seven cents per gallon.

You have to remember that whiskey was selling for twenty-five cents a gallon then in the less settled areas, and for as much as fifty cents a gallon in the more populated areas where distilleries made the whiskey. So, you see who's getting hurt the most with the tax? Because of the wide range in the price per gallon, the tax on the poorer areas equated to around twenty-eight percent as opposed to fourteen percent for the distilleries."

"How did the government justify this?" Stacie asked.

"The same way they justify tax increases today. They say it's for national security. Hamilton tells everyone he wants to raise millions of dollars for defense. One of the ways he proposed to do that was with the whiskey tax. Because the tax was so unpopular, the government had trouble getting people to accept the position of tax collector. Things got ugly and people were hurt. I'm giving you the condensed version," Cheryl said as she leaned over and patted Stacie's arm. "Thomas Jefferson repeals the tax as soon as he's elected and there's no more trouble until the Civil War, when once again the government needed to finance a war. The Confederate government began to confiscate stills for the copper. They needed it to make the percussion caps for muskets. Both the Confederate and the Federal governments established an alcohol tax to finance the war, but guess what? After the war, the tax was never rescinded. Texas currently has five separate taxes on alcohol. That doesn't even count the federal tax. Today we're talking about billions of dollars."

"How do you know all of this?" Stacie asked, amazed.

"That's another story," Cheryl assured her and sipped her wine.

"How does this all relate to your father?"

Again, Cheryl looked at her. "Are you really interested in this?"

"Yes." Stacie held her hand in a Girl Scout's pledge.

"There are several reasons why people make moonshine. My father did it because it's what he knew. His father, grandfather and great-grandfather ran moonshine before him. Right after he and Mom were married, there was a major push to clear the moonshiners out of our county. Dad and Grandpa barely missed being caught. It gave them both a good scare. Dad decided to try the Army. That's the way many of the young people got away from the mountain, but the Army shipped him off to Vietnam. You'd have to know Dad to understand how that nearly destroyed him. He's such a gentle soul. He never hunted for sport. If he picked up a rifle, it was to help put food on the table for his family." Cheryl seemed to become lost in her own memories for a moment.

Stacie waited impatiently. What a fantastic story this would have made. She gave herself a good mental kick for blowing the opportunity she had been given to officially interview Cheryl. *Of course, I wouldn't have heard this story in an interview*, she reminded herself.

"Dad came home on leave before he left for Vietnam. During that time, my mom became pregnant with my oldest brother, Roy. By the time Dad returned from Vietnam, he had a wife and a son to support. The only work he could find was in a factory forty miles from home. The trip was hard enough during good weather, but whenever it rained, or there was ice or snow, the trip was impossible. He carpooled with three other men. One night they were caught in a rainstorm and had an accident. One of the men was injured rather badly. After that, Mom begged him to quit, and Dad turned to the only other thing he knew how to do. He made moonshine."

"Wow," Stacie whispered. "That is amazing. I never dreamed people continued to have stills that far beyond Prohibition."

"Stacie," Cheryl said leaning toward her, "moonshining is a major business throughout the United States today."

Stacie stared in disbelief. "Your dad still makes illegal whiskey?"

Cheryl laughed heartily. "No. He stopped a few years ago."

Stacie felt silly. She kept her mouth shut, allowing her mind time to sort through what Cheryl had told her. Finally, she had to ask a question. "I don't understand why someone would buy this homemade stuff when you can buy whiskey almost anywhere now. I mean, I know there are dry counties scattered around. There are even some in Texas, but it's not as though you have to drive across the country to purchase liquor. So why take the chance?"

Cheryl tilted her head in thought. "I suppose most of the time it's economics. A gallon of moonshine is much cheaper than a gallon from a liquor store. There are people, like tourists, who purchase moonshine for the sheer thrill it brings. They like to take it back home to show everyone. There seems to be this nostalgic rebel image associated with shine. But I think the dominant reason is the taste. Dad made excellent moonshine. People traveled for miles to buy his brew."

"I thought it was dangerous to drink. Can't you go blind or something?"

"You can die from eating chicken if it's not prepared properly," Cheryl scoffed. "There are always a handful of idiots who try to make an extra buck and add something dangerous to their moonshine. Rubbing alcohol or wood alcohol are probably the most common, but I've read about people using formaldehyde, paint thinner, bleach and even lye. You have to remember, most people do this as a means of making money. To do that you have to build up a clientele, and this isn't exactly something that you can run an ad in the local newspaper for."

"How do they sell it?"

"It's all by word of mouth. In Dad's case, people had been buying from his father and grandfather for decades."

"So most people knew what your family did for a living?"

"It was pretty well known around town and maybe a little less known throughout the county."

"How did he keep the news from reaching the local law enforcement?"

"Sheriff Tuttle would never have turned in my dad."

"Your father bribed the sheriff?"

"Lord, no. Sheriff Tuttle and Dad's oldest brother, my Uncle Sonny, went to school together. My grandfather and his father fought in World War Two together. The Tuttle family went back almost as far as my own. Dad's bootlegging was never talked about. If Dad had ever done anything that was harmful to someone else, Sheriff Tuttle would have picked him up in a heartbeat."

Stacie nodded. She understood how deep the roots ran in people who lived side by side for generations.

Chapter Twenty-one

One Wednesday afternoon, after her dinner at Cheryl's, the phone on Stacie's desk rang. It was Estelle asking for the article on the upcoming battle of the bands that Stacie was editing.

When Stacie arrived with the article, Estelle was standing on a chair hanging her latest piece of artwork. "You're either going to have to stop buying art or else build more walls," Stacie teased. During the brief time she had been working there, she had grown to admire the short, feisty editor.

"Then more walls it shall be. I can never get enough of this beauty. Just look at the colors in this," Estelle said, motioning to the whimsical piece of folk art she was hanging. "A woman from Guatemala did this. Isn't it amazing?"

"I admire the way you support women artists."

Estelle's cheeks flamed a dark red as she continued to gaze at her latest piece. "I do what I can. I often wonder what would've become of my family if Mrs. Reilly hadn't taken the time to show my mom's work to her brother-in-law."

Stacie placed the article on Estelle's desk. "Here's the article you asked for. I've already finished editing it and it's ready to go."

"Sorry I didn't catch you sooner. It's been canceled."

"The article?" Stacie asked.

"That too, but I was referring to the event. It seems the promoter was caught with the lead singer of one of the groups and she's underage. All the advertisers are pulling their support, and without sponsors, there's no money for the awards."

"When do I get to move over to reporting?" Stacie asked.

Estelle shook her head and sighed. "You've been working as a copyeditor for less than two weeks."

"But I want to do some real work."

"Why don't we wait and see if you make it through the initial offer of a month?"

A stab of irritation caused Stacie's jaw to tighten. She saw Estelle prepare herself for Stacie's comeback, but she decided not to give her the pleasure. With some difficulty, Stacie swallowed her complaint.

Estelle walked back to her desk. As she went around the corner, she picked up a book and slid it toward Stacie. "Have you read Jean Gray's latest novel yet? I just finished it this morning. Started it yesterday and couldn't put it down."

Stacie turned the book around and read the title, *The Mountain Still Stands*. "No. I like to read mysteries occasionally, but otherwise, I'm not much of a reader."

"Shame on you. How can you expect to be a great writer if you don't read?" Estelle scolded. "This book is a recent release and it's already sold over a hundred thousand copies. I read a review in the *New York Times* yesterday."

Stacie picked the book up and turned it over. "What's it about?"

"The review I just mentioned includes a line that I love. It says the book is about what happens when the Waltons meet the Sopranos. It deals with two families and the choices they make to survive the Depression. Both families run moonshine, but one of the families gets greedy. Making a living isn't enough for them. They want more. Of course, to get more they have to take bigger risks and break more laws."

"They run moonshine," Stacie said as she read the back cover. "This is so weird. I was just talking to someone this weekend who was telling me about her father, who ran moonshine."

Estelle looked up from her desk. "Is that so? Was it someone from around here?"

Stacie flipped the book open. "No. I mean yes. The woman I was talking to lives here, but her father, the moonshiner, lives in Tennessee."

Estelle sat in her chair and tapped the arms. "I wonder if we could get an interview with Jean Gray and maybe tie in your friend's story somehow?"

Stacie glanced up. "No, I don't think my friend would be willing to talk about it publicly. She's sort of gun-shy with the press."

Estelle leaned forward and Stacie realized she had made a mistake. She quickly placed the book back on the desk.

"Who is this friend?" Estelle ask. "If she's had occasion to talk to the press it must be someone of some stature, which would make the story all the more interesting."

"I don't think so," Stacie said. "Listen, I shouldn't have said anything. Can we just forget this conversation ever happened?"

Estelle gazed at her a moment before nodding. "You're probably right, since bootlegging is illegal. All kinds of legal issues are probably involved."

Stacie didn't compound her mistake by informing Estelle that Cheryl's father no longer ran moonshine.

As Stacie returned to her office with the book under her arm, she thought about Estelle's idea. It had occurred to her Saturday night that the story would make a great article, but she was certain Cheryl would never agree to do an interview. *You already have enough of the story for an article*, a tiny voice prodded. *Cheryl is your friend*, her conscience answered back.

Stacie finished reading the book that following Friday morning. As she drove to work, she thought about the vast number of similarities between what Cheryl had told her and what she read in the book. Did the similarities exist because they dealt with the same subject, or could there be another explanation? After arriving at work, she signed online and did a search for Jean Gray. She found a listing for two previous novels and a long list of reviews for the current one; there was nothing on the writer. By noon that day, Stacie felt certain there was something Cheryl had failed to mention.

Not wanting to get into the discussion over the phone or take a chance of someone overhearing and stealing her source, Stacie waited until she got home after work to call and invite Cheryl to dinner. They agreed to meet for Chinese later that evening.

After hanging up, Stacie stared at the book for several minutes before a broad smile broke across her face. The wire service would definitely pick up this article. As the old flame began to rekindle itself, she sat down at her computer with the kittens in her lap and began to type. By the time she had to leave to meet Cheryl, the bones of the article were in place. She printed the draft and left it sitting on her desk. She would start to flesh out the details in the morning.

Chapter Twenty-two

Stacie did a double take when Cheryl walked into the restaurant wearing black jeans with a cobalt blue shirt and black boots. "You look nice," she said as soon as Cheryl slid into the booth across from her.

Cheryl glanced up in surprise. "Thank you."

The waitress appeared to take Cheryl's drink order. Stacie was already sipping her tea. After Cheryl ordered a pot of hot tea, she began to fidget with the menu. "I feel like trying something new tonight. What's good?"

"I've never gotten anything bad here. If you're willing to trust me, we could get the house special for two. It's a combination platter and we can mix and match from the list at the bottom of the menu," Stacie said as she pointed to the list of choices.

"That sounds perfect."

They quickly made their choices and were ready to order by the time the waitress returned with Cheryl's tea.

Cheryl nervously stirred her tea. "Stacie, I need to tell you something. I feel really bad that I've kept something from you," she said and glanced up at Stacie. "I'm ashamed of my reasons for doing so."

"What's wrong?" Stacie asked even though she was certain she knew what Cheryl was going to say.

Cheryl placed her spoon on the table and clasped her hands in front of her. "As you know, we sort of got off to a rocky start."

Stacie's cheeks began to burn. She didn't want to think about their first couple of meetings.

"Because of that," Cheryl continued, "I guess I've been a little reluctant to be completely honest with you." Stacie started to speak, but Cheryl held up a hand to stop her. "I know we don't really know each other, but I like you. As a friend," she hastened to add before leaning back against the seat. "What I'm trying to say is that I've kept something from you and I don't want you to find out later and be hurt."

"Does this have anything to do with *The Mountain Still Stands*?"

The look of shock on Cheryl's face was too much for Stacie. She began to laugh.

"How did you know?" Cheryl asked.

Stacie wiped a tear from her eye. "Believe it or not, my boss was raving about the book after you told me about your father. Since moonshining doesn't appear in many plot lines, it gave me reasons to speculate that perhaps you also wrote using a pen name. You gave me the final clue when you said you had something to tell me."

Cheryl shook her head and smiled. "Now I should probably be twice as nervous. It appears you're a very good investigative journalist."

Stacie thought of the article she had been working on earlier. "Have you considered revealing your family history? It would certainly give you some extra press coverage for the book. I know Estelle is interested in interviewing Jean Gray."

Cheryl shook her head vehemently. "Are you serious? Moonshining is a federal offense."

Stacie frowned. "I thought they went out, chopped up the still and slapped them with a fine for operating without a license."

"There's also the matter of income tax evasion and money laundering," Cheryl said. "I read about a case recently where the man only received five years under the federal liquor laws, but they gave him fifteen years for money laundering."

"Money laundering?"

"Criminals can't exactly take the profits of the family business to the bank each Friday," Cheryl reminded her.

Stacie nodded.

Cheryl looked around and lowered her voice. "My problem goes beyond the law. Dad no longer makes moonshine, and I think he covered his tracks well enough to avoid the law. You have to remember he came from a long line of successful 'shine runners. I can't do anything that might stir up suspicion and get the Feds poking around the county. Besides protecting my father, there are others in the county who continue to depend on it as a source of income. Imagine what it would do to Sheriff Tuttle's career, not to mention all the other folks who would get drawn into the mess just from the backlash."

Stacie decided now might be the perfect time to bring up an issue that had been troubling her. "Is the local law enforcement getting kickbacks? Is that why they look the other way?"

"No. It's not about money, or at least not in the same sense as it is in, say, drug dealing. It's about making a living and maintaining a sense of dignity. Hill people are proud people. Most of them hate government handouts. They want to be left alone to live as they see fit." Cheryl traced a scratch on the table with her fingertip. "Stacie, I don't know how to make you understand what it's like there. We take care of our own. If someone starts running bad moonshine, Sheriff Tuttle shuts them down. The same thing happens if a runner gets greedy and starts making trouble for others. Jobs are scarce in the hills and it's a different world in so many ways." She took a deep breath and slowly exhaled before continuing. "It's about priorities. Maybe the best way to explain it is to tell

162

you something I once heard a news anchor say. He spoke of Americans believing in God, country and family, in that order. Where I come from, we believe in family, God and country. And family for us includes anyone we care deeply for. Although he's no blood kin, Sheriff Tuttle is family to me." She gazed at Stacie. "Does that make sense?"

Stacie nodded. Her family wasn't close, but she did have a slight understanding of what Cheryl meant. The people in Wilburn held a less intense version of those same beliefs.

"Aren't you worried that the book will point a finger back to your father?"

"The book is fiction. There's really no reason it should. If I'd had even the slightest concern that anyone would make a connection between Dad and my book, I would never have written it."

"What if someone eventually discovers that Cheryl Wright and Jean Gray is the same person?"

"Again, it shouldn't matter. I'll simply say that I wanted to branch off from the romance genre and used a pen name in case the book was a flop. I can use Jean Gray's other two novels as a perfect example. Neither of them flew off the shelves." The joking tone left her voice as she gave Stacie a searching look. "Please promise me you won't write anything or tell anyone what I've told you. I had no right to endanger all those folks by telling you."

Stacie felt trapped. She already knew her story would be good. It could possibly give her a shot at a reporting job again. Nevertheless, she didn't want to hurt Cheryl. Looking into Cheryl's eyes, she could see the anxiety building. "I won't," she vowed. She smiled when she realized she meant it. She promised herself she would tear the article up and delete it from her computer as soon as she got home.

"Thank you," Cheryl said as her body visibly relaxed. "I can't tell you how worried I've been all day."

The waitress arrived with their food and they both ate with gusto.

"Oh my," Cheryl moaned as they walked out of the restaurant.

"I can't believe I ate that last egg roll. Why didn't you slap my hand?"

"I was too busy inhaling the last of the sweet-and-sour shrimp," Stacie said as she tugged at her waistband.

"I need to walk," Cheryl said and pointed across the street to the mall. "Let's go window-shop."

Stacie agreed. They left their cars in the restaurant parking lot and darted across the street.

As they strolled through the mall, Cheryl turned to her. "I don't want to bring up bad memories, or embarrass you, but something is really bothering me. Can I ask you a question?"

Stacie nodded, not liking the turn in the conversation.

"That day you came to my house and I wasn't there, why did you break the window? I mean, you seem so calm whenever we talk. You don't seem like the type to explode at a moment's notice."

Stacie rubbed her chin. "It's kind of a long story."

"I'd really like to hear it, if you don't mind telling me."

Seeing the sincerity in Cheryl's eyes, Stacie started by telling her about the disastrous meeting with Congressman Manchester. To her surprise, she continued and told her about being tossed out of Rosie's, although she only skimmed over the cause. She went on to tell her about meeting Trish and in the briefest details told her about Brenda catching them. She finished with the call from Jack firing her.

"I still feel terrible about that," Cheryl said. "I was being such a bitch."

"We're both to blame," Stacie corrected. "But honestly most of it was my fault. I didn't act very professionally."

Cheryl nodded. "So have you gotten things worked out with Brenda?"

Stacie felt the unexpected burn of tears in her eyes. "No." She tried to swallow the lump that had suddenly formed in her throat.

Cheryl looped her arm through Stacie's. "That must have been a horrible time for you. I'm sincerely sorry I added to your problems."

They walked arm-in-arm through the mall. Stacie found the feel of Cheryl's arm against her very comforting.

After several seconds, Cheryl looked at her. "You should go see Brenda and make her listen to your explanation. Friends are too precious to lose over misunderstandings. It's much too easy to lose the people we care about in so many other unavoidable ways."

Stacie nodded. "You're right. I'll camp at her door until she agrees to listen to me."

They continued their window-shopping until just before the mall closed.

"It's too early to call it a night," Stacie said. "We're not far from my apartment. Would you like to come over? We can find a good movie and pop some popcorn."

"Well, all that walking has made me hungry again," Cheryl said and winked. "Can I wake the kittens up and spoil them rotten?"

"Waking them up won't be an issue and unfortunately they're already spoiled rotten. Scout seems to believe any sock she finds is fair game for her to hide. You wouldn't believe some of the places where I've found my socks."

"Wait until they bring you a present. Every time Shakespeare sneaks outside, he comes back with a poor little bird. The first time he did it, I cried for two days."

Stacie shuddered. "Hopefully I won't have to worry about that. Since I'm in the apartment, the only way they'll be able to get out is if I'm with them."

Cheryl rubbed her hands together and gave an evil laugh. "Oh, little do you know."

Chapter Twenty-three

Stacie unlocked the door to her apartment and pushed the door open carefully. The kittens were there to welcome them.

"What a wonderful greeting," Cheryl said as Stacie scooped them up.

"They're trying to make me look bad," Stacie said as she ruffled their fur. "You would think I hadn't fed them for a week." She motioned toward the sofa with her head. "Go ahead and have a seat and I'll get these rascals settled."

"Oh, leave them out," Cheryl pleaded. "They're so cute. Shakespeare is too dignified to play anymore. I threaten to bring home kittens all the time and he gives me that 'oh, bother, why must I humor this human' look that he has perfected."

Stacie laughed and handed over the kittens to Cheryl. "He does seem to have a tad of an attitude."

"When I die, I want to come back as Shakespeare," Cheryl said.

"Why don't you see if you can find a movie while I start the popcorn?" As Stacie reached for the remote control, she noticed the message indicator light blinking on her phone. She selected the call-missed screen and saw her parents' number. They had called shortly after she left to meet Cheryl. A twinge of guilt pricked her conscience; she hadn't returned their last couple of calls. *I'll call tomorrow*, she promised herself. With the rationalization that it was after ten and they would already be in bed, she handed the remote control to Cheryl and headed for the kitchen. As she did so she wondered where she had left the handset to the phone and how long it had been off the charger. "I hope you don't mind," she called from the kitchen. "I don't like microwaved popcorn. I prefer to pop it the old-fashioned way."

"That's fine with me. What kind of movies do you like?"

"Anything that's not gory, scary or loaded down with teenage hormones."

"You sound like my mother," Cheryl said and giggled.

"Hey, watch it. I can be as hip as the next person." Stacie placed a large pan on the stove and added oil.

"As long as there's no boogie man involved," Cheryl teased.

"All right, you just wait—"

The phone rang, interrupting them.

"Shall I bring you the phone?" Cheryl asked.

Stacie quickly turned the burner off from beneath the pan. "No, I can get it." She raced back to the living room. As she slid to a stop in front of the phone, she remembered the handset wasn't on the base. She must have left it in the bedroom. PAY PHONE flashed across the screen. Who would they be calling so late?

Before she could react to the thought, her mother's quavering voice filled the room.

"Stacie Lynn, it's your mama again. I sure wish you'd give us a call. Your sister Junie ain't doin' good. Doc says she may not make it through the night. She's askin' for you. Your daddy and me are pretty near beside ourselves with worryin' about her and not knowin' where you are. We've been tryin' to call you all night. We're at the hospital in Piedmont, so come as soon as you get this here message." There was a slight pause and Stacie could hear muffled voices in the background before her father's voice thundered through the phone.

"Boy, what do you mean worryin' your mama so?" The loud smacking sound of the slap sliced through hundreds of miles of phone cable and sent Stacie to her knees.

"Your brother just got here. Please hurry, honey. Junie needs you," her mother whispered into the phone before hanging up.

Stacie didn't know how long she stayed on the floor or how long Cheryl held her as Stacie cried and clung to her, desperate for the warmth and security being offered.

After Stacie had cried herself out, Cheryl gently lifted her from the floor. "Go pack whatever you need and I'll check the airlines to see if you can get a flight out tonight."

Stacie nodded and stumbled toward her bedroom. She made it as far as the end of the bed and sat down. Junie couldn't be dying. Why didn't they listen to Doc Kurtz? He had told them not to have any more kids after Tommy was born. The comforting sound of Cheryl's voice floated back to her, giving her the strength to go to her closet and retrieve a small suitcase. She pulled clothes from the hangers without paying much mind to what she was selecting. A part of her was screaming for her to hurry, to get to Junie as quickly as possible, but another frightened part knew her father would be waiting for her just as he had been for Danny.

A hand landed on her shoulder, causing her to scream and throw her hands over her head.

"Stacie, it's okay. It's me. Cheryl."

Stacie slowly lowered her arms and turned back to the closet, unable to face Cheryl. "I'm fine," she said quietly. "Why don't you go on home? I'm ready to leave."

"There's not another flight to Lubbock until almost six tomorrow morning but it takes you to Houston first and you'll have to change planes there. You wouldn't get to Lubbock until around ten."

Stacie leaned against the closet door. "That's okay. I can drive it faster."

168

"How long will it take you to drive?"

Stacie struggled to remember how long it had taken her to drive home for the funerals of her grandparents. "Some of the roads are really narrow and there are a lot of curves. Driving at night will be worse. It'll take me about nine hours."

"Then it would be safer for you to wait and fly out tomorrow morning," Cheryl said.

Stacie shook her head.

"I understand. Let me help you pack." Cheryl led Stacie to the bed and sat her down.

Stacie was vaguely aware of Cheryl moving around, but she was too preoccupied with trying to decide how she was going to avoid her parents to pay much attention. She couldn't face her dad's anger. There had to be some way she could talk to Junie without having to see him. Even as she tried to find one, she knew there was no way out for her. She had to be there for Junie. Her suitcase appeared at her feet.

"What's your friend Brenda's last name? Stacie, sweetie, what's Brenda's last name?"

"Evans."

Cheryl patted Stacie's knee. "You finish packing. I need to make a phone call, but I'll be right back," she said.

Stacie nodded and continued to stare at the suitcase full of neatly folded clothes. It finally dawned on her that it was her bag. Cheryl had packed the clothes Stacie had taken from the closet. She grabbed a handful of underwear and socks from a dresser drawer before going to the bathroom to gather the rest of her essentials. With everything packed, she stood staring at the bag. *It's time to go*, she told herself. Closing the suitcase, she took it and headed toward the living room. Cheryl was fidgeting with her key-chain when Stacie entered.

"Are you ready to go?" Cheryl asked.

Stacie nodded.

"Good. Let's go." Cheryl reached for Stacie's bag.

Stacie's hand shot up and pulled the bag from Cheryl's reach.

"No. You can't go." The thought of Cheryl witnessing her humiliation was worse than having to endure it.

Cheryl rubbed a finger over her eyebrow. "You won't wait until morning and you're in no condition to drive that far alone. I'm going to drive you."

"No," Stacie said, shaking her head frantically. "I can't let you. You don't understand." Tears choked off the rest of her argument.

Cheryl stepped forward and pulled Stacie into her arms, hugging her tightly. "There seem to be some issues going on with your family that I don't know about and it's none of my business. However, you're upset and as a friend I can't in good conscience let you drive that far alone."

"Why?" Stacie demanded.

Cheryl pulled back slightly. "Because you're my friend and because I care what happens to you." She kissed her softly. "I would be worried sick if you went by yourself."

Stacie stared at her, unable to believe Cheryl had kissed her. Just as she was beginning to believe her mind was playing games with her, Cheryl kissed her again. This time there was no mistaking the fact that she was being kissed in a manner that left no doubt there was more than friendship involved. As Cheryl's arms tightened around her, Stacie allowed herself to be drawn into Cheryl's passion. The kiss grew more urgent and the suitcase slipped from Stacie's grasp.

The sound of it hitting the floor seemed to break the spell as Cheryl suddenly stepped away. "I apologize," she whispered. "Now is not the time for me to be doing this." Without waiting for her to comment, Cheryl grabbed the suitcase that Stacie had dropped. "Let's go."

Still stunned by the call and by Cheryl's kiss, Stacie complacently followed along and climbed into Cheryl's Jag. She sat staring out the windshield while Cheryl placed the suitcase in the trunk. Thoughts of the feel of Cheryl's lips made Stacie's body tingle, but the memory of the sound of her father slapping Danny drove the pleasant feeling away.

She turned as Cheryl got into the car. "I can't let you do this," Stacie said.

"Then we have a real dilemma because I can't let you go alone." She turned the key and the powerful engine purred to life. "Why don't you try to sleep? If I get tired, I'll wake you."

"You don't understand." Stacie swallowed what little pride she still possessed. "I lied to you about my family."

"Why did you lie to me?"

Stacie studied the face that was in turn scrutinizing her. She would tell Cheryl to mind her own business. If she made Cheryl angry enough she would leave and Stacie would be free to drive home alone. She swallowed before answering and looked directly into those amazing blue eyes. What she saw surprised her. She didn't find the anger or disapproval she expected, but a look of caring and deep concern. "I was ashamed of my family and where I came from." *That's not what I meant to say. What's wrong with me?*

"Why? I've already told you how I grew up. I know what it means to be poor."

"There are worse things than being poor." Unable to meet Cheryl's gaze, she turned to stare out the window.

After several seconds, Cheryl placed a hand on her shoulder. "We have a long drive ahead of us. You can rest, or we can talk. Whichever you're more comfortable doing. Either way, I want you to know that my feelings for you are . . . are . . . strong, and that scares me." Without waiting for Stacie to reply Cheryl drove toward the parking lot exit. "Which way?" she asked as Stacie continued to stare out the window.

"North to Temple. We'll catch Thirty-six from there and take it all the way to Abilene," Stacie replied.

They rode in silence until the city lights fell behind them. Stacie felt the increased output of the powerful motor as the car picked up speed. A quick glance told her they were now going more than eighty-five miles per hour. She felt torn between asking Cheryl to drive faster and begging her to slow down. Somehow, she was going to have to convince Cheryl to drop her off in either

Abilene or Lubbock. She would be able to rent a car there and drive the rest of the way alone.

They had been on the road for over an hour when Stacie's cell phone sprang to life on her belt. Unable to stop the small yelp that escaped her, she grabbed the phone and saw PAY PHONE flashing on the screen, again. It had to be Danny because she had never given the cell phone number to her parents. Her knees went weak at the thought of why he would be calling. Junie must be worse.

Cheryl placed a hand on Stacie's knee. "I'm right here. You're not alone."

Stacie nodded and with her heart in her throat answered the phone.

"It's Danny. Are you okay?"

"I'm on my way," Stacie replied, knowing that would tell him everything she was feeling. "How's Junie?"

"Not too good. She started hemorrhaging and they took her to the county hospital over in Piedmont. They got the bleeding under control, but then it started up again. The doctor came out a few minutes ago and told us that they stopped the hemorrhaging, but now it looks like the baby is having some kind of problems and Junie's going into premature labor. If they can't stop it, they're going to do a Cesarean because they don't want to put any more strain on her body than necessary, but they'll have to wait until Junie's blood pressure stabilizes."

"Where are Mom and Dad?"

"They're here at the hospital," he said.

"Mom called me from the hospital?" she asked, confused. She had heard her father strike Danny and he would never do so in public.

Danny was slow in answering. "Yeah, they were at the hospital when I got here."

Her father *had* struck Danny in public. Something he had never done to any of them. No matter how angry he got, he always saved the whippings until they were safely hidden behind closed doors.

"Danny." The words stuck in her throat.

172

"We're all scared out of our wits. I've never seen Dad so scared."

"She's going to be all right, isn't she?" She heard him take a deep breath.

"The doctor won't say anything more than he's guardedly optimistic. Whatever the hell that means."

Stacie heard the rhythmic clicking of the tires on pavement and the occasional grind of static in the phone.

"How much longer before you get here?" Danny asked.

"We just left. We won't be there until about seven in the morning."

"We?" Danny asked.

"A friend of mine is driving up with me."

Danny was quiet.

"What?" Stacie asked.

"If you're bringing some guy in here, you know the old man is going to go nuts."

Stacie closed her eyes and forced herself not to scream. No one in her family knew she was gay and she didn't feel like talking about her life. "I've got to go. Call me if there's any change." It wasn't until after she disconnected that she wondered how Danny had gotten home so quickly. Coming from College Station, his travel time would have been about the same as from Austin.

"How is she?" Cheryl asked as Stacie slipped the phone back on her belt.

Stacie repeated what Danny had told her and then turned back to the window. As they drove through the darkness, a thousand memories of Junie came racing back and with them the guilt. Stacie had allowed her problems with her parents to spill over into her relationship with her siblings. She stayed in closer contact with Danny than she had Junie, but even that was superficial at best. Unshed tears caused her throat to ache. *I can't keep thinking about Junie or I'll go mad.* She struggled to find something pleasant to concentrate on and found herself remembering the feel of Cheryl's lips and the way her body responded to that kiss. The urge to reach over and touch Cheryl was so strong, Stacie had to tuck her hands beneath her knees. Now was not the time to think about getting involved with anyone.

They drove on several more minutes before Cheryl broke the silence. "Are you angry with me?"

Stacie turned to her. "No. Why would I be angry?"

Cheryl shrugged slightly. "I don't know. I thought you might be upset because of, you know . . . what happened back at your apartment. My timing was way off and I apologize. Or that you were angry that I insisted on coming with you." She rushed on before Stacie could respond. "Listen, I don't want to make this harder for you than it already is. Just tell me what you need from me."

"It's not you," Stacie assured her. "It's me and my relationship with my family." When Cheryl didn't respond, Stacie continued. "I have this love-hate thing going on with my parents. My father handles everything with his fists, and my mom handles everything by looking the other way."

"Is that why you lied about them?" Cheryl asked.

"That's part of the reason. The rest of it was I simply didn't want people to know I grew up poor. It took me three years to get rid of that Texas Panhandle twang, but I did it. Do you know why?"

Cheryl made a small noise that was almost a snort. "Stacie, I'm from Tennessee. I know how people respond to accents."

"Your accent is cute. Everyone loves that soft Southern drawl."

"They may think it's cute, but immediately behind that 'oh, it sounds so cute' comes the assumption that I'm dumb as a stick."

"My family doesn't know I'm a lesbian," Stacie said suddenly, changing the subject.

"Really. That surprises me."

"Why?"

"I don't know. You seem so sure of yourself. I guess I thought you were one of those radical women who shouted it from the rooftops and damn anyone who disagrees."

"Other than Brenda, I've never told anyone."

"Must make getting a date pretty hard," Cheryl teased.

"No. I always found my dates in the gay bars. I guess that's why Rosie's was so important to me. It's strange. I could have gone back a couple of weeks ago, but I don't even think about Rosie's anymore."

"Why do you suppose that is?" Cheryl asked.

Stacie thought about it for a moment. "I don't think I ever really enjoyed going there that much or even dating the women I met there. I mean, the sex was great while it was happening, but after a while it was sort of like eating."

"No pun intended, I guess?"

Stacie blushed. "That's not what I meant. You know how wonderful a really good meal is when you're hungry and everything is cooked to perfection, but after you've had it, you don't really think about it again. It was only important for that short time you were experiencing all of its flavors."

Cheryl nodded. "I guess I can see your point."

"Do your folks know you're gay?" Stacie asked.

"Oh, yeah, they know."

Stacie waited, but Cheryl didn't elaborate. She glanced over once, but Cheryl seemed lost in her own thoughts. Stacie closed her eyes and pretended to sleep.

Chapter Twenty-four

A slight clicking sound of a door opening brought Stacie awake. It took her a moment to remember why she was in a car. Cheryl sat with the door slightly opened.

"I'm sorry I woke you. We needed gas and I was going to run in for some coffee. Can I get you something?"

Stacie looked around her. They were at a large truck stop. "Is this Temple?"

Cheryl smiled as she reached over and brushed a lock of hair from Stacie's forehead. "No. We're in Abilene."

"Abilene!" She tried to focus on her watch. It was almost one in the morning. "Cheryl, I'm sorry. Why didn't you wake me?"

"I was fine and you needed to rest. Would you like some coffee or a soda?"

Stacie nodded. "I'll go in with you."

The truck stop was not much different from others Stacie had seen. The restrooms were clean and the coffee fresh. Stacie found an ATM and withdrew some money. She intended to pay for everything needed for the trip. She bought two donuts and the largest coffee they sold.

Cheryl was pumping gas when Stacie came out. "I can drive for a while if you would like to rest," Stacie offered.

"You should try and sleep as much as you can. It may be a while before you get another chance."

Stacie held up the cup. "After drinking this I won't sleep for a week. Besides, this may be my only opportunity to ever drive something this cool."

Cheryl grinned and nodded. "All right, you drive."

As soon as they were in the car, Stacie handed Cheryl some money.

"What's that for?" Cheryl asked.

"It's for the gas you just purchased."

"I don't need that," she objected.

"Maybe not, but I need for you to take it. I can't let you pay for this trip."

Cheryl hesitated but finally took the bills. "Thanks."

"Now, let's see how this baby drives."

Stacie pulled away from the pumps and was soon making her way toward Sweetwater. The car drove like a dream. "I'll be so spoiled after this that I won't want to drive my poor old Mazda."

They each ate a donut and sipped their coffee as the miles melted away.

"Aren't you going to try and sleep?" Stacie asked.

"I'm not sleepy. The truth is I can't sleep in a car. It makes me nervous. I'm too much of a backseat driver."

"In that case, do you mind if I ask you something that I've been wondering about?"

Cheryl glanced at her. "I guess you can ask."

"Why did you kiss me back there at the apartment?"

Cheryl took a deep breath. "Did it bother you?"

"You can't answer a question with a question."

Cheryl played with the lid of her coffee cup for a second before answering. "I'd been thinking about it since that afternoon when you grilled the steaks. I wanted to kiss you when we were on the patio at my house."

"Why didn't you?"

"There were a couple of reasons. The right time never seemed to pop up and I guess I was a little bit afraid of your anger."

Stacie glanced at her in surprise. "What do you mean? I wasn't angry that night—" She stopped. "I guess you're talking about the incident with the rabbit."

Cheryl nodded.

"Are you still afraid?"

"A little, I guess. I don't want to find myself with another crazy girlfriend."

"Another one? You've had a crazy girlfriend?"

"Do you remember the woman I was telling you about who took me to that . . . that . . ."

"Whorehouse?" Stacie glanced over at her.

Cheryl flinched. "That's not what it was."

"She paid someone to perform a sexual act. I believe that falls under the category of prostitution."

Cheryl waved her off. "I don't want to talk about that. This woman, Wanda, wasn't happy when I tried to break up with her about two years ago. She started stalking me. It got so bad I had to call the police and get a restraining order against her. That's how my parents learned I was gay."

"The police called them?"

"No. Wanda called them."

"Ouch. Not good." Stacie groaned.

"No. Not good at all. My parents are fairly open-minded, but I had allowed Wanda to take some photos."

"Oh, tell me she didn't send them to your family."

"She sent one to my family and one to a sleazy reporter."

Stacie was shocked. "Omigosh. What happened?"

"About what you would expect to happen. I received a call from my mother demanding I come home. When I said no, she and my father arrived on my doorstep in L.A. It took a few hours of tears and heavy conversation, but we eventually worked through it."

"What happened with the reporter?"

"He finally agreed to sell me the photo for twenty-five thousand dollars. Like a fool, I paid him and a week later, I receive an anonymous call from a man telling me to check out a particular Web site."

"He put the photo on a Web site!"

Cheryl shrugged. "I can't be sure if he put it out there or Wanda did. All I know is that it's the same shot I bought from him. It took a lawyer and another bundle of money to have the photo removed."

"Wow. What happened to Wanda?"

"The last I heard she was chasing some golfer around the country."

"Then you move to Austin and a crazy reporter tosses a rabbit through your window." Stacie looked over at her. "I'm so sorry. I must have scared you half to death."

"I have to admit, I was beginning to wonder if there was something in me that attracted women who sadly lacked anger management skills."

Stacie saw the smile on Cheryl's face. "What do you think now?"

"I think we met each other when each of us was going through a rather rough time, and I decided I wanted to give you the benefit of the doubt."

Stacie thought about it for a moment. "I'm not going to be able to think about this until after things get straightened out with Junie."

Cheryl said, "I understand. I didn't mean to make it seem like I was pressuring you."

"You didn't." Stacie was quiet for a couple of seconds while she collected her thoughts. She had no intention of letting Cheryl meet her father. From what she had heard on the phone he was in one of his moods, and if so, it was impossible to tell what he might do next. She took a deep breath and slowly released it. "Things are probably going to get a little crazy at the hospital, especially with my father. It'd be best if you didn't go in."

"If there's a hotel nearby, I could wait for you there."

Stacie shook her head. "I'll be staying at the hospital. If you were to stay, I'd be worrying about you. I think it's best if you go back to Austin."

"I'd rather be nearby but I'll do whatever you need for me to do."

"I really appreciate that. It'll probably be best if you drop me off at the hospital and go back to Austin."

"If that's what you need."

Stacie was surprised to discover that the thought of Cheryl leaving without her made her sad. *That's because you don't want to be there either*, she told herself.

Chapter Twenty-five

Stacie eased the car to a stop in the hospital parking lot. Cheryl had fallen asleep shortly after three and hadn't stirred even when Stacie stopped for gas. Stacie took advantage of the moment to study her face. She really was a beautiful woman. Not in the sense of classical beauty, but rather that of a strong capable woman. Cheryl's eyes slowly opened.

"Good morning," Stacie said.

Cheryl made a soft, almost mewling noise as she stretched. "I'm sorry I fell asleep." She glanced out the window. "I guess we're here," she said, nodding toward the front of the hospital.

"Yeah."

Cheryl turned to her. "I don't mean to embarrass you, but are you going to be all right going in there? I mean, will he . . . ?"

Stacie shook her head. "He won't do anything in front of strangers. He always saved it until we got home." She tried not to think about the sickening sound of the slap she had heard over the phone earlier.

"Don't go home with them." Cheryl clamped her hand over her mouth. "I'm sorry. I shouldn't have said that."

Stacie reached over to squeeze her hand. "It's all right. I understand. I better get on in there and find out how Junie is. Thanks for everything." She ran a hand over her head and squinted. It was going to be another hot day.

"Call me if you need anything or you just want to talk." Cheryl reached into the glove compartment and grabbed a pad of paper and pencil. "This is my cell phone number and I'll just add my home number in case you don't have it with you."

Stacie took the paper with the scribbled numbers. She wanted to say something but didn't know what to say. How could she tell Cheryl what she felt for her when she wasn't even sure herself? "I noticed a motel as we were driving into town. You should probably try to sleep some before you head back."

"I'm fine. I'm one of those lucky people who don't need a lot of sleep. Besides, if I got a room, I'd probably be tempted to keep hanging around." She reached over and squeezed Stacie's hand.

Stacie was hit with an overwhelming urge to start the car and drive away. She was feeling something for Cheryl that she had never experienced before and it both frightened her and at the same time made her want to jump out of the car and dance around in silly circles. "You'll drive careful going back?"

Cheryl nodded.

"Just go back out to the main highway." She pointed in the direction they had just come in from. "Follow that road all the way to Highway Seventy. From there you'll see the signs for Sweetwater. It's a straight shot. You can't miss it. From Sweetwater you'll head toward Abilene."

"I know my way from there," Cheryl said.

They got out of the car and removed her suitcase from the trunk. "I wish I was going back with you," Stacie blurted.

"I wish you were too. Are you sure you won't change your mind about me staying?"

Stacie shook her head. "When I get back, I'd like to call you."

182

"I'd like that," Cheryl said.

"Can I ask you one more favor?"

"Sure."

Stacie reached into her pocket for her keys and began removing her apartment key. "Will you stop by and check on the kittens?"

Cheryl reached out and stopped her. "Brenda is staying at your apartment until you get back."

"Brenda?"

Cheryl nodded. "You may not remember, but I asked you for her last name last night before we left. I found her name on your speed dial and called her before we left. I know it was none of my business, but I gave her a quick replay of what you told me happened with Trish, and I told her about your sister being ill. She said she had a key to your apartment and volunteered to watch both of our places without me asking. I agreed since I wasn't sure when I would get back."

Stacie had a sudden memory of seeing Cheryl fiddling with her keys just before they left her apartment. "You left your house key in my apartment for Brenda?"

Cheryl nodded again. "I decided if she was a friend of yours she must be trustworthy."

"Brenda agreed to watch my place?" Stacie asked, her eyes wide in disbelief.

"Yes. I think you and Brenda need to have a long talk and get things straightened out when you get home. It sounded like she has been as miserable as you were. And again, I'm sorry if I butted in where I shouldn't have, but I didn't know who else to call."

Stacie gave Cheryl a quick hug. "Thank you. I'll call you when I get back." She raced off before Cheryl could see the tears streaming down her face. As soon as she was safely through the hospital doors, she turned and watched the bright red Jag exit the lot, wishing she were leaving with it. She had never felt so lonely in her life. It would have been comforting to have Cheryl nearby but she couldn't take the chance of her father and Cheryl meeting. His anger would ruin everything.

She set the suitcase down and stood gazing at the empty parking space where the Jag had been. She told herself Danny would have called if Junie had taken a turn for the worse.

"Stacie."

She jumped and turned at the sound of her name. Danny was standing behind her. It had been over a year since she had last seen him. He was thinner.

"I didn't mean to scare you," he said as he grabbed her in a bear hug. At an inch under six feet, Danny was the tallest member of her family. He had their father's dark hair and quick temper. Rather than lashing out physically as their father did, Danny turned his anger inward, giving him a dark, sometimes forbidding look. His dark hair was much longer than Stacie ever remembered seeing it. *That's guaranteed to piss Daddy off.*

"How's Junie?" she asked.

He looked at her and shook his head. "The doctor says she's going to be all right, but we almost lost her. She started bleeding Thursday night but didn't say anything. You know how Junie is."

Stacie nodded. Junie had never been a whiner.

"Anyway," he continued, "she didn't mention anything to Bill before he left for work the next morning."

"Yesterday morning," Stacie clarified.

"Yeah. Mom said she noticed Junie was paler than usual when she got up for breakfast, and that she didn't give them a hard time about going back to bed like she normally did. When Mom went in to take Junie her lunch, she went to straighten the bed and saw blood. Mom called Bill at work. By the time he got home and they got her to the hospital she was hemorrhaging pretty badly. They gave her a lot of blood when she came in. Dad and I have the same blood type as her. We both gave blood." He held out his arm to reveal a large bruise.

"Do they need more?" Stacie asked as she tried to remember if she even knew what her blood type was.

"Not unless she starts bleeding again. They did a Cesarean at about four this morning."

"And?" Stacie demanded.

He smiled. "Well, Aunt Stacie, we've got ourselves a brand-new niece. She's a few weeks premature. She only weighed four and a half pounds, but the doctor says she's got an excellent chance."

"Is Junie okay?"

"She's still sleeping. The doctor is a little worried about her not being as strong as she should be. Says it'll take time for her to get her strength back, but he thinks she's going to pull through fine."

"What did they name the baby?" she asked.

He shook his head and grinned slightly. "Junie said she was waiting for you to get here. She even made Bill swear he wouldn't tell."

An awkward silence followed. They stood staring out the hospital doors.

"So where's your fellow?" Danny asked.

Stacie looked at him. "What fellow?"

"The guy who drove up here with you."

"Danny, a female friend drove up with me and she's already on her way back to Austin."

"Oh. I just thought—" He shrugged and picked up her suitcase. "Never mind."

Stacie stared toward the lobby. She didn't want to discuss Cheryl. "Where are Mom and Dad?"

He nodded. "They're in the waiting room with Bill."

"What kind of mood is Dad in?"

Danny took a deep breath. "Walk softly, sister."

Stacie felt the old fear close around her stomach and begin to squeeze. Being in public hadn't stopped him from striking Danny, but perhaps he would calm down now that it looked as though Junie and the baby were going to be all right. She took a deep breath and squared her shoulders. "I guess I may as well get it over with."

Chapter Twenty-six

Danny led Stacie back to the waiting room where their parents and brother-in-law waited. Bill was the first one to see them. His tall lanky form crossed the floor in great loping strides to crush Stacie with a heartfelt hug. Stacie had always liked Bill. He was too skinny, and his prominent Adam's apple always made her think of an old turkey gobbler, but he was good to Junie. That alone put him high on Stacie's list.

"Are you all right?" she asked as soon as he released her.

He nodded. "Stacie, I'll tell you the God's own truth. I've never been so scared in my life."

"How's Tommy doing?"

Bill's eyes lit up. "He's being a real trooper. Mrs. Anderson's keeping him. I guess you remember her."

Stacie nodded, remembering the tall raw-boned woman her mother used to carpool with when they both worked at the chicken-processing plant. Her father tried to step between them, but Bill kept his body firmly planted.

"It's about time you showed up. Where you been that your mama couldn't find you?" her father demanded.

Stacie swallowed her thudding heart. Her father looked much older than he had when she last saw him two years ago. He was a short man with sandy-colored hair that was rapidly thinning. From a distance, he would appear almost timid, but get closer and you would see a harshness in his eyes that made people wary. As a child, Stacie had seen much larger men step around him.

As he came closer to her, she moved back beyond his reach before walking over to where her mother stood.

When she left home, Stacie took with her an old photo of her mother that had been taken the year before her mother married. The photo served as a reminder of what she didn't want to become. The vibrant young woman in the photo looked nothing like the washed-out remnant before her. The long glossy blond curls had been defeated and imprisoned in a tight bun that now possessed the texture and color of faded straw.

"When can we see Junie?" she asked her mother as she gave her an awkward hug. She could hear her father grumbling about her ignoring him. Her back remained stiff as she waited, half expecting to see his fist explode into her peripheral vision. She forced her hands into her pants pockets to hide the trembling.

"Her doctor says we can't see her until after she comes out of the recovery room," her mother explained. Stacie kept her eyes averted from the gap where her mother's front tooth was missing. "We saw the baby already. She's the littlest thing. No bigger than this." She cupped her callused hands together.

Their conversation was interrupted as the men walked back to join them.

Try as she might, Stacie couldn't stop herself from moving out of her father's reach. Maybe she'd be less noticeable if she sat down. Chairs lined the wall and two rows sat back-to-back in the middle of the room. Stacie chose a chair against the wall that had tables loaded with dog-eared magazines on either side. Her parents and Bill took chairs to one side of her and Danny sat on the other. She rubbed a hand over her eyes. Now that she knew Junie was out of immediate danger, she felt the exhaustion roll over her.

"Go and get me and your mama a cup of coffee."

Stacie opened her eyes to find her father leaning forward and staring at her. "I don't want to miss my chance to see Junie," she replied in what she hoped was a nonthreatening voice.

"I said—"

"I'll get it," Danny said, jumping up and moving so that he now stood between Stacie and their father.

Carl Gillette rose halfway from his seat. "I told her to do it."

"Carl, please," her mother begged. "I don't want any coffee."

"Well, I do."

"Then I'll get it," Danny said as he spun on his heels and left the room. Stacie started to follow him but changed her mind. She wasn't here to cater to anyone. She closed her eyes to avoid the glares her father kept sending her way.

"How come your hair is so short?" he barked.

It took her a moment to remember that she had cut her hair after she moved to Austin.

"It's cooler this way," she replied.

"Thought you were a man when you walked in here," he snapped.

I wish to God I was because I'd pound you into the ground, you hateful bastard. She wished she had the nerve to express her thought aloud. *Someday*, she promised herself. She pushed thoughts of him away and pulled the memory of Cheryl's kiss around her. What would happen between them once she got back to Austin? What did she hope would happen? She liked Cheryl. The time they spent together was enjoyable, and once you got to know her, she possessed a sort of understated sexiness that made you want to know more about her. With Cheryl's colorful family background and her quirky sense of humor, Stacie couldn't imagine ever being bored around her. She tried to envision what it would be like to make love to her.

"Are you Stacie?"

Stacie's eyes flew open. A thin, slightly bowed man who looked as tired as she felt stood before her. He was wearing green scrubs.

"Yes." She stood.

"I'm Dr. Abbott. Your sister is asking to talk to you."

Stacie's parents and Bill stood as one.

"I'm only going to allow Stacie to go in now, and only because Mrs. Walker is so adamant that she speak to her," Dr. Abbott said. "The rest of you can see her as soon as we move her to a room. It shouldn't be much longer."

"Now see here, I'm Junie's father and this here is her husband. We ought to be able—"

The doctor stopped him in mid-sentence. "Mr. Gillette, my patient is asking to see her sister. If you'll excuse me." He motioned for Stacie to follow him.

The recovery room he led Stacie to was much smaller than she'd anticipated. There were three beds, but only one was occupied. A nurse with an enormous beehive hairdo sat at a tall desk at the end of the room.

"I'm only allowing you back here because she's so anxious to talk to you. I don't want her upset, so try to convince her to rest. That's the best thing for her now," the doctor instructed before he turned and hurried out of the room.

Stacie approached the bed slowly. A shiny chrome IV pole stood to one side of the bed. On the other side was a large black boxy machine. From the blipping noise it emitted, Stacie deduced it was a heart monitor. Another much smaller machine rested on a shelf at the head of Junie's bed.

The painfully thin woman in the bed was almost as white as the heavily laundered sheets that encased her. Stacie's heart missed several beats when she realized the pale, almost transparent woman was her sister. "Junie, it's me, Stacie."

Bruise-like smudges stained sizeable circles around her sister's dark blue eyes.

"Stacie, I have to talk to you." Junie's raspy voice pained Stacie.

"I'm here. What's wrong?"

"You've got to promise me." She grabbed Stacie's hand in a feeble yet desperate grip.

"What, Junie?" Stacie tried to withdraw her hand, but it was useless.

"Promise me, that if I die, you'll make Bill and the kids move away from here. I don't want my kids growing up with Daddy beating on them like he did us. If I'm not there, I can't stop him."

"You're not going to die," Stacie assured her as she struggled to keep her fear from her voice. "The doctor says all you need is rest."

"Promise me," Junie yelled so loudly the nurse slipped off her stool and started toward them.

Stacie held up her free hand to stop the nurse. "I promise, Junie, but you've got to promise me that you'll stop talking about dying."

"Is everything all right, Mrs. Walker?" the nurse asked.

Junie nodded. "Yes, ma'am. Everything is just fine now." The constricting grip on Stacie's hand eased and Junie's body seemed to collapse in on itself. "Is it all right if my sister sits with me for a while? I ain't seen her in some time now," she asked weakly.

The nurse studied Stacie for a moment before giving a small nod. "I suppose she can stay for a few minutes, if she promises not to upset you."

Stacie nodded and the nurse slowly walked away. "You almost got me kicked out of here, yelling like that," she said, sneaking a peek toward the nurse, who was going back to her desk.

"Why haven't you been coming home or calling?" Junie asked.

"You know the answer to that as well as I do. The man hates everything around him, but for some reason, he seems to hate me the most."

"Why do you reckon that is?"

"If I had the answer to that question, I'd know why we all had such screwed-up childhoods."

Junie nodded slowly. "Your being away makes it harder on

Mama. She misses you. Daddy might be rougher on you, but you were always Mama's favorite."

Stacie gave a small snort. "Danny was Mama's favorite and besides, she never did anything to make it easier on any of us."

"Don't talk like that. You know she always got the worst of his rage." Junie looked at her. "It got worse after you and Danny left. With me married and living in town, Mama was all he had to knock around." Junie took several quick shallow breaths as her body stiffened with pain.

Stacie held her breath until Junie's emaciated body slowly relaxed. "No one was making her stay. She could have moved to Austin with me."

"Did you ever tell her that?" Junie asked.

"Why should I? She'd never leave him."

"She did."

The words fell on Stacie like a sheet of lead. "What! What do you mean, she did? Mama left Daddy?"

Junie nodded. "She came to live with Bill and me before Tommy was born. We told everyone around home that she was there to help me, and she was, after I had to quit working. She stayed with us until after Tommy was born and things got so rough for us. Daddy thinks he talked all of us into going back out there, but I know she saw how we were struggling. She moved back because of us."

"No fucking way," Stacie hissed.

Junie's eyes grew round. "Stacie Lynn Gillette, you better not let Mama hear you say that."

They looked at each other and started to laugh at the childish sound of Junie's words. "Oh, please. Don't make me laugh. It hurts." Junie held her abdomen.

Stacie placed a hand on her arm and felt her trembling. "You should rest."

"I've been in bed so long, I feel like I'm growing to the mattress. I can't wait until I'm able to be up and around again."

"I hear I have a beautiful niece," Stacie said as she pushed the fine hair from Junie's damp forehead.

"They rolled her incubator in here just before you came so I could see her. The doctor says she'll have to stay here in the hospital for a few weeks." Junie gripped Stacie's hand. "I swear, Stacie. We almost lost her. She's no bigger than a minute, but she's the most beautiful baby I've ever seen."

"She should be. After all, she has a gorgeous mother and aunt."

"Ain't that the truth," Junie agreed as she released Stacie's hand. "We named her Stacie Michelle Walker. Stacie is for you and Michelle is for Bill's mother."

A lump formed in Stacie's throat. She swallowed several times before she could speak. "I don't know what to say."

"Just tell me that once she becomes a teenager, she can go to Austin and spend every summer with you."

"Oh, lord. Maybe you should name her Danielle," Stacie said in mock horror. "By then Danny will surely be married and have a home."

"What about you?" Junie asked suddenly. "Don't reckon we'll ever see you in that white dress, huh?"

Stacie froze, not sure what she should say.

Junie gave a small laugh, clutched her stomach and grimaced in pain. "Don't look like you just got caught with your pants down in church. It don't matter none to me and Bill. We talked about it after we saw this show on television about human sexuality and it said that you can't help being that way."

"What way?" Stacie croaked.

"Girl, don't you go stupid on me. I ain't never known of you dating a boy, and just look at you with your short hair and them men's britches. I may not be one of those sophisticated city people you run around with, but who do you think you're fooling?" Junie pulled Stacie closer. "You just watch out that you don't let Daddy figure out what's going on. You know he'll go ape shit on you."

"You really don't mind?" Stacie asked as she struggled to keep her voice from quavering.

"No, I don't care. Heck fire, Stacie. You're my sister and I love you."

"I love you too, June Bug," Stacie said, using the nickname that would have once sent her sister into fits. She ran her hand over her eyes.

"Did I ever tell you that I liked that nickname?" Junie said.

"You could have fooled me. You used to have a conniption every time I called you that."

"Hey, you're my older sister. It was my job to make your life miserable."

"There were times when you certainly did a good job."

Junie's eyes drooped.

Stacie gently squeezed Junie's arm. "I'm going to go so you can sleep. I'll be in the waiting room. If you need anything you just give a holler."

"Most beautiful baby I ever saw," Junie mumbled as she drifted off to sleep.

Stacie stood watching her sister sleep for a long moment before she leaned forward and kissed her forehead.

Chapter Twenty-seven

The nurse with the outdated beehive gave Stacie directions to the nursery. She rode the elevator up one floor, where the doors opened to reveal an oval workstation. A nurse at the station sent Stacie down the hall to a window where she could see her niece resting in an incubator. A few minutes later, a nurse inside the nursery saw Stacie and eased the incubator closer to the window so Stacie could get a better view.

Maternal instinct was not an emotion Stacie had ever experienced, but seeing the tiny infant lying so helpless inside the sterile-looking incubator produced a staggering wave of protectiveness. Gripping the edge of the window, she gazed at the child. *He won't ever hurt you like he did your mother*, she swore.

After several minutes of simply watching the infant sleep, Stacie waved to the nurses and left. She didn't feel strong enough to face her father's hatred. She followed the signs pointing the way to the cafeteria. As she walked along the hallway, she found herself thinking of Cheryl. Stacie wished she were back in the car with her. She thought about how nice it would be to take a long road trip, just the two of them on an isolated stretch of deserted highway. She was shocked when she realized she was becoming aroused at the thought of them alone on the road. Where did that come from? she wondered. Still stunned by the sudden revelation, she made her way to the cafeteria and purchased a cup of coffee and a bowl of oatmeal. She ate the food without paying it much attention. So many things had happened within the last twenty-four hours that she needed time to sit quietly and try to sort through her feelings. She pushed the new feelings for Cheryl into a corner of her mind, to be pulled out and examined at a time when there weren't so many other things competing for her attention.

"Stacie?"

She looked up to find a slightly familiar face smiling down at her. "Angie Kurtz?" They had graduated from high school the same year. They were never really friends since Angie's family lived inside the city limits and the town kids tended to associate with one another. Angie's grandfather was Doc Kurtz.

"It's Angie Dawson now."

Stacie invited her to sit down. As she did, she noticed Angie was wearing a white lab coat with a nametag.

"You became a doctor," she said and pointed to the tag.

A slight flush raced over Angie's fair cheeks. "The doctor title is so new it still squeaks when I use it."

Stacie laughed. "Congratulations on both. Doc Kurtz must be happy."

Angie nodded. "Yes. I think he's finally getting over the fact that he couldn't convince Dad to become a doctor. He's already talking about me moving back to Wilburn and taking over his practice."

"Doesn't seem right to think of him not being the doctor in Wilburn, but I'm sure you'll do a great job."

"Well, I'm not holding my breath on him turning loose of the reins anytime soon. Heck, I don't know how he manages to keep up with everything."

"Does he still make house calls for those who can't get in to see him?"

"Yes. I assisted for him one day in his office, and I swear by three o'clock I was ready to drop in my tracks, then he gets a call that Mrs. Mimms way over on the other side of the county is having chest pains and her son was off working in Galveston. He grabs his bag and that horrible old felt hat of his and off we go. He truly is amazing." She sipped her coffee before adding, "I heard Junie was in here. I went up earlier to see her, but she was still in the recovery room. Have you been able to see her?"

"I just left her. She seems to be very weak. Danny tried to explain to me what's going on with her and the baby."

Angie stared into her coffee. "Her doctor is Dr. Abbott. You know the plant where Bill works makes them see certain doctors. Abbott is one of them. He's a good enough physician. Apparently, he got a burr up his butt and left a six-digit practice in Chicago to come out here and help the poor."

Stacie groaned. "Just what this county needs is another do-gooder."

Angie grinned.

"Do you know what happened with Junie? What caused the hemorrhaging?" she asked Angie.

"I know what I've heard from working around here, and my sister-in-law is a surgical nurse. You know how small this place is. When I went to the recovery room to see Junie earlier, she was still under the anesthesia, but I looked at her chart. First off, she's going to be all right. It's going to take some time for her to start feeling stronger and get her body built back up. Her biggest problem is her body wasn't made to handle childbirth. Her cervix is too small. She has what's known as cervical insufficiency. That just means there are some structural abnormalities of the uterus or cervix. She'd already had a couple miscarriages. To try and prevent another one, Dr. Abbott did a cerclage in Junie's first trimester."

"What's that?"

"It's a precautionary surgical procedure where the doctor goes in and puts a stitch around the cervix to reinforce it. The stitch stays there until the doctor removes it a few weeks before the baby is due. After the surgery, he put Junie on bed rest," Angie said.

"I guess that's when she lost her job."

Angie nodded before sipping her coffee. "The plant let about thirty people go at that same time. They treat their workers like dogs. The working conditions barely pass regulation standards, and the healthcare package they offer is so horrible it shouldn't even be classified as healthcare." She gave Stacie an apologetic smile. "We'd better not let me wander off into that discussion. I tend to get a little irate. I hear you're a newspaper reporter now."

Stacie started to agree, but stopped. "I'm actually a copyeditor for the *Travis County Reporter*."

"You don't mean it! Mother loves that paper. She goes down to San Antonio to visit her sister about twice a year and the first thing they do is find a copy of that paper to see what's going on."

Stacie's shoulders drew back a little straighter. "I'm glad she finds it useful."

Angie stood. "Listen, it was good to see you again, but I've got to get back to work."

"Thanks for explaining what's going on with Junie."

"I'm glad I could help. Don't you worry about Junie." She leaned toward Stacie and lowered her voice. "You might try to encourage Bill to get a vasectomy. I know how weird men around here get when you even mention them having one, but it would certainly make things easier for your sister in the future."

"I'll work on it," she promised.

Stacie remained at the table collecting her thoughts until she finished her coffee. Unable to think of any other excuse to delay returning to the waiting room, she took a deep breath and left the cafeteria.

As she walked through the hospital, she considered calling Cheryl to tell her how Junie was doing. *How pathetic can you get? She's been gone less than two hours and you're already thinking about calling her. You have to get a life.*

As soon as she walked into the waiting room, Bill and her parents rushed toward her. She regretted her childish impulse to hide from them. They were as worried about Junie as she was.

"What did she want?" her father demanded as soon as Stacie joined them.

"She just wanted to talk," Stacie said, looking around, wondering where Danny was. "The doctor assured me she's going to be fine. She's going to need a lot of rest."

"He *assured* you, did he? Well, I guess we can all rest easy now. The city girl has arrived and been *assured*." Her father's mocking tone threatened to sear the final thread of her self-restraint.

"What did he say?" Bill asked.

With some difficulty, Stacie pushed her father's sarcasm away and turned to Bill. "Dr. Abbott didn't say much, but I talked to Doctor Dawson. Do you remember her? She's Doc Kurtz's granddaughter."

"Yeah," Bill said and nodded. "She married Randy Dawson. I knew him in school."

Stacie nodded and quickly told them what Angie had told her about Junie. "She's going to need a lot of rest," Stacie emphasized again as she ignored her father's snide remarks about women doctors. Remembering Angie's parting words, she looked Bill straight in the eye. "Bill, you've got to get a vasectomy. You can't take a chance on this ever happening again."

He paled slightly.

"You almost lost her," Stacie reminded him. "Do you want to take that chance again?"

"You got no business talkin' to a man like that," her father snapped as he stepped toward her.

"No, I don't," Stacie said, sounding braver than she felt and praying he wouldn't strike her when there were others around. "He should have taken care of it after Tommy was born, and then Junie wouldn't be going through this now."

"It's what a woman does," her father replied. He stepped closer to her, his eyes narrowing.

"No, it's not what a woman does," Stacie replied.

"Don't you sass me." He shook his finger in her face.

"I'm not sassing you. I'm trying to save my sister's life." She turned to Bill. "The next time she might not be so lucky."

"Carl, she's right." Bill turned to Stacie. "I promise I'll talk to Doc Kurtz as soon as I get Junie home."

Afraid her legs wouldn't hold her up much longer, Stacie sat down and grabbed a magazine, hoping to discourage anyone from talking to her. When Danny didn't return, Stacie leaned over and asked Bill where he had gone.

Bill glanced at Stacie's father and shook his head slightly.

They must have had an argument. It probably started over the coffee she had refused to go buy. Stacie finished flipping through the magazine and realized she hadn't read a single word. She started over at the front and tried to force herself to concentrate, but her mind was like a box full of fleas and kept hopping around everywhere. She finally gave up even pretending to look at the magazine and set it back on the table.

As soon as her father left the room in search of a restroom, she turned to Bill. "What happened with Danny?"

Bill looked from Stacie to her mother and rubbed a hand over his forehead. "Carl got mad because Danny went for the coffee. He called Danny a sissy."

"What did Danny do?"

Bill gave his head a small shake. "Well, he just looked at Carl and said that if being a man meant being like him, he'd rather be a sissy. Then he left."

Stacie felt like jumping up and down and clapping. Danny had finally stood up for himself. "Did he say where he was going?"

Bill licked his lips and brushed imaginary lint from his leg. "No. Not that I heard."

"He's over at Cutter Taylor's place," her mom replied so softly Stacie barely heard.

"Cutter Taylor. What's he doing over there?"

Bill cut his eyes toward Stacie's mom. "He might have gone over to visit with Cutter."

"He's living with Cutter's twin sister, Connie," her mom said.

"He says he ain't goin' back to college. He got a job over at Desmond's Auto Center and moved in with Cutter. Connie moved in a few days later."

Stacie's stomach gave a sickening lurch. "He dropped out of college? Why?"

"You'd have to ask him," her mom replied as her fingers folded tiny nervous pleats in her skirt.

Carl Gillette stomped back into the room and they all fell silent.

It was almost an hour later before a nurse came to tell them Junie had been moved to a room. As they followed the nurse into Junie's room, Stacie stood back to allow the others a chance to speak with her. Bill went to one side of the bed and her parents to the other. Stacie stood at the foot. The room was a semiprivate room, but the other bed was empty. From where she stood, Stacie could see her own reflection in the large mirror hanging over the bathroom sink. Her hair was a mess and her clothes were wrinkled from the long trip.

"How are you feeling?" Bill asked as he carefully took Junie's frail hand.

"I'm doing fine," she replied and gave him a smile so filled with love that Stacie felt embarrassed that she had witnessed such a private moment. She wondered if anyone would ever look at her like that.

"She's fine. She'll be up and ready to be giving you another son in no time," Carl Gillette boasted as he walked toward the window where a pair of plastic-covered armchairs sat.

Stacie turned, fully intending to tell her father what an insensitive, testosterone-laden jerk he was, when she saw something in the reflection of the bathroom mirror that stopped her cold. There were tears in her father's eyes. She watched as he casually ran a hand over his face and wiped them away. After sitting down, he leaned back and saw her staring at him.

200

"What are you gawkin' at?" he growled.

Stacie shook her head, but found it almost impossible to look away from him. Had she imagined the tears? Confused, she forced her gaze away from him and focused on the ribbing of the thin blanket on Junie's bed. She had never seen her father cry.

Chapter Twenty-eight

Junie drifted off to sleep, as Bill sat on the side of the bed holding her hand.

Stacie's stomach rumbled to remind her that several hours had gone by since she had eaten the small bowl of oatmeal. "Let's go get something to eat while she's sleeping," she suggested.

"I think I'll stay here with her," Bill said. "I'm not really hungry."

"Mom, Dad?"

"It's too expensive to be eatin' around here. We'll wait until we get home and your mama can fix supper," her dad said as he stretched his feet out in front of him.

For the first time, Stacie noticed how tired he looked. In fact, both of her parents looked exhausted. Stacie knew if she offered to buy their meal, he would accuse her of flaunting her money. *Still, he never hesitates to cash that monthly check I send*, she thought with rancor. "All right," she agreed. She turned to her mother, "Would you like to take a walk? I need to stretch my legs."

Her mom threw an anxious glance toward Carl. When he didn't object, she gave a small nod. Stacie ushered her from the room as quickly as possible. "Do you feel up to walking around outside? The air conditioning is set too low in here and I'd like to thaw out a little."

"That would be good. My wrist is hurtin'. The heat will do it good." Years of working in the chicken-processing plant had extracted a price from Lorene Gillette's body.

As soon as they were outside, Stacie casually turned toward town. She was hungry and her mother probably was too. If her dad wanted to sit in there and starve, that was fine with her. As they walked, Stacie's mom suddenly began to talk.

"Do you think it's my fault Junie is so frail?"

Confused, Stacie looked at her. "How could it be your fault?"

"Times were hard when I was pregnant with her. Maybe I didn't take good enough care of myself."

"I'm sure you did the best you could."

She shook her head. "Sometimes I wonder. I shouldn't have let him whip you kids like he did."

"Why didn't you stop him?" Stacie asked. She had needed an answer to that question for years.

" 'Cause I was as scared of him as you were," her mother replied simply.

"But you are our mother. If he didn't protect us, you were supposed to."

"Life doesn't always work out like it's supposed to, Stacie Lynn."

"That's for sure."

"You ain't ever gonna change. You're always lookin' for someone else to blame things on or to make wrong right. What would you have had me do?"

"You could have left him," Stacie said. The late-afternoon temperatures were bouncing off the sidewalk and causing her to sweat.

"You make it sound so simple."

"It was simple," Stacie snapped, harsher than she intended.

"You were working full-time. We could've gotten by on what you made."

Lorene exhaled noisily. "We barely got by on what me and your daddy made combined. We did the best we could by you kids. You never went to bed hungry, and you had clean clothes."

"And we lived in daily fear of our father beating the crap out of us. Don't you know why I don't come home? I can't stand the knot my gut gets tied into from merely thinking about being around him. It's easier for me to stay away than it is to walk around on pins and needles wondering if the next thing out of my mouth will be what sets him off."

Her mother stopped suddenly and dropped down to sit on the curb.

Stacie glanced around to make sure no one was watching them. "Mom, what's wrong? Why are you sitting on the curb like that?"

"Because I want to," she replied stubbornly.

"What do you mean you want to? Come on, people are staring."

"I don't care if people are starin'. I feel like sittin' right here."

Stacie scratched her head in frustration. "Why? What are you trying to prove?"

"Not a thing, Stacie Lynn. I'm sittin' here because I want to."

Stacie considered leaving her sitting there and going on to find a restaurant alone, but her mom's sudden defiance baffled her. Stacie gave up. *What the heck? No one knows me here anyway.* She dropped down on the curb beside her mother. "Okay, I give up. What the hell is wrong?"

"Me," her mother began. "My whole fuckin' life is what's wrong."

Stacie was eternally grateful that she had sat down; otherwise, she would surely have fallen down upon hearing her mother utter the word *fuck*. Before she could recover, her mother was rushing on.

"I left my parents' house when I married your father. I've been with him for nearly thirty years. I had you three kids and I raised you as best I could. When I married your father, he was so sweet. He used to pick wild daisies and bring them home in his lunchbox."

Stacie stared at her. "What changed him?"

Lorene looked at her. "Things happened. There wasn't just one thing. It was me, you, Junie, Danny, and all the things he couldn't control. He woke up one day and found himself in a world he wasn't prepared to live in."

For the second time in as many minutes, her mother shocked her. "Are you saying it's our fault he beat us?"

She shook her head and looked off down the street. "No. I'm just sayin' the carefree boy I married didn't know how to grow up to be a man. When life didn't go as he thought it should, he got sour on life." She turned her gaze back on Stacie. "Did you learn anything in college? Your father beats us because he can't beat the world that has beaten him. Did it ever occur to you that maybe he and I had dreams, just like you kids do?"

Stacie felt the first inkling of shame starting to creep up her spine. "I guess I assumed you were doing what you wanted to do."

Her mother gave a harsh laugh and said, "You thought I liked rippin' out chicken guts? Can you even begin to imagine what it's like hearin' you're too old to do a job? I'm only forty-five." Her voice broke. She turned her face away.

Stunned by the bitterness in her mother's voice, Stacie stared at the smashed beer cap lying between her feet. She struggled to get a hold on her mother's confession, her father's tears, Junie nearly dying, the four-and-a-half-pound miracle lying in an incubator and Cheryl Wright's kiss.

"I shouldn't have said those things," her mother said finally. "You kids aren't responsible for the way me and your daddy's life turned out. Fact of the matter is, you all are the only good things that ever happened to us."

"Did you really leave Daddy?" Stacie asked.

Lorene massaged her wrist. "Arthritis. The only thing I got for all those years workin' in that danged old chicken plant."

"Mama?"

Her mother continued to rub her wrist. "Carl and me never should have gotten married. I was barely seventeen. You were born five weeks before my eighteenth birthday. I was twenty when Junie came along and twenty-three when Danny was born. Carl's only nine months older than I am. When I was seven, my daddy got a job in Dallas. He was a bricklayer and there wasn't any work around here. He and your Uncle James would drive home every Saturday afternoon, then turn around and go back the next afternoon. One weekend Daddy brought me a music box. It was one of those with the little ballerina girl on top. She wore a pretty pink costume and had a little painted-on tiara with a teeny-tiny little pearl. Every night when I went to bed, I would wind that music box up and watch the ballerina spin round and round. I decided I wanted to be a ballerina when I grew up." She laughed suddenly. As she did so, she covered her mouth with her hand as she always did when she laughed.

Stacie realized the missing tooth embarrassed her mom. *Why didn't I ever notice that before?*

"I was such a silly kid," her mom said. "I would spin round and round until I'd get so dizzy I couldn't stand up. Can you just imagine someone with these big clodhopper feet wanting to be a ballerina?" Her mother thrust her tennis-shoe-clad feet out in front of her.

"Your feet aren't big," Stacie said.

Lorene's voice went soft. "When I was a young girl, people used to tell me I had pretty feet. They were so narrow. Look at them now. They're as wide as a flatbed truck. I can't find a decent shoe that doesn't hurt my feet."

"Why did you marry Daddy?" Stacie asked.

"When your daddy was younger, he was a handsome man, and he made me laugh. You probably can't remember, but before Junie was born, we used to go to dances all over the county. Sometimes we would leave you with Grandmother Gillette, and other times, we'd take you with us. Your daddy used to dance you around the dance floor. He would put your feet on top of his and you would stare up at him like he was a god." She started massaging her wrist again. "I guess he was a god to you then."

"What happened? Why is he so angry? When did he start . . . ?"

Lorene tucked her aching wrist against her stomach and hunched forward slightly. "Junie and Danny don't know what I'm about to tell you. Maybe we should have talked about it years ago. Maybe it would have helped him. You weren't quite two yet and I was pregnant with Junie. Me, you, your daddy and his youngest sister Nelda were drivin' home from a dance over in Garza County. You don't remember your Aunt Nelda, but when she was around, you wouldn't leave her side. We used to have to trick you just to get you in the car to go home."

Stacie recalled the photos of her Aunt Nelda scattered throughout her grandmother's house.

"On that night, your daddy and Nelda had been drinkin'. We were in that old 'sixty-five Mustang that Carl rebuilt." She looked over at Stacie. "That's what he wanted to do—rebuild old cars. He was pretty good at it too." She shook off the memory. "Anyway, Carl and Nelda were both too drunk to drive, but you know how stubborn he can be. It had been rainin' off and on most of the day. I was sick. I had eaten something at the dance that didn't agree with me and was lyin' down in the backseat. You were kneeling on the floorboard talking to me. You always seemed so much older than you really were."

Stacie felt an odd tingling sensation creeping along her spine and shivered.

Her mom looked over at her. "Are you sure you want to hear the rest?"

Stacie nodded.

"Your daddy and Nelda were singing. Neither one was any good at it, but it sure didn't keep them from trying." She smiled briefly before a look of sadness crossed her face. "A cat ran out into the road and your daddy tried to dodge it. He lost control of the car. It seemed like that car just kept flipping over. When it finally stopped, it was on its side with the driver's side up in the air. You were so scared. You were screamin' and cryin'. We all started yellin' about the same time, and it seemed like everyone was all right. Nelda said her foot was caught under the dash.

"Carl was trying to help Nelda get her foot loose, but she told him to get us out first, so you wouldn't be so scared. He managed to get out and pull the back door open. I was way too big to crawl over the seat. He lowered himself back down into the car and helped me out, and then he lifted you up and sat you on the side of the car. I couldn't get off the car by myself because I was so big with Junie. He told you to wait and he'd be right back for you. Then he helped me down off the car. That's when we smelled the gasoline. Your daddy ran back for you, but you had crawled back into the car to help Nelda. You told me later that you heard your Aunt Nelda cryin'."

A shiver ran down Stacie's spine. As a child, she had experienced a recurring dream of a woman calling out to her in the dark, but Stacie could never find her. The dream had eventually stopped and she had forgotten about it.

"He got back down into the car, and by that time, I was screamin' for them to hurry up and get out. I guess with everything that had happened, you sort of panicked and started fightin' him. You wouldn't let him get you out of the car. You were a fightin' and hangin' on to everything you could grab onto. Finally, Nelda convinced you to let him get you out and she promised she would be right behind you." Her mother paused for a moment. "He couldn't let you go because you were still not too sure you wanted to leave. He had you all wrapped up in his arms. He jumped off the car and ran over to where I was, to hand you to me and all at once, the car blew up. All of this stuff was flyin' around us. Your daddy threw himself over us. He has a scar on his back where a chunk of metal hit him."

Stacie felt the air leave her lungs. "If I hadn't caused him so much trouble, he could have gotten her out," she whispered.

Her mom looked at her. "You don't know that. They both could have been killed. You were a kid. Don't go blamin' yourself.

For years, I blamed myself for not being stronger and drivin' home. Carl blamed himself for being drunk and drivin', and so did your Grandfather Gillette." She shook her head and sighed. "When he found out Nelda had been killed, he almost beat your daddy to death. Carl never raised a hand to stop him. Carl thought he deserved that beatin', but still it shamed him. He was never the same afterward. I know I should be ashamed of myself, but I thank God every day that selfish old bastard is dead."

"Was that the only time he ever hit Daddy?"

"Lord no, girl. That old man was the devil himself."

"There's research that suggests abused children often become abusers themselves. Do you think that will happen to us?"

In a rare display of affection, her mother reached over and patted Stacie's arm. "No. I don't worry about you girls. Danny's temper sometimes worries me, but he seems more bent on beatin' up hisself."

Stacie watched as a woman with two small children walked down the street. "Mom, you never answered my question. Did you leave Daddy?"

"Yeah. I went to stay with Bill and Junie for a while. Your daddy ain't an easy man to live with. Or maybe I'm just lookin' for something that I can't seem to find."

"What kind of something?" Stacie asked, wondering if her mom was looking for a new man in her life.

"I want something of my own," she said and then stopped suddenly. "I forgot you were hungry." She stood up and brushed the back of her skirt off. "Let's see what we can find. I don't ever come here unless I have jury duty. Which ain't very often."

"There's a sign down there for the Rib Shack," Stacie said as she pointed down the street.

They walked into the small rustic building. From all appearances, it was doing a booming business. They were quickly ushered back to a long picnic table.

"If all these people are any indication, the food must be great," Lorene said.

209

"I can't believe it can be any better than your spareribs. We all love your barbecue," Stacie said.

"My daddy taught me how to barbecue. The secret is all in the sauce. Someday I'll show you how to make it."

Stacie agreed but she doubted that day would ever come.

They ordered and the food was quick to arrive. One bite told Stacie it wasn't great food that packed the place. After taking a bite, her mother looked at her and frowned. "Must be the only place in town to eat," she whispered. "Maybe I should come over here and open up a restaurant and give them a little competition."

It wasn't until they were about to go back into the hospital that either of them spoke of their earlier conversation. "Mom," Stacie began. "If you ever need a place to stay, you know you're welcome to come to Austin. I have a small one-bedroom apartment, but I have a comfortable couch and you would have the place to yourself during the day."

She gave a slight nod. "Thanks, honey. Let's hope it don't have to come to that."

Chapter Twenty-nine

Junie was sleeping when they returned. Danny was standing by the windows that looked out over the hospital parking lot.

"Where's Carl and Bill?" Lorene asked quietly.

"They went to the cafeteria. Bill wanted to get something to eat," Danny replied.

"Have you eaten?" his mother asked.

"Yeah. I grabbed something before I got here."

"Has she been asleep this entire time?" Stacie asked. What she really wanted to ask him was why in the heck he had dropped out of college.

Danny gave a slight shrug. "I guess so. She has been since I came in."

"I'm goin' to go find me a soda," Lorene said. "Those ribs are makin' me thirsty."

Stacie waited until their mother had left the room before walking over to stand by Danny.

"I know what you're going to say," he said, anticipating her lecture.

"Good. That'll save me a lot of energy. Now tell me why you dropped out."

He continued to stare out across the hospital parking lot.

"Danny, answer me. I know how much college meant to you. What happened? If it's something I can help you with, I will."

He ran his hand over the back of his neck. "Look, I'm sorry. You have every right to be mad at me. You've sent me a lot of money and I blew it."

"Blew what?" she asked. "The money or the opportunity?"

"Opportunity."

"It's not too late. You just have to tell me what's happened and we'll find a way to fix it."

He whirled and Stacie couldn't stop her arms from flying up in a defensive manner. She saw the look of horror cross his face.

"God, Stacie. I wasn't going to hit you. I'm not like him."

She dropped her arms and tried to calm her pounding heart. "I'm sorry. I didn't mean to do that. I know you'd never hit me."

"Do you?" he demanded. "How can you be so sure I'm not just like him?"

"I know you, Danny. You'd never hit anyone."

"What makes you so sure you know me?"

"Because she changed your shitty diapers forever," Junie said. "Mama didn't think she was ever going to get you potty-trained."

Danny and Stacie turned to the bed. "I'm sorry we woke you," Stacie said as she walked over to stand by Junie's bed. "How are you feeling?"

"Like someone threw me in the dryer and turned it on high," Junie replied.

Danny joined Stacie. "I saw the baby. She's beautiful," he said.

Junie's face brightened. "That's what I told Stacie. Now, before Mama and Daddy get back, tell me what's going on between you two?"

Neither Stacie nor Danny spoke.

"And I thought Tommy was a handful," Junie said with a sigh. "I reckon I'll just have to stand each of you in a corner until you decide to talk."

"Stacie's mad at me because I dropped out of college," Danny said.

"Well, I'm mad at you too," Junie said. "Why did you do it?"

"That's what I was trying to find out when he pulled his clam routine," Stacie said.

Danny gave a crooked smile before answering. "Man, just like old times with both of you ganging up on me."

Junie shook a finger at him. "It took both of us to keep up with you."

"He's trying to change the subject," Stacie warned her sister.

"Okay, okay. You win. I dropped out because I need to get a job."

"Did you lose the job at the restaurant?" Stacie asked.

"No."

"Then why do you need another job?" Stacie demanded. "Your scholarship should be paying for almost everything you need, and between what you make at the restaurant and the little extra you get you should have plenty." She didn't know if Junie knew she was sending Danny monthly checks and she didn't want to embarrass him by mentioning it directly.

Danny pushed his hands into his pocket and began to fidget.

"Does this have anything to do with Connie Taylor?" Junie asked.

"She's pregnant," Danny admitted before glaring at Stacie and adding, "Yes, it's mine."

Stacie bit her tongue to keep from saying something she would later regret. She couldn't afford to increase the amount she was sending him.

"What's that got to do with you dropping out of college?" Junie asked. "I thought you were supposed to be graduating in December. This was going to be your final semester, right?"

"Yeah. Look, I can always go back and finish later on," he said.

"But you won't," Stacie said, angry and hurt by his decision to quit. "You know as well as I do that if you drop out now you'll get caught up in day-to-day living and you'll never go back."

"How far along is Connie?" Junie asked.

"Four months," Danny replied.

Junie released a loud snort. "Danny Gillette, you are the biggest fool I ever met." She waved him off. "In fact, I don't even want to talk to you anymore. Get out of my room."

Stacie and Danny both stared at their sister as if she had taken leave of her senses.

"What's wrong with you now?" Danny asked. "Are you on some kind of weird medication?"

Junie looked at him. "Danny, if she's only four months pregnant, the baby isn't even due until February."

"I can count to nine," he said. "But I couldn't let her continue working out there at the plant. You know how dangerous that place is. Now, she has no healthcare at all. She even lost her apartment and had to move in with Cotton."

"Can't she move over to College Station with you and look for a part-time job?" Stacie asked.

"I live in the dorm," Danny protested.

"Find a small apartment somewhere around there?" Junie said.

"Apartments cost money," he said and threw up his hands.

Stacie looked at Junie and shook her head. "Leave him alone. He's lazy and just wants to whine."

"I am not lazy," he snapped. "And I'm not whining. I'm trying to tell you what's going on."

"No, Stacie's right," Junie said. "When Stacie was going to school, she worked three, sometimes four jobs. Here you are with one little job and four months to go before graduation. Wow, Danny, that's a sad story and I really feel sorry for you."

"I thought you two would be more understanding."

"I'll tell you what I understand," Junie said. "If you don't finish college, you're cheating yourself and you're cheating that baby." She reached out and touched his hand. "Bill and I are struggling

214

because we weren't smart enough to better ourselves. Bill graduated from high school and went to work at the plant just like his parents did. I never even graduated from high school and that's the biggest regret of my life. If I could change anything about my life, it would be my education. Somehow I would get through college so I could provide a better life for my kids."

Before any of them could respond, Bill and their parents returned.

Chapter Thirty

The green glow-in-the-dark clock on the dashboard read ten forty-seven as Stacie paid the cab driver. Since Junie and the baby were out of immediate danger, Stacie had decided not to test Estelle's warning of being fired if she was ever late for work during the first month.

Danny and Connie Taylor drove her to Abilene, where she caught the last flight of the day out to Austin. On the trip to Abilene, she quickly learned she wouldn't mind having Connie Taylor as a sister-in-law. Connie was as mad at Danny about his intentions to drop out of college as Stacie and Junie were. By the time they arrived at the airport, the two women had managed to convince him to consider other options, at least, before taking such a drastic step.

Due to the lateness of the flight's arrival, she decided not to call Cheryl but to grab a cab instead. She had considered calling several times during the weekend but hadn't. There was just too much going on with her family and there was no energy left to handle another issue. As she walked toward the building, she could see a light shining in her living room window. As she trudged up the steps to her apartment, she surveyed the vehicles in the parking lot and finally spotted Brenda's car.

Stacie picked up her pace on the stairs. As she reached her door and started to put the key into the lock, she hesitated. What if Brenda wasn't alone? Stacie hadn't called to let her know she would be back tonight. A hollow sense of dread hit her. What if Trish was in there with Brenda? The awkwardness of that situation was almost enough to send her down to her car. This was silly. This was her apartment. *I'll just knock on the door.*

Stacie knocked on the door and stepped back slightly so that the reflection of the security lights would illuminate her. The door opened quick enough to let her know Brenda didn't have to take time to get dressed.

"Hi," Brenda said as she pulled the door open and stepped aside to let Stacie enter. "If I'd known you were coming home tonight, I would have gotten out of your way."

"You aren't in the way," Stacie said. "I really appreciate you watching the kittens for me." As if on cue, Jem and Scout came tearing out of the kitchen. Stacie dropped her bag and scooped them up. "Hey, you little mutts. I've missed you guys." She used her foot to close the door.

"I guess it's true," Brenda said. "Miracles really don't cease to occur. I never thought I'd see the day you owned an animal."

"That's where you're confused," Stacie teased. "I don't own these guys. They own me."

"How's your sister and the baby?"

"Both are doing well. Junie's doctor says she'll probably be able to go home around midweek. He wants her to be a little stronger. The baby was about seven weeks early, so she'll have to stay a while longer."

"They're probably worried about infection," Brenda said. "Preemies can't fight them off as well as full-term babies. Is Junie breastfeeding?"

217

"Yes. There was some concern for a while because the baby wouldn't nurse, but she caught on with a little coaxing."

"Good. With preemies it's always better if they're breastfed."

Stacie looked at Brenda over the heads of the kittens. "I sometimes forget you're a nurse."

Brenda shrugged. "Listen, Cheryl told me about what happened with Trish and I'm really sorry I went off on you like I did. It's just that when I saw—"

"It's my fault. You tried to tell me that night at Rosie's and I was being an asshole and blew you off. I feel bad about the entire mess. I'm willing to forget it ever happened if you are," Stacie said as she carried the kittens over to a chair and sat down.

"I'd like that. I've missed talking to you," Brenda said.

Stacie looked at her and grinned. "I've missed you."

Brenda sat down on the couch. "So, what's going on between you and Cheryl Wright?"

"I wish I knew. Before I tell you about that there are a couple of things I need to straighten out."

Brenda eyed her for a moment before nodding.

"I've always lied about where I'm from. My family doesn't live in Lubbock. I grew up in a little town, Wilburn. Lubbock is the closest city, but I lied about living there."

Brenda stared at her with a puzzled look on her face. "Why?"

"I was ashamed of growing up poor, and my family wouldn't exactly qualify for a Family of the Year award."

"Hell, Stacie, that's what makes friends so much fun. If everyone liked their family, we wouldn't need to go out and find new friends."

Stacie wasn't sure she agreed with Brenda's logic but was eternally grateful Brenda wasn't angry with her.

"Now, the good stuff," Brenda said. "What's going on between you and Cheryl? I went by her house Saturday to feed her cat. She has a kick-ass place."

Stacie quickly filled Brenda in on everything that had occurred after their fight.

"Wow, Jack fired you. I can't believe that. But it sounds like you're doing okay in this new job," Brenda said.

"It's actually better than I first thought it would be. The people are nice and they're funny. I just wish I could get back to being a reporter."

Brenda said slowly, "If she went all the way home with you, she must be at least a little serious."

It took Stacie a moment to catch up with Brenda's sudden subject change. "Maybe. I don't know."

"What about you? How do you feel about her?"

Stacie took a deep breath. "I like her, and I think about her when she's not around."

Brenda chuckled and rubbed her hands together. "Could it be you're finally falling in love?"

Stacie frowned. "No. I'm not falling in love. I just like her. I would like to be friends with her."

Brenda slapped her hands. "I knew it. You are falling in love."

"You are so full of shit. We've been friends for years, and I'm not in love with you."

"Well, heck. You do have a point there," a crestfallen Brenda agreed.

"What about you?" Stacie asked.

"They cut my overtime hours at work, so I ended up having to get a roommate."

"Yuck. Is it at least someone you like?"

Brenda nodded and stretched out on the couch. "Yes. It's Zoey. The bartender at Rosie's."

"Trust me, I know who Zoey is." Stacie cringed. She didn't want to talk about Zoey. It brought back the night she had tossed Stacie out of the bar.

"The timing was right for us both. Her latest girlfriend kicked her out and Zoey was living in the back room of the bar."

"I didn't know the bar even had a back room," Stacie admitted.

"They usually use if for storage." Brenda stopped. "You know, Zoey really likes you."

"Yeah, right," Stacie replied.

"She does. She thinks you're wasting your potential."

"What potential?" Stacie asked as she set the kittens on the floor. "You want something to drink?"

"No. It's late. I should get on home so you can rest."

"I'm too wound up to sleep. It's late. Why don't you stay here tonight?"

Brenda seemed to consider the offer for a moment. "Okay. I don't have to be at work until eleven tomorrow, so I'll have plenty of time to go home and change."

"Is there anything to drink, except that horrid wine you like so much?" Stacie asked.

"Yeah. There's beer."

Stacie went to the kitchen and returned with two cold beers. The kittens stayed at her heels through the entire trip.

"Are you still seeing Trish?" Stacie asked, handing Brenda a beer before taking a long drink of her own.

Brenda began to scratch at the label on her beer bottle. "Yes. I know I probably shouldn't, but I don't know. I can't seem to walk away." When Stacie didn't comment, Brenda continued, "I hope you don't mind, but I invited her over last night to play cards. Now that Zoey's at the house and Trish has all those roommates, we don't have a chance to be alone very often."

Stacie thought it was a little freaky but didn't say so.

They continued to chat for several minutes until Stacie's eyelids began to droop. "I shouldn't have had this beer. I'm suddenly so sleepy I can barely keep my eyes open." She stood. "I'd better get on to bed. I have to be at work by seven tomorrow." She started toward the bedroom and stopped. "I'm glad you're not still mad at me."

"Me too. And for what it's worth, I think you should give serious consideration to pursuing Cheryl a little bit harder before someone else snatches her up."

"We'll see," Stacie said as she retrieved her suitcase and headed for her bedroom. As she prepared for bed, she realized she didn't like the idea of Cheryl dating someone else.

Stacie woke up several minutes before the alarm went off. The beer she had consumed before going to bed was straining her bladder. Hopping out of bed, she made her way to the bathroom as quietly as possible so as to not wake Brenda. The kittens kicked up a ruckus the minute she walked through the door. After she was done, she took the kittens back into the bedroom with her and placed them on the bed before turning on the bedside lamp.

She took a moment to find the old stuffed bear the kittens loved to play with, and then went to her closet to see if she could locate clean clothes to wear to work. She didn't have a large wardrobe, but what she had was of good quality. Flipping through her meager selection, she realized she would have to do laundry when she got home that afternoon. That would be a good time to call Cheryl. The thought sent a faint fluttering through her stomach. While trying to determine what the fluttering meant, she finally found a pair of slacks and a blouse that would do.

The kittens were still begging for attention, so she ignored the suitcase that needed to be unpacked and sat on the bed playing with them. As she glanced around the room, something kept bothering her, but she couldn't pinpoint exactly what it was. The only furniture in the room was a bed, a nightstand, a small dresser and her desk. There wasn't a lot of clutter sitting about. A clock and a water glass were on the nightstand. The usual knickknacks on her dresser all seemed to be in place. Her laptop was on her desk. Everything seemed to be where it belonged, but something was wrong. After a while, she forgot about the nagging feeling and gave the kittens her full attention until it was time to get ready for work.

Chapter Thirty-one

Stacie was so tired her bones ached when she walked into her bedroom after work that day. She felt like crying when she remembered she still had to do laundry.

"I'll sleep for an hour," she promised herself, "and then I'll do laundry and call Cheryl."

She was drifting off to sleep when she realized what was different in her bedroom. Sitting up in bed, she stared at her desk. Hadn't she printed the article she had written about Cheryl's family making moonshine? She tried to remember if she had actually printed it or just intended to, but too much had happened in the last few days. She leaned over the edge of the bed to see if perhaps the kittens had knocked it off while playing. There was nothing on the floor.

"You dreamed it," she muttered as she lay back down and went to sleep.

It was after eight when she woke up. Gathering her dirty

clothes and cell phone, she headed down to the laundry room. She got her laundry started before calling the hospital and talking to Junie.

"How are you feeling?" Stacie asked once Bill had passed the phone to Junie.

"A lot better. They got me up and made me walk some today. That wasn't much fun, but Dr. Abbott says I'll only get sorer if I stay in bed."

Stacie listened as Junie told her about the baby's progress and that Mrs. Anderson had brought Tommy in to see her. Junie's last bit of good news brought tears of joy to Stacie's eyes. Danny would be returning to A&M for the fall semester. By the time she got off the phone with Junie, her clothes were almost ready to be tossed into the dryer. Stacie waited until the clothes were in the dryer before she dialed Cheryl's number.

"I didn't think you were going to call," Cheryl said after Stacie had answered all her questions about Junie and the baby.

"I'm sorry. I needed time to think about some things," Stacie admitted.

"And what did you decide?"

Stacie watched a pair of jeans flying around and around in the dryer. "I think I'd like to see you again."

"I like the way you think," Cheryl teased.

"I've never been in a serious relationship."

"It's kind of like walking. Once you get beyond the initial faltering steps, it's easy."

Stacie laughed. "We probably should stay at the crawling stage for a while."

"There's no hurry. We can take it as slow . . . or as fast . . . as you want," Cheryl said.

A warm rush of desire ran through Stacie. "When can I see you again?"

"I'm free tomorrow night," Cheryl said. "Since I'll be home all day, why don't I throw a roast on and you can come by after work for dinner?"

"It's a date," Stacie said.

They continued to talk until the dryer buzzer sounded. Stacie felt a sense of loss after they hung up.

She folded the clothes before going back to her apartment and quickly putting everything away. After kicking her shoes off, she went to the kitchen and made a sandwich. She took the sandwich to the bedroom and turned on her laptop. She no longer wanted to do anything that might jeopardize her budding relationship with Cheryl. She searched for the article and deleted it from her hard drive. As she did so, she was once more struck with the feeling that she had printed the article and left it on her desk.

She was distracted when Scout attacked her bare ankle. "Ouch, you little demon," she yelped as she pulled the kitten off her ankle.

After playing with the kittens until they collapsed in exhaustion, Stacie crawled into bed and fell asleep thinking about her upcoming evening with Cheryl.

The following day was unmercifully long. Stacie found herself glancing at her watch every five minutes.

Estelle came by right after lunch to talk to her about one of the articles Stacie was editing.

"Are you taking medication or something?" Estelle asked.

"No. Why?" Stacie asked puzzled.

"You've looked at your watch a half-dozen times since I came in here."

"Sorry. I guess I'm a little excited." She groaned to herself when she saw Estelle's sudden interest.

"Really? What's going on?"

Stacie tried to backpedal. "Nothing really. I'm meeting a friend for dinner tonight."

"Is this a friend or a *friend*?" Estelle asked, wiggling her eyebrows.

A blush heated Stacie's cheeks. It spread all the way down her neck when Estelle burst out laughing.

"Oh, what I wouldn't give to be so young again." She patted

Stacie on the shoulder before turning to leave. "Have fun, but remember."

"I know. I have to be here by seven."

Stacie shot out of her office as soon as the clock hit five. She tried to control her impatience, but it seemed as though every car on the freeway was determined to go twenty miles per hour. Once she reached her apartment, she took a quick shower and changed into a yellow sleeveless pullover and a pair of white shorts. Less than an hour after getting to her apartment, she hugged the kittens and made them a promise of a trip to the park come the weekend and headed for Cheryl's.

The minute Cheryl opened the door Stacie knew something had happened. "What's wrong?" she asked.

Cheryl wiped her tearstained eyes and motioned for Stacie to come in. Cheryl didn't speak until they were seated in the living room.

"I have to ask you something," Cheryl said. "I don't mean to offend you, but I have to ask."

Stacie nodded slightly as a sick feeling began to ooze into her stomach.

"Did you tell anyone what I told you about my father and moonshine?" Before Stacie could respond, Cheryl held up her hand. "Please don't lie to me. This is too important."

Stacie shook her head. "I told Estelle some of the things you told me, but I never mentioned your name. Remember? I told you. It was when she was talking about your book."

"Are you certain you didn't mention my name?"

"I'm absolutely positive."

"And you didn't say anything that would allow her to guess who I am?"

Stacie shook her head adamantly. "As far as I know, Estelle Vargas doesn't have a clue that I'm even acquainted with you. Has something happened?"

Cheryl leaned her head against the back of the sofa. "A guy

225

named Ron Bauer from the *Juice* called me today. He wanted to know if I was interested in commenting about my family's moonshine business."

Remembering the article he wrote about her caused Stacie's blood to boil. "The man is scum. Maybe he was bluffing."

"No," Cheryl said. "He had enough details to convince me he knew what he was talking about."

"Who else knows Jean Gray is your pen name?"

"My publisher, agent, publicist, and I guess their office personnel. I've used the name for two other novels. I use it when I write something other than romance. Gray was my mother's maiden name." She pounded the sofa arm. "I'm so stupid. It never occurred to me that anyone would go to the trouble to do an extensive background search on Jean Gray."

"You think that's what happened?"

"What other explanation is there?"

"What about someone where you grew up? You said everyone around there knew your family. Isn't it possible that someone remembered your mother's maiden name and put the pieces together? Maybe someone saw a chance to make a buck and spilled their guts."

"That's always a possibility, but why would someone from Tennessee call this Bauer guy from the *Juice*. If they wanted money, wouldn't they be better off calling a national magazine?" Cheryl shook her head. "I'm telling you it doesn't make sense." She covered her eyes. "Stacie, my parents are going to get pulled into this mess. Hell, half the county at home will be." A tear ran out from beneath her hand. "Why did I write that stupid book?"

Stacie stared at Cheryl and felt her heart break as she slowly accepted the truth. *I did print the article*, she cried to herself. Could Brenda have found it and taken it? She was the only person Stacie knew who read the crap the *Juice* printed. *She's still pissed about Trish and she's doing this to get even with me.* Stacie came off the couch so quickly Shakespeare shot off his ottoman and disappeared into the kitchen.

"What?" Cheryl asked, startled by Stacie's sudden move.

"I have to go do something. I'll call you later." She leaned down and kissed Cheryl softly. "I'm really sorry about all this." Without giving Cheryl time to ask questions, Stacie ran to her car.

Brenda's car wasn't in the driveway when Stacie arrived. She walked to the front door and pounded on it, hoping Zoey would know where Brenda was. There was no answer. Stacie glanced at her watched and cursed. It was almost seven-thirty. Zoey would already be at the bar.

Stacie went back to her car and debated whether she should start driving around looking for Brenda or stay here until she returned. Before she could make up her mind, Brenda's car pulled into the driveway. Stacie jumped out, ready to get answers.

"Do you want to tell me what's going on?" Stacie demanded.

Brenda reached inside the car and removed a bag of fried chicken carryout. "You seem a little pissed. What's up?"

"If you wanted to get even with me, that's fine. You didn't have to drag Cheryl and her family into the mess."

Brenda turned from locking her door, confusion clearly written all over her face. "Stacie, I've had a rough day. Normally, I would humor you and let you vent, but one of my patients died today and I'm really not in the mood for dyke drama, so what's your problem?"

"My problem is you stealing stuff out of my apartment and selling it to that sleaze hound at the *Juice*."

Anger followed by pain flashed in Brenda's eyes. "You better have something to back that accusation up with."

"I left an article on my desk. You found it and decided to use it to get even with me for that little incident with Trish. You sent it to Ron Bauer over at the *Juice*. You probably remembered his name from the article you mailed me on his last hatchet job on me."

Brenda leaned against her car. "Yes. I mailed you a copy of the article about you spending the night in jail, but I haven't mailed anything to this Bauer guy and I can't believe you would think I'd steal from you." Her voice broke as she turned her head aside.

Some of Stacie's conviction melted. "It had to be you. I left the article on my desk. I worked on it the night before I left to go to Wilburn. When I got back, it wasn't there. At first, I thought I'd been mistaken about printing it, but now Bauer is calling Cheryl." She let out a frustrated growl. "The bastard has my article."

"If the article is so damaging to Cheryl, why did you write it?" Brenda asked, glaring at her.

"I thought it might be the boost I needed to get back as a reporter, but that was before."

"Before?" Brenda pushed.

"Before I realized I cared about her," Stacie softly admitted.

Brenda walked to the corner of the garage, removed the lid to a garbage can and dumped the bag of carryout into it. She returned to the car and unlocked the doors. "Come on, let's go."

"Where are we going?"

Brenda motioned impatiently for Stacie to get into the car.

Stacie raced around the car and climbed in. She couldn't remember ever seeing Brenda looking so grim. "Do you want to tell me where we're going?"

"I wasn't the only person in your apartment."

Stacie fell back against the seat and closed her eyes. Brenda had mentioned having Trish over. "Brenda, I'm so sorry. God, I'm such an ass."

"Yes, you are, and right now, I don't want to talk to you. So please shut your fucking mouth."

They drove the remainder of the way to Trish's apartment in silence. Brenda parked the car beneath a large shade tree.

"I don't want you to go in," Brenda said.

"Look, I'm getting my article back." Stacie reached to open the car door when Brenda's hand clamped down on her wrist.

"I'm going to say this one more time," Brenda muttered

between clenched teeth. "You keep your ass in this car or so help me . . ." Her glare left no doubt of her seriousness.

Stacie swallowed and finally managed a nod.

When Brenda stepped out of the car, she slammed the door so hard the vehicle rocked.

Stacie waited until Brenda disappeared around the side of the building before opening the door to allow a breeze inside the car. As the minutes crawled by and the sweltering heat continued to build within the car, Stacie got out and paced alongside.

Nearly a half-hour went by before Brenda reappeared. Her pounding footsteps indicated her anger hadn't abated, but it was the slump in her shoulders that made Stacie feel like a first-class jackass. She was standing by the trunk of the car when Brenda walked by and slapped the folded sheaf of paper into her hand.

"There's your article," she said in a voice so thick with pain Stacie barely recognized it.

Neither of them spoke on the excruciatingly long drive back to Brenda's apartment.

Unable to face Brenda, Stacie kept her eyes glued to the folded pieces of paper in her hands. Why had she written the article? Her greedy ambition and disregard for others had done nothing but hurt the two people she cared for the most. In disgust, she ripped the pages into several pieces and stuffed them into her pocket. She stole a glance at Brenda. Tears were streaming down her cheeks. Empathy for her best friend filled Stacie with a pain so profound she found it difficult to breathe.

"Brenda, I'm so sorry."

A small sniffle was Brenda's only response.

As soon as the car came to a halt in Brenda's driveway, she killed the engine and, staring straight ahead, said, "I'm the one who should be apologizing. I brought Trish into your house. She used me to get to you."

"You're not responsible for what she did."

"To some extent I am. I shouldn't have taken her there when

you weren't around." She took a deep breath and slowly exhaled. "I can't talk about this right now. Can I call you in a few days?"

"Yeah, sure." Stacie started to get out of the car. "Is everything okay between us?"

Brenda gave a sharp sob. "It's been a bad day. I let myself get attached to a patient at the nursing home and she died today. I shouldn't have kept seeing Trish, and I definitely shouldn't have ever taken her to your apartment. I'll really sorry I've caused all this trouble."

"You didn't cause the trouble. I shouldn't have written the article to begin with. I violated Cheryl's trust."

Brenda opened her door.

"Brenda, you deserve someone better than Trish," Stacie said suddenly. "We both deserve something better than what we were getting at Rosie's. Let's change our Thursday night get-together to some other place. I'm tired of playing that game."

Brenda gave a slight nod. "I'll call you soon."

Stacie walked slowly to her Mazda and started the long drive back to Cheryl's house. It was time to confess her part in all this.

Cheryl stared at her, clearly shocked by the news.

Stacie told Cheryl everything. She explained that she had written the article, about Trish stealing it, the horrible accusations she'd made against Brenda, and finally about Brenda retrieving the article from Trish. "So, you see," Stacie ended, "it's entirely my fault."

"What possessed you to write the article to begin with?"

Stacie closed her eyes and took a deep breath. "I thought I could use it to worm my way back into a reporter's position."

"You used me."

Stacie shook her head. "That's not what happened. I didn't come here the first time looking for an article."

"But I was gracious enough—no, let me rephrase that—stupid enough to lay one at your feet, and there was no way you could pass up such an opportunity." Cheryl stood and began to pace the length of the living room. "How could I have been so stupid?"

"I had already decided not to submit the article," Stacie said. "I promised you I wouldn't use the information. I just hadn't gotten around to throwing it away." She cringed at the lameness of the statement.

Cheryl sat down suddenly. A long silence stretched between them before Cheryl finally spoke. "Maybe you did me a favor."

Stacie sat back in surprise.

"I've worked so hard trying to keep Cheryl Wright and Jean Gray from being connected that I sometimes get confused about which one I am."

"Which one are you?" Stacie asked with a nervous glance toward the door. How much did she really know about this woman?

Cheryl laughed and threw up her hands. "I'm both and I'm neither." She moved to the sofa and sat beside Stacie. "If my grandmother were still alive, do you know what she would be saying right now?"

Stacie shook her head.

"She would point her finger at me and say 'Oh, what a tangled web we weave.'"

"'When first we practice to deceive,'" Stacie finished.

They both laughed.

"Our grandmothers were both smart ladies," Stacie said as she reached for Cheryl's hand. "Can you ever forgive me?"

"I don't think you wrote the article with any intention of hurting me or my family. I'm more upset that you betrayed the trust I placed in you."

Stacie started to protest, but Cheryl held up her hand.

"I believe you when you tell me you didn't intend to go through with trying to publish the piece."

The tension began to ease from Stacie's muscles.

"The book is fictional and although it takes place in Tennessee, the setting is only loosely based on my hometown. There's noth-

ing even vaguely similar between the characters and my family."
She stopped and gave a small shrug. "Other than their chosen pro-
fession."

"Then why are you so concerned?"

"I guess I'm afraid of what would happen if the press decides to
make this their story of the month. You know what happens. They
take a bump in the road and turn it into a mountain." She rubbed
a hand over her eyes. "I'm worried about dragging Dad and all his
friends into this. He hasn't made moonshine for a few years, so I'm
positive there's no tangible evidence on the property for them to
find. I'm certain the only evidence they could find now would be
hearsay. I know he never had a bank account until recently and all
the money in it is from his legitimate business. The bank records
are on the up-and-up and he's meticulous in his bookkeeping.
Whatever money he has in the bank can be legally accounted for.
My parents have always lived a very frugal lifestyle. They're the
'cash and carry' type. They don't have credit cards and they don't
borrow money. The house and land in Tennessee have been in the
family for generations. As I told you before, I truly believe he's
covered his previous activities as much as he possibly could." She
glanced at Stacie. "But you know if the government gets a big
enough burr up its butt and really goes after him, it's going to get
hairy. It's always the little things that put you away."

They sat in silence for several seconds.

"Stacie, I can't let this become a feeding frenzy. I know Dad was
in the wrong legally, but he's in a legitimate business now. He had
a family to support and he did what he knew best. I won't fault him
for that."

"What does he do now?"

"You won't believe me," Cheryl said and smiled playfully. "He
designs Web sites."

Stacie frowned. "Web sites? As in Internet Web sites?"

"It's the perfect occupation for him. He works from home and
sets his own hours."

"How did he get started in that?"

"About seven years ago, I went home for a visit and I took my laptop with me. I needed to check my e-mail one night, so I took my laptop to the kitchen to use the phone jack there. Dad has always been Mr. Curiosity. He asked me what I was doing and I showed him. He spent the rest of my vacation playing on the Internet. A few weeks after I left, I got an e-mail from him." She shook her head. "That was one of the biggest surprises of my life. He had bought a computer and his fascination with the Web continued to grow. He got books from the library and taught himself how to construct them. From there he ended up starting his own business."

Stacie couldn't help comparing him to her own father, who still refused to try anything other than planting the same tired fields of onions each year.

A clock from somewhere in the house chimed. Stacie glanced at her watch, shocked to see it was already eleven. "I should probably get going. I have to work tomorrow."

Cheryl simply nodded.

"Are you angry with me?" Stacie asked

"I'm more disappointed than angry. Trust is a big issue for me, Stacie."

"I understand. Can I call you tomorrow?"

Cheryl stood. "Why don't you give me a couple of days? I'm going to need some time to talk to my parents. I may even fly out to see them."

Stacie tried not to let her disappointment show. Cheryl and Brenda had forgiven her, but neither wanted to talk to her anytime soon.

Chapter Thirty-two

Stacie was on the verge of nodding off when Estelle came into her office. Thoughts of how she hurt Cheryl and Brenda had kept her awake most of the night.

"I wanted to ask you about the suggestion you made for the article on the balloon festival." Estelle stopped. "Are you all right?"

The touch of concern in Estelle's voice was Stacie's undoing. She tried to turn away to hide the fat teardrops pouring down her face.

"Hold on a minute," Estelle said as she turned and closed the door to Stacie's office. "One of the great things about this old building is that all of the offices have doors. I can't stand those new open cubicles." She took a seat beside Stacie's desk. "Now, what's going on?"

Stacie was crying so hard, she couldn't have talked even if she had wanted to.

"Do you really hate the job that much?" Estelle asked, misunderstanding Stacie's tears.

"It's not the job," Stacie wailed as she yanked a fresh handful of tissues from the box.

"That's a relief, because I've kind of gotten used to having you around."

Stacie glanced over to see if Estelle was making fun of her. "Really?" she asked.

"Yeah, you're proving to be a much better worker than I thought you'd be. I honestly didn't think you'd last a week."

"Then why did you hire me?"

Estelle looked down at her hands. "Ralph Manchester and I are old friends. He heard about you getting fired and called me."

"Why?" Stacie asked and blew her nose.

"He thought I should hire you. He told me you were green as goose shit, but he thought you had moxie."

"Why would he do that? He walked out on the interview."

"He walked out because you were trying to bully him into taking a stand on something he was not ready to take a stand on. My guess is, he heard about Jack letting you go and assumed the interview you didn't get with him was the reason you were fired. I probably shouldn't tell you this, but for all his bluff and bluster, Congressman Ralph Manchester is an old softie at heart."

"Strange, I heard almost the same words used to describe you," Stacie said with a tired smile.

"Whoever told you that was obviously mistaken."

"I don't think so."

Estelle waved her off. "We're not talking about me now. What has gotten you so upset? You don't seem like the sort to cry because you broke a nail."

Stacie started telling her about Junie and the baby and didn't stop until she had told her about the article she had written about Cheryl's family and the entire sordid mess associated with it, only leaving out the nature of her relationship with Cheryl.

Estelle blew out a long breath when Stacie finished. "No one can accuse you of leading a boring life, that's for sure." She rested her elbow on the chair arm and raised one finger. "First, you should have called me and told me about your sister."

"I didn't want to be fired," Stacie argued.

"Don't be a silly goose. I wouldn't have fired you over missing work for a valid family emergency, and before we continue this conversation, I should warn you that in addition to counting Ralph Manchester among my friends, I also consider Jack Conrad to be a good friend. I called him before I called you."

Stacie grimaced.

"Exactly," Estelle said at Stacie's reaction. "You weren't fired without reason, were you?"

"No. Jack probably gave me more chances than he should have," Stacie admitted.

"I'm glad you understand that. Now, my second point is, Cheryl Wright has every right to be angry with you. What you did was inexcusable." Stacie started to defend herself, but Estelle stopped her. "I'm not finished yet. The fact that you had already decided not to use the article says something for your character, but then you turn around and tell Cheryl's story to me, another newspaper person. Didn't it occur to you that doing so might be a little risky?"

"No," Stacie answered honestly.

"An interview with an author would be right up my alley. You even knew I was interested in doing an article on Jean Gray. Then you disclose to me that Cheryl Wright and Jean Gray are the same individual. How could you be so sure I wouldn't jump on this story myself? I could have written it up and printed it before the *Juice* had a chance to."

"You wouldn't do that."

Estelle looked at her for a long moment. "No, I wouldn't, but, Stacie, you need to start thinking before you open your mouth. Your actions have caused a lot of pain for several people. You do realize Cheryl's father could be prosecuted?"

"I do now. I didn't think anyone would care."

"If there's a dollar involved, someone always cares. I'm not well versed in tax laws, but I do know there are numerous ones relating to alcohol. My guess is Cheryl's father wasn't paying the tax on the income he was earning from this homemade whiskey. While the law might overlook the illegal distillery manufacturing, I can't see the IRS forgiving his failure to pay income taxes."

"I don't know how to make things right," Stacie said, her tears threatening to start again.

"Well, sitting here bawling won't fix the problem."

"I've got to think of a way to stop him from printing that article," Stacie said.

"You can forget about that. Ron Bauer has a story and he's going to run it. The thing you have to worry about is how much of your story can be verified, and was he able to dig up more on his own."

"Cheryl is never going to talk to me again."

Estelle stood up. "Things will look much brighter once you've gotten some sleep." She glanced at her watch. "It's almost lunchtime. I'm going to give you the rest of the afternoon off."

"No," Stacie protested.

"Let me finish," Estelle said, holding up a hand. "There's an arts fair downtown this weekend and I need someone to cover it. So much is going on that we're finding ourselves short-handed. Go down Saturday, take a few photos, interview a couple of artists and give me a small write-up." When Stacie didn't immediately respond, Estelle put her hands on her hips. "Well, do you want the assignment or not? If you do, then get out of here. You're on an hourly wage and I don't want to have to pay you overtime."

Stacie jumped up. "Sure I want it. I'll have it for you first thing Monday morning."

"You bet your boots you will." Estelle opened the door and turned back to Stacie. "Go see Cheryl and get this mess ironed out."

"She doesn't want to talk to me for a few days."

"Then you'll have to respect her wishes. But I'll bet you she's feeling about as low as you are over this."

Stacie watched as Estelle disappeared out the door. Was Estelle referring to the article or had Stacie's deepening feelings for Cheryl somehow been revealed?

Chapter Thirty-three

The ringing of the alarm clock pulled Stacie from the warm embrace of a dream. Not yet ready to face the start of another day, she fumbled for the shut-off switch. The ringing stopped only to begin again before Stacie could remove her hand.

"Phone," she mumbled as she struggled to wake up enough to stop the irritating noise. Thoughts of Junie and the baby brought her fully awake. She answered without taking time to check the identification of the caller.

"Stacie, this is Estelle. I'm sorry to disturb you, but something has come up. I need you to come back to the office. Can you come in right away?"

"Yes," Stacie replied as she kicked the tangled sheet away.

The sudden movement attracted the attention of the sleeping kittens. They instantly attacked her feet. Sharp claws and teeth sank into the tender skin around her ankles. She shook the attackers loose and buried her feet beneath the safety of the bedcovers. "I can be there in about forty-five minutes." Stacie fumbled with the clock and was surprised to find it was only a little after three. It took her a second to remember she had left work early, gone home and lain down for a nap.

After hanging up, she sat up in bed and rubbed her ankle. "You guys are getting too big for that. It's starting to hurt," she said while shaking a finger at them.

Scout's response to the reprimand was to pounce on the waggling finger. Jem attacked Scout's back leg.

"I'm glad to see you understand who's in charge here." Stacie threw the end of the sheet over the kittens. She made her escape to the bathroom and closed the door while they fought their way out.

After splashing water on her face to chase away the last traces of sleep, she brushed her teeth and tried to comb her hair into some semblance of order. She opened the bathroom door slowly, expecting the little marauders to charge her, but there was no sign of them. Walking into the bedroom, she found them perched on the corner of her bed.

Jem was lying on his back slapping empty air while Scout licked her paw and washed her face with the utmost dignity.

Stacie kept a watchful eye on them as she dressed.

When the duo continued to ignore her, she stepped closer to the bed. "Oh, I get it. I'm being ignored." She glanced at her watch. "I bet I know a way to get your attention." She went into the kitchen and pulled a can of tuna from the pantry.

As soon as the electric can opener began to hum, Jem came tearing around the corner in eager anticipation. Scout followed at a more leisurely and dignified pace but was still quick enough to be standing by the food dish when the tuna arrived.

"You are so easy," Stacie chuckled as she scratched the kitten's ears.

A minute later she was out the door.

She caught a break in the afternoon traffic and stepped into Estelle's office ten minutes early. "I'm a little early, but I—" The sight of Cheryl sitting across from Estelle brought her up short. She glanced from one to the other. "What's going on?"

239

"Close the door, please," Estelle said as she motioned for Stacie to have a seat. "I believe you two know each other."

Stacie nodded, slowly glancing between the two women for an explanation. She noticed a copy of *The Mountain Still Stands*, the novel Cheryl had written under the pen name of Jean Gray, lying in front of Estelle.

"Cheryl, if you wouldn't mind repeating your proposition so that Stacie will know what's going on," Estelle said.

Cheryl turned to face Stacie. "I want to try and neutralize the story in the *Juice*. I asked Estelle if she would be open to the *Reporter* doing a story to reveal the connection between my two writing identities. I've talked to my publicist and my publishers. Everyone agrees that maybe it's time for Cheryl Wright and Jean Gray to go public."

"What about your father? Aren't you concerned about him getting into trouble?"

"That's the fly in the ointment," Estelle said. "We need to know exactly how much Ron Bauer knows. The problem is, if anyone starts calling him and showing an interest in the story, he's going to smell a bigger story and really go looking for dirt. Whether it's true or not won't matter much."

Stacie gave them the highlights of what she had written in the article.

"Do you know if this Trish woman gave Bauer the article?" Estelle asked.

"She didn't give him the original. Brenda got that back from her," Stacie said. "But she could have faxed it to him or made a copy."

Estelle leaned forward on her desk. "Can you find out what she gave him?"

Stacie's stomach gave an unpleasant turn. She didn't want to talk to Trish, but she certainly couldn't ask Brenda to do so. "Maybe. I'm not sure Trish will talk to me, but I can try."

"Can you call her now?" Estelle asked.

"I'll try." Stacie stood, intending to go to her office to make the call. She was going to have to call Brenda for Trish's number and she didn't want Cheryl or Estelle to see her grovel, assuming she'd have to beg Brenda for the information.

Estelle pushed her phone to the edge of the desk. "Here. You can use mine."

She dialed Brenda's number and woke Zoey up. "She's working a double shift," Zoey grumbled. Stacie didn't have Brenda's work number and it took her a while to persuade Zoey to give it to her. By the time she had gotten the number from Zoey and then convinced the receptionist at the nursing home that it was urgent that she speak to Brenda, Stacie was already starting to have doubts about the wisdom of calling. Getting her to give out both Trish's home and work number took another ten minutes.

Stacie glanced at her watch. It wasn't yet five. Trish might still be at work. She almost shouted with joy when Trish actually answered her own line. She would have preferred talking to Trish in person, but she didn't have time. While working as a reporter, she had found she could usually watch people's eyes and know if they were lying to her. Talking to Trish over the phone robbed her of that opportunity.

"What do you want?" Trish asked suspiciously.

"I'm calling to inform you that I'll be filing criminal charges against you." She turned away from the shocked looks she received from both Estelle and Cheryl.

Trish snorted. "Yeah, right. What are they going to do? Slap my hand for taking a few pieces of paper?"

Stacie continued her bluff and prayed Trish didn't know anything about copyright laws. "In case you forgot, I make my living as a reporter. You stole an article from me with the intent to sell the contents. That's illegal under the copyright law. I'm filing criminal charges against you for stealing it from my home, and I'm filing charges against Ron Bauer for plagiarizing my work."

"How can he plagiarize your work when he hasn't even read it?" Trish asked.

Stacie was certain Trish didn't sound as sure of herself as she had originally. "You gave him my article."

"I did not."

"Well, you didn't exactly hand it to him, but you read it to him over the phone or gave him a copy."

"Did he say that? Because if he did, he's lying."

Stacie forced herself to sound exasperated. "Then how did you get the article to him?" All she really wanted to know was exactly what Trish had told Bauer.

"I called him and asked him if he was interested in doing a story on a well-known author with a daddy who ran moonshine. He asked me who the author was and I told him Cheryl Wright."

"Then what?" Stacie asked, almost afraid to breathe.

"He asked me what evidence I had and I told him about the story I found in your bedroom."

"He didn't ask you to read it to him?"

"No. He wanted me to bring the article to his office down-town."

"You didn't take it to him?"

"No."

"Why not?" Stacie asked, not sure whether she should believe Trish or not.

Trish didn't answer.

"Trish, why didn't you take the article to Bauer's office?"

"I didn't take it because he's an asshole. I asked him how much he would pay and he said twenty-five dollars. I argued it was worth more and he said—" She stopped short.

"He said what?" Stacie prompted.

"He said he wasn't interested because no one really cared about what some lesbian writer's daddy did. He said the article he did on you was a big flop. No one cares what lesbians do anymore."

Stacie tried to think of some way to end the call.

"So how much trouble am I in?" Trish asked with a slight catch in her voice.

"It's up to the district attorney." Stacie hung up before Trish could say anything else. She felt a little twinge of guilt for scaring Trish, but it quickly abated when she thought about the trouble Trish's greed had caused Cheryl.

Estelle and Cheryl looked at her expectantly.

"She didn't give him a copy of the article. She says she spoke to him on the phone. He only offered her twenty-five dollars for the article. She said the meager payment hadn't been worth meeting him. She also said he didn't seem that interested."

Estelle ran her finger over the edge of her lip. "He might have been trying to get the story cheap. I can't believe he's not interested in the article."

"He was interested enough to call me," Cheryl reminded them.

"It's a perfect follow-up on the other article he did on your little rampage with the bunny through the window," Estelle said with a glance at Stacie.

"Don't tell me you read the *Juice*," Stacie said and groaned.

"I read everything," Estelle reminded her before turning to Cheryl. "What do you want to do? There's a slim possibility he won't do anything with the information."

Cheryl closed her eyes and took a deep breath. "I'm going to give you the story of my pseudonym, and if Bauer releases the story about Dad's activities—"

"I was doing a book review," Stacie cut in.

They both turned to look at her. "What?" Estelle asked.

"If anyone asks me about the article that was stolen from my house, I'll tell them it was a rough draft for a review of *The Mountain Still Stands*. Think about it. If Bauer writes a story identifying Cheryl Wright and Jean Gray as the same person, and then tells about Cheryl's father being involved in making illegal whiskey, all Cheryl needs to say is Bauer used the book's *fictional* plot as background information."

Estelle stared at Stacie for a long moment. "Did your friend Brenda read the article?"

"No."

"Are you sure?" Estelle pressed.

Stacie thought back to how upset Brenda had been about her patient dying. "I don't think she would have. She was already upset about something that had happened at work. Having to go to Trish

243

and confront her would have been hard. No. She wouldn't have read the article."

Estelle nodded and turned to Cheryl. "If the government gets pissy and the case goes to court, it will be Stacie's word against that of the woman who stole the article from her apartment and a reporter who writes for a tabloid."

"I don't want to put either of you in an awkward position," Cheryl said. "And I certainly don't want to bring a government lawyer down on your heads."

Estelle waved her off. "Truthfully, I don't think it'll ever get that far. Ron Bauer is lazy. He's not going to pursue anything unless he's sure it's going to get him a story," she said and leaned back. "Here's what we're going to do. Stacie will write a review and I'll run it along with the article unveiling the identity of Jean Gray. There's no reason that I can see that anyone in their right mind would assume your fictional characters have anything to do with your real life. But what has been discussed here doesn't leave this room." She turned to Stacie. "Can you keep your mouth shut?"

"Yes," Stacie assured her.

"You can't even tell your friend Brenda," Estelle said. "This will forever remain between the three of us."

Cheryl and Stacie nodded in agreement.

"Good." Estelle hopped off her chair. "Stacie, I'll hold space for you, but I have to have both items no later than noon tomorrow. Can you handle that?"

"Yeah, I've already read the book. I'll need to skim through it again to refresh my memory on the details, but I can do that and write a review by noon tomorrow. Are you going to write the article revealing Jean Gray?"

Estelle looked at her and frowned. "No, I'm going to a play tonight. You're writing both pieces."

Stacie's mouth dropped. "Both!"

"Yes, both. You started this mess and I expect you to clean it up," Estelle said with her hands on her hips. "Are you going to have a problem handling that?"

Stacie's head came up and her shoulders straightened. "Not at all, boss. You just make sure you save me plenty of space." She nodded to Estelle. "If you'll excuse me, I have work to do." She reached across and picked up the copy of *The Mountain Still Stands* from Estelle's desk. "Can I borrow this, again?" she asked before turning to Cheryl. "Ms. Wright, if you would be so kind as to join me in my office, I have a few questions."

Chapter Thirty-four

Stacie sat in a circle of warm light at her desk waiting for the printer to spit out the final copy of the article derived from the interview with Cheryl. Rather than waste precious time in traveling home and back, Stacie had decided to complete the work in her office. She had no intention of leaving until both pieces received Estelle's approval.

After the interview, Cheryl had gone home with a reminder that Stacie should call her if she had any other questions or needed additional verification on any of the information obtained during the interview. "No matter what time it is," Cheryl added as she left.

Stacie couldn't help but wonder what Cheryl would look like sleeping. A familiar warmth rushed over her, but she quickly pushed it away. There was too much work to be done to allow her thoughts to drift off to those memories.

Stacie had a rough first draft by the time Estelle came by just before seven to announce she was leaving for the day.

"Here's my cell phone number," she said, scribbling on a pad of paper. "If it looks as though you're not going to be able to complete the assignment, give me a call."

"All right. Have a good time. I'll see you tomorrow," Stacie said without taking her eyes off her computer. After Estelle left, Stacie revised several attempts before she was satisfied with the final product.

She set the article on the corner of her desk and stretched. The clock on the wall read twelve minutes after eight. Her stomach reminded her she hadn't eaten lunch or dinner. Digging through her desk for change, she ran to the break room and grabbed a soda and a bag of chips before going back to her office and starting to review *The Mountain Still Stands*.

Originally, she intended more or less to skim the book, but she quickly found herself immersed in the lives of Cheryl's vivid characters. Sometime around three the following morning, she heard the distant laughter of someone coming in. They would be starting the layout. Today would be a long day for most of the staff. She quickly scribbled a DO NOT DISTURB sign and taped it to her door. Using the last of her change, she went to the break room one last time for a cup of coffee before closing her door and returning to her reading.

It was nine-thirty that morning before she finally closed the book and sat back down at her computer. At ten forty-eight, she handed Estelle the final drafts of both pieces.

"You look pretty pleased with yourself," Estelle said as she took in Stacie's wrinkled attire. "I take it you spent the night here."

"I didn't want to waste time driving back and forth," Stacie explained.

Estelle nodded. "Go get yourself some breakfast while I read these over."

Stacie shook her head. "I'm not hungry. I'll be in my office whenever you're finished."

A few minutes later, Stacie's phone rang. It was Estelle. "E-mail me a copy of the interview and book review, please."

Stacie did as she was asked and waited. Another twenty-five minutes went by before Estelle came into her office.

"Great job on both pieces. Why don't you go on home and get some sleep?"

"What about revisions?" Stacie asked.

"There aren't any. I've already sent the copy over for the layout people to start working on." She glanced at her watch. "We had minutes to spare. That was good work." She turned and started to leave. "You're going to make one hell of a reporter someday."

Stacie was too tired to argue. "If I live that long," she called after Estelle.

"Oh, you will. There's true printer's ink running through your veins. Now, get out of here. I already owe you a fortune in overtime."

Chapter Thirty-five

Stacie went back to her apartment but was too revved up to sleep. She took the kittens to Zilker Park and found a shady spot away from the main flow of hikers to let them play. After spreading a blanket on the ground, she teased the rambunctious duo with a bird feather and a loose piece of binding on the blanket.

It wasn't long before Jem curled himself in a tight knot and fell asleep. When Scout couldn't coax him out of his nap, she curled up beside him. Stacie stretched out beside them on her back and stared up into the massive canopy of a pecan tree. Slowly she allowed her thoughts and feelings for Cheryl to work their way to the top of her mental list of things bothering her.

It was useless for her to pretend she wasn't developing strong feelings for this complex woman from Tennessee. The issue was how far was she willing to let the emotional attachment develop. Her life plan didn't include a serious relationship until after her career was securely established. If she allowed her emotional involvement with Cheryl to blossom and one of those once-in-a-lifetime job offers came her way, would Cheryl be willing to pull up stakes and move? Did she even have a right to expect Cheryl to move?

If she were to pull back gradually from Cheryl now, Cheryl probably wouldn't even notice. *I would miss her.* The thought ricocheted around in her mind until she accepted it as true. She would miss spending time with Cheryl. The truth was she wanted to kiss Cheryl again and maybe even move beyond a kiss. She shifted, suddenly feeling uncomfortably warm.

Here she was making plans for a future with a major newspaper, and it might never happen. When did she stop thinking about writing a book and start thinking about making it big in the newspaper industry? Would she be happy in New York? Or Los Angeles? She sat up and gazed across the wide green expanse of the park. She loved living in Austin. Brenda was here, and despite the irritating stairs, she liked her little apartment. Maybe someday she could convince her siblings to move to Austin.

Family. That was another issue. The conversation with her mother continued to bother her. She tried to imagine what it must be like to be her mother, trapped in a dead marriage, in an even deader town. As usual, thoughts of her father quickly skittered away, but this time she grabbed hold of the slippery demons and held them up for closer inspection. Losing a sister, as he had, would be horrible enough, but to have your father condemn you as being responsible for her death would compound the pain beyond measure. As a young man, he dreamed of rebuilding old cars. He had set aside that dream and watched it decay into dust as he toiled on the Garrison farm to feed his young family. When fate snatched even that sad consolation prize and he faced unemployment, he continued trying to do the only thing he could remember—farming. For the first time, she wondered if he even enjoyed planting those pathetic fields of onions. Maybe he continued to do so because he felt he had no other choice. She recalled the dark days of her own unemployment and the bone-numbing moments of doubt when she wondered if she would ever get another newspaper job. She tried to imagine how she would have felt had she been forced to move to another career. A deep chill sent a ripple down her spine. She would never be able to forget how her father had treated them, but for the first time she saw the tiniest glimpse of what it must have been like for him all these years.

Junie and Bill were caught up in the same trap as her parents. It was only a matter of time before Bill was laid off or the plant shut down completely. What would they do then? What would become of their kids? What kind of future was there in Wilburn for any of them?

The cell phone on Stacie's belt jangled, making her jump and causing the kittens to open their eyes and stretch.

Stacie smiled when she saw the caller was Cheryl.

"I hope I didn't wake you," Cheryl said.

"No. I'm over at Zilker Park. I brought the kittens over here. They've been closed up in the apartment for days."

"I spoke to Estelle. She's really happy with the article and book review you did. She read me a few of the highlights. The review made me want to read the book." Cheryl's rich laugh teased Stacie's ear.

"The book is really awesome. Estelle was right. It should be a movie."

"That's just a rumor, you know."

"Why did you go to Estelle? Any paper in Austin would have snatched up the opportunity to print your story."

"I liked what I heard about her from you."

Stacie grinned and shook her head. "I didn't even realize I had talked about her to you."

"She's the kind of person you can always depend on, no matter what."

Stacie agreed that Estelle was very special.

"I was wondering, if you're not too tired, maybe you'd like to get together for dinner tonight. I know you're probably exhausted, so we could make it an early evening."

Stacie sensed she was standing at a crossroads. If she followed the pathway leading toward Cheryl, would she limit her chances of the career she had dreamed of for so long? Or would that road lead her to the love and happiness she had been unconsciously seeking all these years?

Impatient paws pushed against her leg. Stacie looked down to find Scout, her head tilted slightly to the side, staring at her. Stacie held out her hand, fully expecting Scout's usual attack. Instead, the kitten crawled into Stacie's hand and curled up to sleep.

Stacie couldn't keep from chuckling. "Dinner would be great. Can you pick me up? I kind of like riding in that snazzy car of yours."

After agreeing that Cheryl would pick her up at five, Stacie disconnected and slipped the phone back onto her belt, being careful not to disturb the sleeping bundle in her hand.

Chapter Thirty-six

Stacie and Cheryl sat in the empty parking lot of the Mexican restaurant Stacie had recommended.

"I can't believe it has gone out of business," Stacie said.

"When was the last time you were here?"

Stacie shrugged. "I don't know. A few months ago, I guess."

"Any other suggestions? I'm kind of in the mood for enchiladas now."

"There are several other places, but to be honest, I always came here when I wanted Mexican food."

Cheryl looked at her and grinned. "How tired are you?"

"I slept most of the afternoon," Stacie reminded her. "Why?"

"I know a great place, but it's a ways from here."

"Let's go."

As Cheryl pulled out of the parking lot and drove toward the interstate, Stacie tried to anticipate where they were going. It wasn't until the Jag continued south that she realized they were headed toward San Antonio. "Are we going to San Antonio?" Stacie asked.

"Is that all right?"

"You bet it is."

They remained silent until Cheryl maneuvered the car through the congested afternoon traffic. "How's your sister doing?"

"Good," Stacie replied. "She still tires easily, but she'll be fine. They think the baby will be able to go home sooner than expected. She's gaining weight and all her tests look good."

"You never told me what they named her."

"Stacie Michelle."

Cheryl glanced at her and grinned. "What a pretty name. I'm sure she'll be just as beautiful as her namesake."

Embarrassed, Stacie shrugged. "Let's hope she's smarter."

The traffic flow slowed drastically. They found themselves caught in between several eighteen-wheelers. "I hate those things," Cheryl said, nodding toward one of the trucks. "I'm always terrified they won't see me alongside them." Cheryl took her time and carefully wove the Jag through the confusion. As soon as they were in the open, she let out a loud sigh. "Do you mind if I ask you a personal question?" she asked before Stacie could comment on the trucks.

"Okay."

"Is your dad abusive?"

Stacie looked at the window. She knew the time would come when she would have to tell Cheryl about her family, but she had hoped it wouldn't be so soon.

"I'm sorry. You don't have to answer that. It's none of my business."

"It's all so complicated. I try to hate him, but then I remember those rare moments that would happen when we'd all be so happy." She started to tell Cheryl about her childhood and suddenly it all began to pour out of her. She didn't intend for it to happen, but once it started, she couldn't stop.

Cheryl let her talk and occasionally handed her a fresh tissue.

It wasn't until Stacie saw the sign for Ackermann Road that she realized they were already in San Antonio. "Damn. I'm sorry. I didn't mean to unload all that on you."

Cheryl put a hand on Stacie's arm. "I'm glad you told me. It helps me to understand you better."

"You mean you now know where I got the violent gene that hurled a stone rabbit through your window."

Cheryl shook her head as she shifted lanes and took the exit ramp leading to downtown. "No. I meant I now understand why you don't let yourself get too emotionally involved with anyone."

Stacie felt a stirring of irritation. She didn't want her actions to be second-guessed. "His hitting me doesn't dictate who I am," she argued.

"No, but it affects how you relate to others."

Stacie started to disagree, but knew that what Cheryl said was true. Before she could say anything else, Cheryl changed the subject.

"Have you ever been to the Great Smoky Mountains?"

"No," Stacie answered, somewhat disoriented by the sudden switch in topics.

"You should go sometime. It's absolutely beautiful, especially in the fall. You have to see it to believe it. The colors are incredible." She pulled into the parking lot of Los Amigos.

Stacie took a deep breath and leaned her head back. "Maybe you could take me sometime."

Cheryl parked the car and shut off the motor. She sat gazing at Stacie for a long second. "I think I'd like that."

Stacie held her breath, certain that Cheryl was about to kiss her. Instead, she simply squeezed her hand.

"I hope you'll like the food here," Cheryl said as she opened the car door.

"I'm sure it's great." Stacie tried not to let her disappointment show in her voice as they walked into the restaurant. She waited until they were seated before asking, "How did you find this place?"

Cheryl started telling her something about a book signing, but Stacie found herself unable to concentrate on anything but the sensual shape of Cheryl's mouth and the fullness of her lips. Afterward, Stacie wouldn't be able to recall what she had eaten. All she could think about was touching Cheryl. She fantasized about touching her. How she would feel in her arms. How she would taste. Would she come quietly or would she be loud? In Stacie's fantasy, she was loud and wet and . . .

"Stacie. Stacie."

Cheryl was leaning forward, staring at her with concern.

"What?" Stacie managed.

"Are you all right? I've been talking to you and you haven't heard a word I've said."

"I'm sorry," she stammered as blood rushed to her face.

"You didn't like the food?" Cheryl asked and pointed to Stacie's nearly untouched plate.

"I was so enthralled with what you were talking about."

Cheryl leaned back in surprise and suddenly started laughing.

"What's wrong?"

"I was telling you about a horrible signing that should have bored you to tears." Cheryl shook her head. "What were you thinking about? You wouldn't believe how happy you looked."

Stacie ducked her head and pretended to be interested in her food, when all she really wanted to do was take Cheryl to bed.

Cheryl parked the Jag in a visitor's parking slot at Stacie's apartment. "It's already after eleven. I'm sorry it's so late. I promised I'd have you home early."

Stacie stretched and ran her hand over the luxurious leather seat. "I'm fine. I slept most of the afternoon. Besides, I had a great time."

Cheryl laughed and rolled her head across the headrest. "Can you believe we drove all the way to San Antonio just to have dinner? It seems kind of decadent to travel so far to eat."

"There's nothing wrong with being a little decadent some-times," Stacie replied.

Cheryl looked at her and said, "You can be a lot of fun."

"And that surprises you?"

"Yes and no. Most of our time together hasn't been under the best of circumstances."

"That's true," Stacie admitted.

"I know we haven't known each other very long, but I like you a lot. In fact, I think I'm falling in love with you."

Stacie's heart pounded. No one had ever told her they thought they might be falling in love with her. How was she supposed to respond to a statement like that? She tried to speak, but her tongue refused to work.

"That's not the response I was hoping for," Cheryl said with a sigh. "I'm sorry. I shouldn't have said anything."

"No," Stacie blurted. She turned toward Cheryl and forced herself to concentrate on expressing her feelings. "I like you a lot. Maybe I'm falling in love with you, too. I don't know. I've never been in love. I think about you all day long, and I can't wait until I see you again. When I'm around you I feel something warm and sometimes kind of scary right here." She placed her hand over her heart. "I want to . . . I want . . ." She kept thinking about the fantasy she'd had at the restaurant.

"What?" Cheryl asked in a voice husky with emotion.

Stacie leaned across the seat. She teased Cheryl's warm moist lips with the slightest of touches. "I want to make love to you," she murmured as the pressure of her kisses increased slightly. "I want to hold, kiss, touch and taste your passion. I know it's there. I can see it barely hiding beneath the surface." Stacie's hand slipped across Cheryl's shoulder and closed around the back of her neck, drawing Cheryl's mouth to hers. "Don't tease me," she insisted as her lips claimed Cheryl's warm mouth. The kiss grew in urgency until Stacie practically had Cheryl pulled on top of her. "Let's get inside while I'm still able to walk," she said as she let her hand casually brush down the back of Cheryl's thigh.

They didn't make it any farther than the foot of the stairs before Cheryl pulled Stacie to her and kissed her deeply. Before Stacie could protest, she found herself against the wall of the stairwell with Cheryl's thigh pushing between her legs. Cheryl's kiss grew hungrier.

Stacie tried to control the frantic need building within but found she was unable to stop her hips from beginning a slow grind against Cheryl's thigh.

Somewhere down the way, a door slammed. Cheryl pulled back enough for Stacie to catch her breath. "Get me inside and finish what you've started," she begged.

Cheryl grabbed Stacie's hand and together they flew up the stairs.

Stacie fumbled with the keys, unable to get them to work.

Cheryl took them from her and opened the door, pulling Stacie in behind her and shoving the door closed.

Stacie heard the keys fall to the floor as Cheryl began kissing her and running her hands down Stacie's back. As their kisses deepened, Stacie found herself pushed against the closed door. Cheryl's hands slipped beneath Stacie's shirt and caressed her skin. A warm tongue circled her nipple. She groaned in pleasure as Cheryl eased Stacie's slacks and underpants down. Stacie tried to protest that she couldn't stand, but it was too late. Cheryl was on her knees, pushing Stacie's legs apart, and then Cheryl's mouth was already between Stacie's legs, sucking, licking and teasing until a primeval howl of pleasure ripped from Stacie's throat as she buried her hands into Cheryl's soft hair and allowed herself to surrender to Cheryl's desire.

Stacie lost track of time, but at some point, she felt her noodle-like muscles give way and she started sliding down the door.

Cheryl stood and pulled Stacie into her arms, supporting her. "This is just the beginning," she whispered as she led Stacie to the bedroom.

Chapter Thirty-seven

Stacie raced into her apartment and scooped up the rapidly growing Jem and Scout. She was home a little earlier than usual. Estelle had let her leave early as a bonus for making it through her first month without being late or quitting. The fifty-dollar bet Estelle had made with her on her first day at the *Reporter* sat proudly in her pocket.

Even more important than winning the bet was the call she'd received just before leaving the office. It was the result of something she had been working on for over a week. She felt the first flutter of nervousness as she dialed her parents' number. The old fear surfaced as soon as her father answered.

"What's wrong?" he asked as soon as he heard Stacie's voice.

"Nothing. I'm calling to see how you guys are doing."

"Same as we've been doing all along."

Stacie couldn't think of a discreet way to begin the conversation, so she simply jumped in. "Dad, I'd like for you and Mom to move to Austin. There's an auto body school here that I think you would love, and I know Mom could find something she would enjoy doing. After you guys get settled, maybe we can get Junie and Bill to move here with the kids." She held her breath, waiting for him to start screaming at her or hang up.

"Why would we want to live in Austin?" he asked with no trace of anger in his voice.

His calmness frightened Stacie more than his yelling. "I live here and it would be good to have you and Mom closer." She took a deep breath to slow her thudding heart. "Dad, I want a family."

"Took you long enough to figure that one out."

"Your beating on me didn't help," she snapped and instantly regretted her outburst. "Look," she said, trying to keep her voice calm, "I know there are problems we need to work out between us, but I think it's worth a try."

"Why now?" he asked.

If there were going to be changes made it had to start with honesty. The phone grew slippery in her hand. She dried first one palm and then the other. "I've met someone," she said. "She has shown me how important family is."

"She," he repeated.

"Yes. Dad, I'm gay." She squeezed her eyes and braced for his outrage. All she heard was silence. "Dad?" There was no answer. *What if he'd had a heart attack?* "Dad!" she yelled.

"I'm not deaf," he replied gruffly.

"Then say something."

"Don't get smart with me or I'll—"

"You'll what?" she yelled. "Hit me? Hit Mom? What will you do? How much longer do you think we're going to keep coming back for you to smack us around?" Her anger got the better of her. "When Junie was in the hospital you asked me what she said to me in the recovery room. Well, Dad, she begged me to get Bill and the kids out of your house if she died. She didn't want you beating her kids the way you did us. You've already lost Danny. You're about to lose Mom. Is that what you want? Do you want to spend the rest of

260

your life alone? We would have all been better off if the car had exploded while you were in it."

Her words shocked her into silence. Only the occasional sound of static could be heard in the phone.

"I'm sorry," she said as soon as she could speak. "That was a cruel thing to say."

"You enjoyed it, didn't you?"

"No, I didn't. Unlike you, I take no pleasure in causing other people pain." She hung up the phone, praying she hadn't made things worse for her mom.

She made her way to the bedroom and slowly changed clothes. She and Cheryl were having dinner together as they did most evenings. Tonight, Cheryl was cooking. Stacie took a small overnight bag. Since it was Friday, she would probably spend the night.

After dinner, they cuddled up on the couch and Stacie told Cheryl about the call to her father and its disastrous ending.

"I shouldn't have ever made the call," Stacie said as she wiped the tears from her eyes.

"Sometimes we have to try even if we know it won't work. What's the deal with the auto body shop?"

Stacie repeated the story her mom had told her about how Stacie's father had once loved to rebuild cars. "I called the school and they have openings for a class that's starting next month. I had this stupid idea that Dad could go."

Cheryl hugged her tighter. "You have such a big heart. That's one of the reasons why I love you so much."

Embarrassed, Stacie tried to shrug it off. "What's the other reason?" she asked.

"You write great reviews. Do you have any idea how the sales on the book have skyrocketed in the local stores since your review was published?"

Stacie stuck out her tongue.

"Honey, don't make promises you can't keep."

"I think I can manage to carry through with this." She ran her tongue slowly across Cheryl's bottom lip, eliciting a soft sigh from her.

"Come on." Cheryl took Stacie's hand, pulled her up from the sofa and led her down the hallway to the bedroom.

Stacie slowly removed Cheryl's blouse, planting tender kisses across her bare shoulders and back. As Cheryl's bra dropped away, Stacie reached her hands around to cup Cheryl's breast. Her thumb and forefinger caressed taut nipples. She slid Cheryl's shorts off her hips and down until they fell to the floor.

Cheryl kicked them away.

With her hands and lips, Stacie tried to cover every inch of Cheryl's body. "I love you," she whispered. When Cheryl began to arch her body toward Stacie's wandering hand, Stacie eased her lover down onto the bed and stretched out beside her. With little urging, Cheryl's legs parted, allowing Stacie complete access. She started with wide, soft circles drawing them ever smaller as Cheryl's desire grew.

When Cheryl finally came in an explosive burst, Stacie held her tightly until Cheryl rolled over and pulled Stacie into her arms.

They made love until they both fell into an exhausted slumber.

Stacie woke during the night and eased out of bed. She pulled on Cheryl's robe before opening the blinds. A full moon cast a soft glow across the bedroom floor. Stacie stood staring out the window. Her first try at a reconciliation with her father hadn't gone very smoothly. She stared up at the moon and straightened her shoulders. She wasn't going to give up. As long as there was any hope, she was going to keep trying.

Cheryl stirred and turned toward Stacie. "What's the matter? Can't you sleep?"

"No."

Cheryl got out of bed and pulled a long-tailed shirt from a dresser drawer. "Come on," she said, reaching for Stacie's hand.

"I'll make you some warm milk with cinnamon. My mom used to make it for me when I couldn't sleep."

After Cheryl, Stacie and Shakespeare had all enjoyed a cup of warm milk, Stacie crawled back into bed and snuggled into Cheryl's arms. As the soft cocoon of sleep wrapped around her, she felt a sense of peacefulness unlike any she had ever known. In her last conscious moment, she understood what it meant to be loved.

Publications from
BELLA BOOKS, INC.
The best in contemporary lesbian fiction

P.O. Box 10543, Tallahassee, FL 32302
Phone: 800-729-4992
www.bellabooks.com

NO SISTER OF MINE by Jeanne G'Fellers. 240 pp. Telepathic women fight to coexist with a patriarchal society that wishes their eradication.   ISBN 1-59493-017-1 $12.95

WICKED GOOD TIME by Diana Tremain Braund. 224 pp. Does Christina need Miki as a protector . . . or want her as a lover?   ISBN 1-59493-031-7 $12.95

THOSE WHO WAIT by Peggy J. Herring. 240 pp. Two brilliant sisters—in love with the same woman!   ISBN 1-59493-032-5 $12.95

ABBY'S PASSION by Jackie Calhoun. 240 pp. Abby's bipolar sister helps turn her world upside down, so she must decide what's most important.   ISBN 1-59493-014-7 $12.95

PICTURE PERFECT by Jane Vollbrecht. 240 pp. Kate is reintroduced to Casey, the daughter of an old friend. Can they withstand Kate's career?   ISBN 1-59493-015-5 $12.95

PAPERBACK ROMANCE by Karin Kallmaker. 240 pp. Carolyn falls for tall, dark and . . . female . . . in this classic lesbian romance.   ISBN 1-59493-033-3 $12.95

DAWN OF CHANGE by Gerri Hill. 240 pp. Susan ran away to find peace in remote Kings Canyon—then she met Shawn . . .   ISBN 1-59493-011-2 $12.95

DOWN THE RABBIT HOLE by Lynne Jamneck. 240 pp. Is a killer holding a grudge against FBI Agent Samantha Skellar?   ISBN 1-59493-012-0 $12.95

SEASONS OF THE HEART by Jackie Calhoun. 240 pp. Overwhelmed, Sara saw only one way out—leaving . . .   ISBN 1-59493-030-9 $12.95

TURNING THE TABLES by Jessica Thomas. 240 pp. The 2nd Alex Peres Mystery. *From ghosties and ghoulies and long leggity beasties . . .*   ISBN 1-59493-009-0 $12.95

FOR EVERY SEASON by Frankie Jones. 240 pp. Andi, who is investigating a 65-year-old murder, meets Janice, a charming district attorney . . .   ISBN 1-59493-010-4 $12.95

LOVE ON THE LINE by Laura DeHart Young. 240 pp. Kay leaves a younger woman behind to go on a mission to Alaska . . . will she regret it?   ISBN 1-59493-008-2 $12.95

UNDER THE SOUTHERN CROSS by Claire McNab. 200 pp. Lee, an American travel agent, goes down under and meets Australian Alex, and the sparks fly under the Southern Cross.   ISBN 1-59493-029-5 $12.95

SUGAR by Karin Kallmaker. 240 pp. Three women want sugar from Sugar, who can't make up her mind.   ISBN 1-59493-001-5 $12.95

FALL GUY by Claire McNab. 200 pp. 16th Detective Inspector Carol Ashton Mystery.
ISBN 1-59493-000-7 $12.95

ONE SUMMER NIGHT by Gerri Hill. 232 pp. Johanna swore to never fall in love again—but then she met the charming Kelly . . .   ISBN 1-59493-007-4 $12.95

TALK OF THE TOWN TOO by Saxon Bennett. 181 pp. Second in the series about wild and fun loving friends.   ISBN 1-931513-77-5 $12.95

LOVE SPEAKS HER NAME by Laura DeHart Young. 170 pp. Love and friendship, desire and intrigue, spark this exciting sequel to *Forever and the Night*.
ISBN 1-59493-002-3 $12.95

TO HAVE AND TO HOLD by Peggy J. Herring. 184 pp. By finally letting down her defenses, will Dorian be opening herself to a devastating betrayal?
ISBN 1-59493-005-8 $12.95

WILD THINGS by Karin Kallmaker. 228 pp. Dutiful daughter Faith has met the perfect man. There's just one problem: she's in love with his sister.   ISBN 1-931513-64-3 $12.95

SHARED WINDS by Kenna White. 216 pp. Can Emma rebuild more than just Lanny's marina?   ISBN 1-59493-006-6 $12.95

THE UNKNOWN MILE by Jaime Clevenger. 253 pp. Kelly's world is getting more and more complicated every moment.   ISBN 1-931513-57-0 $12.95

TREASURED PAST by Linda Hill. 189 pp. A shared passion for antiques leads to love.
ISBN 1-59493-003-1 $12.95

SIERRA CITY by Gerri Hill. 284 pp. Chris and Jesse cannot deny their growing attraction . . .   ISBN 1-931513-98-8 $12.95

ALL THE WRONG PLACES by Karin Kallmaker. 174 pp. Sex and the single girl—Brandy is looking for love and usually she finds it. Karin Kallmaker's first *After Dark* erotic novel.
ISBN 1-931513-76-7 $12.95

WHEN THE CORPSE LIES A Motor City Thriller by Therese Szymanski. 328 pp. Butch bad-girl Brett Higgins is used to waking up next to beautiful women she hardly knows. Problem is, this one's dead.   ISBN 1-931513-74-0 $12.95

GUARDED HEARTS by Hannah Rickard. 240 pp. Someone's reminding Alyssa about her secret past, and then she becomes the suspect in a series of burglaries.
ISBN 1-931513-99-6 $12.95

ONCE MORE WITH FEELING by Peggy J. Herring. 184 pp. Lighthearted, loving, romantic adventure.   ISBN 1-931513-60-0 $12.95

TANGLED AND DARK A Brenda Strange Mystery by Patty G. Henderson. 240 pp. When investigating a local death, Brenda finds two possible killers—one diagnosed with Multiple Personality Disorder.   ISBN 1-931513-75-9 $12.95

WHITE LACE AND PROMISES by Peggy J. Herring. 240 pp. Maxine and Betina realize sex may not be the most important thing in their lives.   ISBN 1-931513-73-2 $12.95

UNFORGETTABLE by Karin Kallmaker. 288 pp. Can Rett find love with the cheerleader who broke her heart so many years ago?   ISBN 1-931513-63-5 $12.95

HIGHER GROUND by Saxon Bennett. 280 pp. A delightfully complex reflection of the successful, high society lives of a small group of women.   ISBN 1-931513-69-4 $12.95

LAST CALL A Detective Franco Mystery by Baxter Clare. 240 pp. Frank overlooks all else to try to solve a cold case of two murdered children . . .   ISBN 1-931513-70-8 $12.95

ONCE UPON A DYKE: NEW EXPLOITS OF FAIRY-TALE LESBIANS by Karin Kallmaker, Julia Watts, Barbara Johnson & Therese Szymanski. 320 pp. You've never read fairy tales like these before! From Bella After Dark.   ISBN 1-931513-71-6 $14.95

FINEST KIND OF LOVE by Diana Tremain Braund. 224 pp. Can Molly and Carolyn stop clashing long enough to see beyond their differences? ISBN 1-931513-68-6 $12.95

DREAM LOVER by Lyn Denison. 188 pp. A soft, sensuous, romantic fantasy.
ISBN 1-931513-96-1 $12.95

NEVER SAY NEVER by Linda Hill. 224 pp. A classic love story . . . where rules aren't the only things broken. ISBN 1-931513-67-8 $12.95

PAINTED MOON by Karin Kallmaker. 214 pp. Stranded together in a snowbound cabin, Jackie and Leah's lives will never be the same. ISBN 1-931513-53-8 $12.95

WIZARD OF ISIS by Jean Stewart. 240 pp. Fifth in the exciting Isis series.
ISBN 1-931513-71-4 $12.95

WOMAN IN THE MIRROR by Jackie Calhoun. 216 pp. Josey learns to love again, while her niece is learning to love women for the first time. ISBN 1-931513-78-3 $12.95

SUBSTITUTE FOR LOVE by Karin Kallmaker. 200 pp. When Holly and Reyna meet the combination adds up to pure passion. But what about tomorrow? ISBN 1-931513-62-7 $12.95

GULF BREEZE by Gerri Hill. 288 pp. Could Carly really be the woman Pat has always been searching for? ISBN 1-931513-97-X $12.95

THE TOMSTOWN INCIDENT by Penny Hayes. 184 pp. Caught between two worlds, Eloise must make a decision that will change her life forever. ISBN 1-931513-56-2 $12.95

MAKING UP FOR LOST TIME by Karin Kallmaker. 240 pp. Discover delicious recipes for romance by the undisputed mistress. ISBN 1-931513-61-9 $12.95

THE WAY LIFE SHOULD BE by Diana Tremain Braund. 173 pp. With which woman will Jennifer find the true meaning of love? ISBN 1-931513-66-X $12.95

BACK TO BASICS: A BUTCH/FEMME ANTHOLOGY edited by Therese Szymanski— from Bella After Dark. 324 pp. ISBN 1-931513-35-X $14.95

SURVIVAL OF LOVE by Frankie J. Jones. 236 pp. What will Jody do when she falls in love with her best friend's daughter? ISBN 1-931513-55-4 $12.95

LESSONS IN MURDER by Claire McNab. 184 pp. 1st Detective Inspector Carol Ashton Mystery. ISBN 1-931513-65-1 $12.95

DEATH BY DEATH by Claire McNab. 167 pp. 5th Denise Cleever Thriller.
ISBN 1-931513-34-1 $12.95

CAUGHT IN THE NET by Jessica Thomas. 188 pp. A wickedly observant story of mystery, danger, and love in Provincetown. ISBN 1-931513-54-6 $12.95

DREAMS FOUND by Lyn Denison. Australian Riley embarks on a journey to meet her birth mother . . . and gains not just a family, but the love of her life. ISBN 1-931513-58-9 $12.95

A MOMENT'S INDISCRETION by Peggy J. Herring. 154 pp. Jackie is torn between her better judgment and the overwhelming attraction she feels for Valerie.
ISBN 1-931513-59-7 $12.95

IN EVERY PORT by Karin Kallmaker. 224 pp. Jessica has a woman in every port. Will meeting Cat change all that? ISBN 1-931513-36-8 $12.95

TOUCHWOOD by Karin Kallmaker. 240 pp. Rayann loves Louisa. Louisa loves Rayann. Can the decades between their ages keep them apart? ISBN 1-931513-37-6 $12.95

WATERMARK by Karin Kallmaker. 248 pp. Teresa wants a future with a woman whose heart has been frozen by loss. Sequel to *Touchwood*. ISBN 1-931513-38-4 $12.95